THE TWO MASTERS OF SINANJU
LEFT THE EDGE OF THE RUNWAY

Chiun broke to the right, tearing off after the newer plane. Remo stayed on course, running at full speed.

Wind caught the tail, fluttering it ferociously as he outpaced the rear of the plane. A line of ragged grass sprouted up before them.

The end of the runway. Beyond that, a three-hundred-yard drop to the rocks below. Remo doubted he could stop on time. There would be only one chance at this.

He leapt from the runway and spread-eagled himself on the lower left wing of the large biplane.

The plateau surface suddenly dropped out from beneath him. Far below, frothy waves crashed against basalt rock.

Other titles in this series:

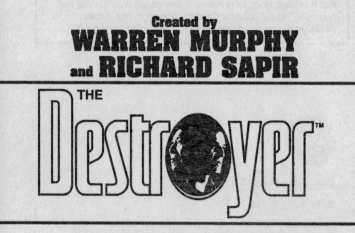

Created by
WARREN MURPHY
and RICHARD SAPIR

THE Destroyer™

THE EMPIRE DREAMS

A GOLD EAGLE BOOK FROM
WORLDWIDE®

TORONTO • NEW YORK • LONDON
AMSTERDAM • PARIS • SYDNEY • HAMBURG
STOCKHOLM • ATHENS • TOKYO • MILAN
MADRID • WARSAW • BUDAPEST • AUCKLAND

First edition November 1998

ISBN 0-373-63228-2

Special thanks and acknowledgment to James Mullaney for his contribution to this work.

THE EMPIRE DREAMS

Printed in U.S.A.

AN IMPORTANT MESSAGE FROM CHIUN

Remo eats beef Stroganoff!? Chiun watches soap operas!? What has happened to our beloved Destroyer series?

These are but a few of the many questions inspired by some of the recent entries in the books, which have for years chronicled the adventures of the Master of Sinanju and a few other lesser characters. In one novel in particular (was it number one billion and eighty-three?) I am depicted as a White-hating old man obsessed with daytime dramas. This is simply not so. I am neither old nor a fan of these programs. Oh, at one time I enjoyed them. But it has been many years since cruel fortune stripped this single pleasure from my bleak life.

Is there an explanation for this lapse, you now ask?

The answer is yes. There is an explanation.

The explanation? Sloth.

This story obviously was from an earlier time in my dubious association with Remo Williams, my slug-brained pupil and purported "star" of this series. Somehow the fools at Gold Eagle (whose gold is scarce and whose eagles, I believe, are actually pigeons) mixed in an old manuscript with the new. What should have been billed as a "classic" Destroyer novel was thrown in with the rest.

Do not bother to ask me how such a thing could happen. Just look at the copyright page of the book you now hold.

Canadians. Need I say more?

Apparently there were modern elements added to the old story to update it. Again, do not bother to ask. If these nitwits were to publish a biography of Nero he would doubtless be wearing Air Jordan sneakers and racing around Rome in a dune buggy.

Oh, what will happen next!? Master of Sinanju, help us!

Although you are undeserving and have never done anything nice for me, I shall honor your request.

To those of you who care about such things, the problem has been addressed. I have enlisted the aid of a particularly dim American to relate my epic adventures. Apparently he has been hovering like a servile dog at the periphery of this dreadful series for many years, and so understands what has gone on before. This new scribbler is quite dense. As Americans weaned on "The Gong Show," you should be very happy with him. And do not despair; if he fails in his duties, I will flay him and move on to the next. There are many more where he came from. Unfortunately. You Americans have yet to understand the term "family planning." (A suggestion from one who has been forced to live among you for many years: Look it up.)

As for Remo's diet in the book that inspired the most mail, it was awful, was it not? Omelettes, stews, fried eggs, bread, coffee... Back then he would have eaten a yak on a stick as long as it was first dipped in Twinkies.

There. I have addressed your inane questions and silly concerns. You may go back to using your typewriters to pester the editorial departments of your local newspapers. One parting suggestion. Change the ribbon.

> I am, with moderate tolerance for you,
> Chiun, Reigning Master of Sinanju

With love, for Kathleen A. Mullaney,
who never lost faith. And for James T. Mullaney, Jr.
(December 28, 1928–June 15, 1986).
I got in the truck and drove.

And finally, once more, for the Glorious House of Sinanju.
E-mail address: Housinan@aol.com

It's been too long...

PROLOGUE

He watched the old men climb the bitterly cold, windswept beaches, proudly reliving memories of their hazy youth.

And he remembered.

He watched tired soldiers, teary-eyed and long-retired, grow maudlin and weepy in the midst of row-upon-row of whitewashed crosses and fluttering flags.

And his resentment spread.

He watched presidents and prime ministers—too young or cowardly to have participated in those dark events themselves—laud the sacrifices of those who had fallen in the conflict, old now by many decades.

And he seethed.

He watched hours upon hours of documentaries and news reports retelling the horrors of a struggle that could not possibly be understood by an outsider.

And the hatred grew....

1

He had decided long before that he preferred being feared to being liked. It was his experience that people who were liked were not respected. He wanted respect. And fear—when used judiciously—always, always bred respect.

Not that fear did Nils Schatz much good these days.

He was retired. Not by any choice of his own. It had been a forced retirement.

Those who had inflicted this malady of inactivity on him weren't fearful of him. The young ones were like that these days. They knew his past, yet they didn't care. And of all the young ones, Kluge was the worst.

Adolf Kluge was the current head of IV, and it was Kluge whom Nils Schatz was meeting with this morning. Regrettably he couldn't hope to inspire fear in the IV director. But Schatz did hope that the young man would listen to reason.

The air of the village was cold in his throat as he made his way down the tidy cobbled streets. The gleaming bronze tip of his walking stick clicked a relentless, impatient staccato on the perfectly shaped gray stones.

He passed between narrow passageways designed only for single-lane traffic. Most people either walked or used bicycles to get around the village.

As he strolled along, several people on bikes passed by in either direction. The older ones facing him nodded politely as they slipped by. The impertinent young ones didn't even pay any attention to him. Coming from the other direction, those his age hunkered down over their handlebars and kept their backs to him.

The older ones understood who and what Nils Schatz had been. They still feared him.

But it was no longer enough.

Schatz quickened his pace. His meeting with Kluge was at eight o'clock. He checked his watch. He would be ten minutes early.

The whitewashed buildings smelled of freshly baked bread. They were lined up in perfect cookie-cutter formation along the narrow lane. There were no front yards. The stoops opened out directly onto the street.

Schatz could see dumpy elderly housewives moving just inside the immaculate windows that looked out to the lane.

The whole village was supposed to remind everyone in it of a picture-perfect Bavarian town. From the gaily painted shutters and window boxes to the neatly tiled roofs. The spotless streets and orderly

shops were meant to give the impression that a chunk
of Europe had been transplanted somehow to the
mountains of Argentina.

But that was not the case.

What the IV village represented was an admission
of failure. Those who lived there had been forced to
flee the land of their birth and were now deluding
themselves into thinking that they had brought some
of that land with them.

The sorry fact was, this was not home. And for
Nils Schatz, it hadn't been home for more than thirty
years.

His breath made fragile puffs of mist in the crisp
mountain air. Each puff brought him closer to his
last. Soon, there would be no more. It was as if his
life were mocking him—floating out before him in
this land of his exile.

The last of the neat little houses broke away into
a wide-open field. The cobbled path led into a much
older stone road.

A vast shadow cast the ancient roadway in shades
of washed-out gray. Through rheumy eyes Schatz
followed the shadow to its origin.

Up ahead loomed Estómago de Diablo, the "Belly
of the Devil." That was what the locals called it. It
was an ancient fortress of mysterious origin. Some
thought it was Aztec, while others argued that it was
Mayan. No one knew for certain who had built the
huge stone edifice.

The palace, the ancient roads and the terraced

fields in the surrounding terrain were all that remained of an empire that had peaked and died more
than one thousand years before.

The irony that the IV village had sprung up in
what was essentially the ruins of a dead thousand-
year empire was not lost on anyone there. For Nils
Schatz, it was a lack of respect for the old ways that
had brought them here at all.

The huge stone structure squatted on a separate
mountain peak from the rest of the village. Schatz
crossed the perfectly preserved rock bridge that
spanned the chasm between the peaks.

He did not reflect on the remarkable engineering
accomplishment the bridge represented. It was just
something for him to tap his highly polished cane
impatiently upon as he crossed into the bowels of the
massive fortress.

There were four guards within the gigantic old
archway. All were blond haired and blue eyed with
muscular physiques. They also were each indistin-
guishable from one another. They stared, mute, at
Schatz as he passed.

The guards were not simply being polite. The men
were incapable of speech. They had been genetically
engineered by the late Nazi scientist, Dr. Erich von
Breslau. Some DNA glitch had robbed them of the
ability to speak. In an earlier time, they would have
been rightly executed as imperfect. In IV they were
kept as soldiers.

So unlike the old days, Schatz thought, not with sadness but with bitterness.

His face creased in severe lines, he found his way down the vaulted stone corridor to the office of Adolf Kluge.

KLUGE READ THE PROPOSAL without a hint of expression.

He scanned each line with patient eyes, occasionally wetting his lower lip with the tip of his tongue. It was a habit he had developed years before in school. He didn't even realize he was doing it.

When he was finished, he tapped the sheaf of papers into a tidy bunch. He set them neatly aside.

"Interesting," the head of IV mused, looking up.

Nils Schatz sat in a too comfortable chair on the other side of Adolf Kluge's desk. He had waited impatiently for half an hour as Kluge carefully read the proposal—a proposal he should have read weeks before.

"How soon can we begin?" Schatz pressed.

Kluge raised an eyebrow. "This isn't the regular way we do things around here, Nils," he said. "There are committees that sort through this kind of thing." He indicated the stack of papers with a wave of his hand.

"Committees," Schatz spit angrily. "Everything in this infernal village is governed by committees. No one wants to *do* anything anymore. We just fill out forms and pass them up to others, who throw them away. We *must* start this, Adolf. Soon." His eyes were fearsome with just a hint of desperation. His balled fist shook with pent-up rage.

Kluge sighed. He drummed his fingers delicately on his desktop as he looked over at the picture that hung from the mahogany-paneled wall of his large office. The eyes of Adolf Hitler—Kluge's name-sake—glared arrogantly from beneath a sheet of gleaming glass.

"How old are you, Nils?" Kluge asked gently.

Schatz stiffened. "I fail to see the relevance of that question."

"*I* think it may be relevant, my old friend."

"I am not old," Schatz insisted, seething. He stopped short of saying that neither was he Kluge's friend.

Kluge nodded thoughtfully. "I suppose it may be a matter of perspective. You appear to be in very good physical condition."

"I exercise daily."

"Nonetheless," Kluge pressed, "you must notice that there aren't many like you left. You are one of the few people left in the village from the old school."

"Again, I fail to see the relevance."

The leader of IV smiled wanly. "This proposal of yours is from another era," Kluge said, pressing his palm to the stack of papers. "IV simply does not have the physical resources it once had to mount a campaign this...ambitious. Perhaps your efforts

would be better spent here at the village. I understand
you have a garden.''

"Do not dare patronize me, Kluge," Schatz
growled. "I am not some mental defective."

In days gone by, his tone would have sent men
scurrying like frightened mice—desperate to apologize. Not anymore. Adolf Kluge merely looked at
Schatz with the patience the young reserved for old
men with foolish dreams of glory.

"I am not patronizing you, Herr Schatz," Kluge
replied slowly. "I am merely telling you the financial
realities of IV's current situation. You know of the
events surrounding the failure of PlattDeutsche?"

"I know that the company failed. While *you* were
in charge here," Schatz added icily.

Kluge almost laughed at him at that point.

Almost laughed! The impertinent toad had the
nerve to snicker. Nils Schatz resisted the urge to leap
across the desk and throttle the much younger man.

"Yes, I was the one who left Lothar Holz in
charge during the company's brush with the men
from Sinanju. Had I known the threat they posed, I
would have taken different measures. Or instructed
Holz to back away. Slowly."

"Instead you pressed ahead. Holz died along with
Dr. von Breslau. And the company failed as a result
of the lawsuits generated by the computer-to-brain
uplink system they had developed. All of this could
have been construed by some to stem from a lack of
leadership here at IV.''

"You made that clear at the time."

"With me, there are no secrets," he said. This time it was Schatz who resisted the urge to smile.

"That may be true," Kluge said, "but as a result of that misadventure, IV lost a very lucrative company. We still have other assets, obviously, but in the current market we need to take a step back and recognize our long-term fiduciary responsibilities. Take you, for instance. There are not many left of your generation, but there are many more only a decade or two younger than you. I need to think of their future well-being. It is not as if they can go out and find work elsewhere. IV is responsible for their retirement expenses. You need to understand, Nils, that these are not the old days."

Schatz's eyes were hooded. When he spoke, the words were lifeless.

"You are more concerned with walkers and bedpans than you are with fulfilling the mission of this village?" he asked flatly.

"I am sorry, Nils, but I see our mission from an entirely different perspective. If I am able to care for these people in their infirmity, then I see that as a fulfillment of our original charter. Of course, there are other concerns. But the events at PlattDeutsche America are only a few months old. I will address the interests of our founders as soon as IV is financially able."

That was it. The meeting was over.

Schatz stood. When he spoke, his tone was ice. Every word dripped menace.

"You may remove me from the rolls of those for whom you feel responsible to care."

His eyes chips of flinty rage, he wheeled around, heading for the door. He collected his metal-tipped walking stick from its resting spot against the heavy wooden frame.

"Nils, be reasonable," Kluge begged patiently. He stood, as well. "You *must* see this from my perspective. Your goals are too high. This plan of yours would never have worked."

It was too much to bear. Schatz spun back around, eyes mad. He aimed the blunt end of his cane at Kluge.

"Silence! You shame me! You shame *him!*" He stabbed his cane wildly toward the portrait on the wall. "You shame the people who built this haven! You are a disgrace, Adolf Kluge. To everything the movement represents. A disgrace and a coward."

The cane quivered in the air. It was not merely for effect. For a moment Kluge actually thought the old man might attack him.

Whatever thought Schatz might have had, passed quickly. The cane snapped down to the floor with an authoritative crack.

Spinning on his heel, Nils Schatz marched from the room, slamming the huge oaken door behind him. As the noise rumbled off through the old fortress, Kluge could hear the old man's cane tap-tap-tapping along the echoey stone floors of the cavernous corridor.

The sound died in the distance.

Alone in his office, Kluge sat back down, frowning deeply.

He drew the stack of papers detailing Schatz's proposal across his desk.

The words on the cover sheet were in German. Kluge was surprised at the difficult time he had reading his native tongue these days. Most of the business he conducted for the village was in English. He read the words again. Carefully.

"Der Geist der stets verneint."

"The spirit that never dies."

Kluge smiled wanly.

"My poor old Nils," he mused. "Pity you don't realize your day died more than half a century ago."

Gathering up the sheets of paper, Adolf Kluge dropped them in the trash barrel next to his tidy desk.

2

His name was Remo and he liked nuns.

It was a drastic change from the earliest opinion he could remember having. There was a time in his youth when he had hated nuns. More often than not, he had feared them.

But that was a long time ago. Back when Remo Williams was a ward at Saint Theresa's Orphanage in Newark, New Jersey, the nuns told him when to go to bed, when to get up, when to go to school and, most important of all, when to go to church. Hate and fear went hand-in-hand during those years.

Now, on this cool summer night, as he walked the darkened streets of Nashua, New Hampshire, Remo was surprised at how completely his attitude had changed. The respect he felt for the women who had raised him was not grudging but absolute. But even though Remo's opinion of these "brides of Christ" had evolved over the years, he knew with sickening certainty that there were some who did not share his enlightened attitude. He was after one in particular.

Curved street lamps gathered swarms of flitting flies and moths around their dull amber glow. What little weak light that managed to carry down to the sidewalk on which he strolled illuminated the funereal lines that traced Remo's cruel features. He was deep in thought.

Remo was a man of indeterminate age. Most who saw him placed him somewhere in his thirties. His short hair and deepset eyes were as dark as the night through which he passed like a vengeful shadow. His T-shirt and chinos were black.

Remo was here this night because of a simple news report. One like so many others that had interrupted regular television programs of late.

Back in the days after Saint Theresa's, when Remo had been a beat patrolman living in a dingy Newark walk-up, such break-ins by news anchors were rare. They heralded only the most dire tidings. Back then, when Walter Cronkite appeared, Mr. and Mrs. America sat up and took notice.

Over the years, as the uncommon of America's subculture slowly and insidiously became the norm, the anxiety traditionally brought on by a special news bulletin gradually washed away. Now, an entire generation was desensitized to the violence that spilled regularly from their TVs like coins from a one-arm bandit. When the anchorman appeared these days, America now hoped he wouldn't be on too long into "Friends" just before they hurried out to the fridge for a snack.

But this night, Remo had been paying attention. And when the blow-dried anchor spoke of what had happened across the border from where he lived in Massachusetts, something in his frigid soul cracked like ice settling on a pond.

The sound of sirens that had filled these same streets on television had echoed to silence up the Merrimack Valley by the time Remo had arrived in Nashua. He left his car on a residential side street in the south end of town.

Like metal to a magnet, Remo was drawn to the buzz of activity in the center of town.

He found the vans first. Call letters and painted logos identified them as members of the Boston media. Satellite dishes atop their roofs pointed south as the men and women farther ahead reported the gruesome details of the day's events back to their home stations.

The gaggle of reporters squeezed in around a small building that seemed out of place for such attention. The Nashua police station. To Remo, the press there represented an intrusion on the simpler world he had known as a child.

"...was once a small town has grown into the era of urban violence," a reporter with a serious voice was announcing into a mushroom-shaped microphone as Remo slipped past.

"...are telling me they can't remember the last time such a violent act was committed in Nashua, Peter," another was saying.

"Good eeee-vening!" screeched a third. "I'd like to give a big hello out there for all the kids in Sister

Mary Bernice's first-grade class at Nashua's St. Jude Elementary. Hi, kids! You're gonna be happy to know that you've got the day off tomorrow! Whoopee!''

The hapless reporter was a local weatherman who had been conscripted into fieldwork when no one else could be found to cover this particular story. Completely out of his element on television on an ordinary day, he was flapping his arms and yelling excitedly in the same squealing, girlish manner he always used on his bizarre weather forecasts. Unfortunately, the grating personality that had made him a local curiosity if not an institution for the last ten years was woefully misplaced today.

The camera feed to the New Hampshire network affiliate was rapidly shut down. A half-dozen representatives of the station quickly tackled the panicked-looking weatherman, wrestling the microphone from his frightened grip.

As the group rolled around in a frantic, grunting pile of arms and legs, Remo continued on.

He was careful not to stray into range of the many television cameras. A specter in black, he followed the deepest shadows to the rear of the police station.

There were no reporters here. Several members of the Nashua police department milled anxiously around a dozen or so parked police cruisers. Most of the men in blue were engaged in conversation with one another.

Although he passed within arm's length of two

police officers, neither man saw Remo. He slipped through the police lines and up to the rear brick wall of the building.

Fingers immediately sought the rough texture of the wall. The instant his sensitive pads brushed the surface, his shoes shot off the ground. A silent wraith, he stole up the side of the police station with impossible swiftness.

He was up and over the roof ledge seconds later. On his feet the instant he reached the surface, he moved in a swift glide over to the dented ventilator unit.

It was a curving tin device that jutted like a crooked finger from the pebbled roof surface.

There was a wire-mesh grate across the square opening that was meant to prevent birds and squirrels from entering the building below.

Hard fingers stabbed through the interwoven mesh. Remo peeled the covering back like the top of a tin of sardines. His face was harsh as he deposited the tight curl of wire grating to the cool roof surface.

A moment later, Remo had melted through the opening, vanishing from the roof. His roiling thoughts were filled with images of death.

LINUS PAGGET had started screaming for a lawyer the minute the tear gas canister crashed through the stained-glass window of the St. Jude convent. As the police flooded through the smoke-choked chapel—faces covered in masks more menacing than any Star

Wars costumer could have envisioned—Linus screamed that he had rights that must not be ignored. He uttered the words while cowering behind the base of the statue of the Virgin Mary, hands clasped in a mockery of supplication atop his greasy head.

Linus screamed himself hoarse as he was dragged down the rows of empty pews and out into the waiting paddy wagon. Even though his throat was raw, he had screamed as the big truck tore through the press lines to the police station.

But the screaming had paid off. It was now some three hours after the incident that had caught national attention and Linus Pagget had gotten what he wanted. His court-appointed lawyer had just left his cell.

His attorney was already formulating a strategy. There was no pleading innocent, as Linus had initially wanted. Dozens of nuns were witness to his depraved acts. And no American outside the White House would be believed when his word was placed against that of a line of wimple-wearing, rosary-clutching witnesses.

They were going with either an insanity or "drug rage" defense. There was also the possibility that his childhood doctor could be blamed for the anti-hyperactivity medication he had prescribed in Linus's youth, but that possibility—his lawyer had told him—was a long shot at best.

No matter what case they presented, Linus knew as he shifted on his uncomfortable cot that he would not receive the kind of justice that would have been dispensed years before. He had committed acts that would have granted him immortal infamy in any other day, so abhorrent were they. And for a moment now, he had been awarded the stature of ignominious celebrity. But by next week, the revulsion of the nation would fade. In a month? No one would remember his name.

It was only a matter of time before the world forgot all about him. And when they did, he would be paroled.

For now, Linus would have to sit in his cell.

He shifted again as he stared at the drab gray wall of the Nashua jail. The cot couldn't have been less comfortable. He jammed a balled fist several times into his cardboard-flat pillow in an attempt to fluff it.

With a grunt, he rolled over.

He was startled to find a face staring back into his. Linus jumped back with a start, banging his head on the painted cinder-block wall.

"Dammit!" he growled, slender fingers grabbing the injured spot at the back of his head. "Who the hell are you?" Linus demanded.

He failed to note that the cell door was wide open. Nor did he notice the lack of guards in the block.

Standing before Pagget, Remo didn't respond. His deep eyes—as cold and limitless as the farthest reaches of space—were locked on the weak brown eyes of Linus Pagget.

Remo had been struck by the ordinariness of the man lying on the plain jail cot the instant he stepped before the old-fashioned cell. Pagget could have been any thug summoned from central casting for any gritty reality TV show.

The man was in his late twenties. He had the emaciated mien of a full-time drug or alcohol abuser. Probably both. Bloodshot eyes darted with furtive suspicion around black-rimmed lids. His scraggly blond beard did not match the greasy hair atop his balding head.

Still on his cot, Linus struggled to a sitting position. His pale features pulled into an injured knot. The wiry stubble of his goatee jutted forward accusingly.

"I said who the hell are you?" he snapped.

Remo's hard face was a block of frozen obsidian. He straightened up, fixing Pagget with a look of pure malice.

"Death," he replied, voice soft.

And suddenly, Linus Pagget felt his entire world collapse into the boundless fury of the intruder's dark, accusing eyes.

Before the criminal could cry out for help, a thick-wristed hand shot forward. In a breathless whisper, night fell on Linus Pagget.

HE HAD NO WAY OF KNOWING how long he had been out.

When Linus awoke, he felt something hard against

the back of his head. For a minute, he thought he had dreamt the whole thing and that he was leaning against his cell wall. But when he opened his eyes, he found that he was no longer in his cell.

A chill night wind blew across his prone form. All around, crickets chirped.

Linus struggled to a sitting position.

Remo was a few feet away from him, perched atop a chunk of carved granite. He was staring off into the unseeable depths of the night. Somewhere far distant, an owl hooted.

There were other objects, like the one Remo sat on, lined up beyond him. Their shape was familiar to Linus.

Twisting sharply, Linus saw that he had been propped up against yet another of the familiar objects.

Headstones. The stranger from his cell had brought him to a cemetery.

Linus gulped. "What do you want from me?" he asked, hoarse voice tremulous.

Remo's answer was a puzzling non sequitur.

"I was sentenced to die once," Remo said. His gaze remained far off. As if by staring alone, he could peel back the years to view his younger self. "Just like you."

"Hey, I haven't even been tried yet," Linus insisted.

The evil smile that cracked the wistful veneer of Remo's face sent an icy frisson up the young man's spine. As quickly as the smile appeared, it scurried off, leaving in its wake the death's skull mask that was Remo's usual expression. Night shadows painted eerie streaks across the sunken patches of his face.

"I was framed for murder. They strapped me into an electric chair. Believe me, Linus, you don't know fear until you have that done to you."

Linus wanted to dispute that, but remained mute. He began listening for the sound of police sirens. *Hoping* their piercing cry would rise up from the deathly still night.

"I thought the world had ended when they pulled the switch. But it didn't. When I woke up, they'd given me a new face and a new life. I was supposed to rid the world of scum like you."

At this, Linus felt his head begin to swim. He pushed himself carefully to his feet. Eyes darted to his left. In the far-off distance, the wrought-iron cemetery gate jutted from the crooked earth. Linus inched toward it.

Remo continued to speak, seemingly unmindful of what was going on three yards to his left.

"You ever hear of CURE, Linus?" Remo asked.

The killer was shocked to be addressed. He sniffled at the cold. "No," he said. He had begun to shake in fear.

"I'm not surprised. Only a handful of people have. They were the group that was supposed to clean up America. Work outside the Constitution in order to preserve it. They drafted me. And I've been a loyal foot soldier for them, more or less, for a long time now. But I've failed, Linus. You want to know how I *know* I've failed?''

When he turned his attention on Pagget, the scrawny young man froze like a deer caught in headlights. He had been attempting to tiptoe away through the damp night grass.

Linus wheeled, leaning casually against the nearest moss-covered headstone.

"No," he announced. "Uh, no. Why?"

"Because in America now, a piece of slime can break into a convent wielding a gun, Linus. He can steal the prescription drugs from convalescing nuns and hold a one-man party for twelve hours straight while police negotiators try to talk him out. He can rape a nun, Linus. He can get a butcher knife from the convent kitchen and hold it to her throat and force himself on her. Then he can carve up her body like a Halloween pumpkin. In the America I was supposed to be preserving, that sort of thing wouldn't happen.''

By this time, Linus could not stop his shaking legs.

His ears strained for police sirens.

Where were they? Didn't they miss him by now? They *had* to be looking for him.

"And no one cares." Remo's voice was somewhere else. Lost in the hazy images of days long past. "You know what, Linus? I wish *I* didn't care. But I *do*. And even though I've tried, I don't know what to do to *stop* caring.''

Still sitting atop his stone perch, Remo's head drooped, as if pressed down by both great sadness and awesome responsibility.

That single moment of intense introspection by his captor was the break Linus Pagget had been waiting for.

He turned and ran. Ran for all he was worth.

His lungs burned. His raw throat bled.

He ran, and ran, and ran.

The cemetery gate rose up before him. He grabbed the cold iron with shaking hands. As he shoved it open, slipping on the wet grass, a face appeared on the other side.

Linus screamed.

"I can only do what I know is right, Linus," Remo said as he reached through the gates and grabbed the whimpering man by the throat. "But between you and me, I don't think it makes a difference anymore."

"You don't have to do anything!" Linus pleaded.

Remo said not a word. Although it would bring him no satisfaction, the decision had already been made.

Two hands reached out for the sides of Linus's head.

The pain was incredible. Brilliant. Blinding. It was a more excruciatingly intense crystallization of sheer agony than Linus Pagget could ever have imagined in his twenty-seven long, but useless years of life. And then it was over.

The official report would eventually say that Linus Pagget had been spirited from the Nashua Police Station by forces unknown. Whoever had liberated him from his cell possessed equipment that was somehow able to exert hydraulic force of incredible proportions. The bones of his skull had literally been fused into a single, tight mass no larger than a baseball. Somewhere in that tight ball of pulverized calcium phosphate, the evil brain of the late Linus Pagget had been compressed into a gray knot the size of a Ping-Pong ball.

But even though a machine of incredible force had to have been used to do such a deed, there were no signs of such a killing device, nor of the tracks it would have left near the spot where Linus's body had been found.

There were many who believed his death was an act of God. But those who had suffered most at his hands, the nuns of St. Jude, did not speculate on the thing that might have brought the man who had terrorized them to his violent end. They merely prayed for Linus Pagget's eternal soul.

AFTER HE WAS DONE, Remo let the lifeless body drop to the cold earth.

He felt nothing about what he had just done. In fact, he felt nothing at all. About anything. And the emptiness within him was almost unbearable.

As he looked down at the body, he shook his head sadly.

"And another hundred will flood in to take your place," he said, hollow of voice.

Remo turned from the twisted remains of Linus Pagget. He left the cemetery, intense desolation slowly flooding the gutted pit that was his very being.

3

The Banque de Richelieu was tucked away between a pair of old brick buildings on a small street between the Boulevard du Montparnasse and the Avenue du Maine.

The bank was just shy of one hundred years old, and most of its architecture and its interior reflected its long history. Beyond the foyer of gleaming marble and polished wood, however, invisible to the eye of the average customer, the old bank had been forced to make some concessions to the modern era.

There were now motion-sensitive beams that activated a silent alarm. Bulletproof glass had replaced the steel bars at the tellers' cages. Paint bombs set to explode if a single franc was touched improperly were set in bags and vaults and at each teller's drawer.

The main vault of the Banque de Richelieu was a fortress. The walls were three feet of reinforced steel encased in a tomb of poured concrete. It would have taken two hours of sustained cannon fire directed against a single spot in a side wall of the vault to even crack the facade.

Today the thickness of the vault didn't matter. Today the massive door was wide open.

Ordinarily the whirring, remorseless eyes of surveillance cameras scanned the interior of the bank. This afternoon they had been disabled. Every precaution had been taken to ensure that there would be no evidence of what would transpire here today.

Monsieur d'Ailerons, the manager of the Banque de Richelieu for the past thirty years, had seen the last of his employees through the doors at a little after five that afternoon. When he was alone, clucking and fretting, he had moved nervously about the building, disabling security systems with a quick professionalism.

He had finished early.

Taking a seat in a hard-backed chair near the door, Monsieur d'Ailerons waited. Legs crossed sharply, back straight, eyes forward, d'Ailerons was one of those rare people who appeared to be standing at attention even when sitting down.

He was panting lightly, though not from his exertions. Nerves made his heart and lungs thunder in his chest.

It didn't take long before he started to wish he had gone through his routine more slowly. He had nothing more to do now but sit. And wait.

As he studied the front door, Monsieur d'Ailerons drew a precisely folded silk handkerchief from the interior pocket of his impeccably tailored suit bought in a small medium-priced shop on the Rue de la Verriere. Dabbing with slender fingers, he mopped away the sheen of nervous sweat that had formed on his pale, broad forehead.

The cloth came back drenched. He hadn't realized he was perspiring so much. With a crisp snap of his wrist he replaced the handkerchief in his suit pocket.

He checked his Swiss watch.

It was time—6:00 p.m. sharp.

Unusual. They were always on time. Perhaps something had happened to them.

Pushing his small bifocals back up his long nose, Monsieur d'Ailerons allowed himself the hope that they wouldn't arrive after all.

His hopes were dashed two seconds later when there came a sharp rap of knuckles on the glass at the front door. It was not yet 6:01 p.m. They were still on time.

A fresh stream of sweat began trickling from beneath his arms. Moving swiftly on short legs, he went to answer the door.

In the hallway between the two sets of double doors, the banker drew a key from the pocket of his trousers. Reaching up, he quickly unlocked the dead bolt at the top of the door frame. Squatting, he flicked open the hand lock at the door's base.

He opened the door, stepping back obsequiously. Nils Schatz and his ragged entourage bustled into the ornate entryway of the Banque de Richelieu. The IV renegade didn't even look at the Frenchman as his group moved into the depths of the bank.

Rapidly d'Ailerons relocked the doors. He hurried back inside the bank. As expected, the men were waiting for him in his office.

It was the same procedure they had gone through every time during the past several months of secret meetings. Tonight it would be different, however. Monsieur d'Ailerons need only work up the courage to make it so.

"Hurry up, d'Ailerons," Nils Schatz demanded impatiently.

The German was standing in front of d'Ailerons's spotless desk. He held his walking stick in one hand and was tapping it relentlessly on the faded carpeting.

Schatz's men stood behind him. There were six of them altogether. Four were of Schatz's generation—though like their leader they were in remarkable physical condition. The other pair was much younger. Though concealed mostly by black winter hats, the heads of these two were shaved and spotted with tattoos.

It had been d'Ailerons who had suggested to Schatz that the young men wear some sort of hats when accompanying the old German on these trips to the bank. After all, they hardly looked like ordinary Banque de Richelieu patrons. Surprisingly Schatz had agreed.

Ordinarily d'Ailerons would peer disapprovingly down his long nose at such a lowly twosome. But under the circumstances he wouldn't dare. Not considering the company they kept.

The banker crossed behind his desk and carefully unlocked the long top drawer. He removed a few slips of paper tucked deep in the back and passed them across the desk to Schatz.

Schatz examined the slips of paper. Bank notes. As good as cash. Withdrawn from several special accounts. This was the way the transactions had been conducted all along. Schatz was holding several hundred thousand dollars in his hands. It was the most he had ever gotten at one time.

Monsieur d'Ailerons was blinking and swallowing like mad. He wanted to speak—knew he *should* speak—but no words would come. He twitched and perspired, struggling with how he should broach the subject.

He finally gave up the thought that he would mention the irregularities to Schatz. Let the others find them. It would be their problem, not his.

No, it *would* be his. That was what had been troubling him since he found out. He *must* find the courage to speak. Must tell what he—

"You are more fidgety than usual," Schatz said abruptly.

The banker jumped in his seat, shaken from his trance.

When he looked over, he saw that Schatz was peering up at him. The German didn't lift his head from the handful of checks, but had merely rolled his eyes up to the tops of their sockets. His eyes, hooded beneath his brow, lent his face a demonic cast.

The banker glanced at the others. They were all staring at him, expecting him to speak, but he wasn't sure he wanted to any longer.

He swallowed again, hard.

"It is just—" D'Ailerons hesitated, fearful of what he was about to say. He closed his eyes. Perhaps it would be easier if he didn't have to look at Nils Schatz. "Does Mr. Kluge know of all this?" he blurted.

His question was met with silence. After what seemed like an eternity of utter quiet, Monsieur d'Ailerons opened his eyes. Nils Schatz was staring at him with those icy, washed-out blue eyes.

"What do you mean?" the German asked flatly.

D'Ailerons swallowed again. His throat had turned to dust.

"With respect, Herr Schatz, you informed me when we began these transactions many months ago that this operation had the blessing of Herr Kluge," the banker said.

"And?"

"I have learned of some irregularities in the accounting methods of my subordinates. These were per your specific instructions, I am told."

"And?" Schatz repeated coldly.

"The way it has been done lends one the impression of someone attempting to cover his tracks," d'Ailerons suggested. "There has been much money taken from IV accounts but in a most secretive manner. It is almost as if you are...*embezzling* the funds, Herr Schatz.''

Schatz finally lifted his head completely. Frigid eyes stared fully at Monsieur d'Ailerons.

''That is a very interesting conjecture,'' Schatz said thoughtfully. ''Do you realize, d'Ailerons, that in my younger days I might have killed you with my own hands for even suggesting that I was a thief?'' Some might have treated the words as a joke. Not Nils Schatz. Schatz never joked. He stared, unsmiling, at the banker.

D'Ailerons shrugged helplessly. ''I did not mean to insult, surely. If you give your word that Herr Kluge knows of this, then I consider the matter settled.'' He nodded emphatically. He suddenly noticed that his desk drawer was still open. He made a great show of closing and locking it once more.

''I have already told you Herr Kluge approved of the appropriation of funds,'' Schatz said slowly.

''Indeed,'' d'Ailerons said with a carefree motion of one shaking hand. ''Absolutely. That is that.'' He clapped his hands together to brush off the last remnants of some imaginary dust.

''Who have you mentioned this to?'' Schatz pressed.

''Pardon me?''

''This—'' Schatz waved his cane in the air ''—this notion of yours?''

D'Ailerons was suddenly deeply offended.

"No one, sir, certainly. It was only a thought. I am certain Herr Kluge has his reasons for conducting business in this manner. Remember, the Banque de Richelieu has had a history with IV going back to the war."

"I am aware of your fine history, Frenchman," Schatz offered contemptuously.

"Yes." The banker fussed with his desktop, not making eye contact with any of the men in the room.

D'Ailerons was uncomfortable now for an altogether other reason. He knew of the bank's shaky history prior to World War II and of its sudden revival immediately after the war. Back then, through circuitous means, IV had bailed the bank out of its immediate financial difficulties. In the time since, the Banque de Richelieu had been more indebted than its owners would have liked to the secret organization.

"I will let you in on a little secret, d'Ailerons," Nils Schatz whispered. He leaned over the desk. His cane—clenched in his fist—rested parallel to the desk surface. "Your assumptions are correct. The money you have given me these many months? All stolen from the coffers of IV."

D'Ailerons was taken aback by Schatz's candor. He began fussing at his desk more furiously. He straightened his blotter, pen and pencil holder, and a small bronze barometer that had been a gift from his sister.

"I am certain you have your reasons." The banker

nodded sharply. The pounding of his heart made his ears ring.

He had suspected Schatz was stealing. Now, confronted with an admission of guilt, he wished more than anything he had kept his suspicions to himself.

"Oh, I have a reason," Schatz said, voice still low.

"Of course," d'Ailerons agreed. He studied the corners of his blotter.

"Look at me!" Schatz screamed, his voice suddenly loud and shrill in the tiny office. Even his own men were startled by the sudden jarring change.

D'Ailerons's head snapped up as if shocked by electricity. Schatz leaned back and aimed the bronze end of his walking stick accusingly at d'Ailerons.

"I mean to finish what was started more than fifty years ago by a visionary the world has chosen to blindly vilify. Kluge does not appreciate the importance of the goal. *We* do," he said, indicating with a swirl of his cane the other men in the room. "You have given us the funds we need to see this vision to fruition."

Schatz still clenched the bank notes in his other hand. He held them aloft. One of the older men dutifully collected them and tucked them away in the pocket of his black suit jacket.

D'Ailerons didn't know how to respond. In the next moment it didn't matter.

"I suppose I should thank you for your generous help these many months," Schatz said with an indifferent shrug. "I think, however, that I will not."

The cane was up in an instant, held firmly in the German's hands. Using a batter's grip, he swung the metal tip at the man behind the desk. It met with the side of Monsieur d'Ailerons's head with a resounding crack.

The banker's bifocals were thrown from the tip of his nose. They clattered across the floor.

Schatz brought the cane back and swung.

Another crack. This shattered the bone into the brain and brought blood to the surface. D'Ailerons fell forward.

Again.

Swing and hit.

D'Ailerons was sprawled across his desk by now. Blood seeped out, staining his blotter.

Feverishly, wildly, Schatz pounded him again and again. His eyes sparked with an internal rage as he brought the cane repeatedly down atop the battered head of the banker, dead now for minutes.

Blood spattered across Schatz's clothes and around the walls of the office. His men backed away at first, avoiding the spray. Eventually they stepped in, pulling Schatz away from the mangled corpse.

He allowed himself to be restrained.

The end of the cane was covered with blood and gore. D'Ailerons's face was an unrecognizable pulp.

Panting, catching his breath, Schatz went around the desk. He used the tail of the banker's jacket to clean the reddish slush from his walking stick. Once it was clean, he pulled his handkerchief from his pocket.

"The Frenchman always shuts off all of the alarms and cameras. Perhaps now we should liberate what we can from the vault?" He wiped at the blood on his face with his handkerchief. "I believe, after all, that this may be our last chance for a withdrawal."

"Go," one of the older men ordered. The two young men with the shaved heads left as directed. One of the older men went along, as well, in order to keep an eye on them.

As the rest of them were leaving the office, Schatz cast a last glance at the late Monsieur d'Ailerons. He tipped his head pensively.

"I have always found the company of the French to be invigorating," he said without malice or humor. He glanced at his men. "For their sakes let us hope they feel the same."

Still breathing heavily, Schatz left the office.

The lifeblood of Monsieur d'Ailerons ran in drizzly red rivulets from the gleaming desk surface.

4

Before the morning sun had even peeked over the easternmost horizon of the continental United States, Harold W. Smith was snapping off his alarm clock. As usual, he had shut off the alarm a minute before it was due to sound.

Sitting up on the edge of the bed, Smith slipped his feet into his ratty slippers. Behind him his wife continued to snore lazily beneath the covers. He left her there in the dark, oblivious to her husband's movements.

While his wife and his nation slept on, Smith made his careful way across the cold floor to the bathroom.

As a boy there was an expression common to his native Vermont. "Up with the sun," people used to say. Even as a child Smith had always considered to be slugabeds those whose day began only with the inevitable arrival of a star.

Smith was always up before the sun. After all, there was always much to be done.

This had been Smith's guiding principle his entire life. There was always much to be done. And, he noted ruefully, more and more these days there seemed less time in which to do it.

He shut the creaking bathroom door behind him. Only then did he turn on the light.

For a time a few years before, he had thought that the dull fluorescent glow of the light was casting unflattering shadows across his gray features. It was giving him the appearance of an old man. Eventually he had realized that the light was only reflecting reality. Smith *was* old.

Somehow age had taken firm hold of Dr. Harold W. Smith and—like a dog with a tattered rag—refused to let go.

He felt old now as he took his antiquated straight razor from the medicine cabinet.

Smith wasn't a man given to extravagances of any kind. He considered shaving cream to be just such an unnecessary expense. First lathering up his face with soap, he went to work with the sharp edge of the razor.

The cost of heating the water was avoided simply enough. Harold Smith set the tap on Cold.

Miraculously Smith somehow managed to get through the same ritual every morning without slicing in his gaunt, gray flesh. It required a knack that few men had. Nor were there many men who would want to develop this skill.

He allowed himself tepid water in the shower. Smith had had difficulties with his pacemaker-equipped heart in recent years and didn't wish to jar his system any more than was absolutely necessary. Ice water from the showerhead—no matter how bracing he had claimed it to be in youth—could easily give him a heart attack at his age.

His morning bathroom ritual over, Smith reentered the bedroom.

As always he had laid his clothes out the night before. It was easy enough getting dressed in the dark.

His wife continued to snore softly from beneath the massive pile of bedcovers. He watched her sleep as he drew on his gray three-piece suit.

How many mornings have I left her like this? Smith wondered.

He knew how many years it had been. Fifty.

Fifty years of marriage. Quite an accomplishment in this day and age.

They had married young. After Smith had returned from the war.

Maude Smith had stuck by him during those early days when the war's Office of Strategic Services was being transformed into the peacetime CIA. She had been a dutiful wife up to and beyond the time of Smith's "retirement." When he had settled in as director of Folcroft Sanitarium, a private health facility here in Rye, New York, Maude Smith had gone with him. Just as any good wife would.

What Maude never knew—could never know— was that Harold Smith hadn't retired from the intelligence service.

His appointment as head of Folcroft had been a cover. The sleepy sanitarium on the shores of Long Island Sound was in reality the headquarters of the supersecret government organization CURE. Smith had been its one and only director for more than thirty-four years.

As the incorruptible head of CURE, Smith directed vast amounts of information to covertly aid law-enforcement agencies in their fight against crime. Set up as an organization whose mandate was to rescue a country so endangered that the Constitution had become an impediment, CURE used extralegal means to achieve its ends.

If his quietly sleeping wife only knew the power wielded by the nondescript gray man who had shared her bed for the past five decades, she would have been shocked. And Maude Smith would have been even more stunned to learn that her seemingly un-assuming Harold would have liked nothing more than to level the most fearsome power at his disposal directly at the woman whom Mrs. Smith had considered to be her best friend for the past fifteen years.

The lump beneath the mound of blankets stirred. The snoring grunted to a stop.

"Are you going to work, Harold?" Her voice was hoarse in the early-morning hours.

"Yes, dear."

"Don't forget our flight."

"I won't, Maude."

Maude Smith was already rolling over. Already going back to sleep. The snoring resumed.

Smith left her in the predawn darkness. Let her enjoy the rest he couldn't. He made his quiet way downstairs.

Two minutes later, Smith was backing his rusting station wagon out of his driveway.

Four houses down he passed the sleeping home of Gertrude Higgins, a matronly widow who had made it her business to regularly poke her nose into the affairs of everyone else in the neighborhood.

Gert Higgins was the person against whom Smith had—however fleetingly—contemplated employing the most lethal power in CURE's arsenal.

Of course, it had only been a flight of fancy. Brought on by...what?

Not anger. There was little that could get Smith truly angry these days. He had seen so much that inspired anger in his long life that he had become desensitized to much of it.

What Smith felt was just a hair over the other side of perturbed. This peevishness had surfaced the day Maude Smith had presented him with the plane tickets.

It was for their fiftieth wedding anniversary, she had said. He worked so hard. Other people had vacations. They had never gone anywhere together.

The list was well-rehearsed. It was unlike Maude Smith to do anything as spontaneous as purchasing airline tickets to Europe. Even to celebrate fifty years of marriage.

It hadn't taken Smith long to learn that it was Gert Higgins who had pushed Maude along. She was the one who had encouraged Maude to buy the tickets without "bothering poor, overworked Harold."

Of course, his first impulse was to return the tickets.

Maude had prepaid for them.

He was going to cash them in just the same. He had even gone so far as to contact the airline from his computer at Folcroft. But at the last minute he hesitated.

Fifty years.

There was a small part of Smith that felt a pang of guilt for the many years of deceit. For the years of placing his own life in danger without concern for his family. For years of being a bad husband.

In the end Smith had kept the tickets.

His wife had been overjoyed. Her reaction had produced even more guilt. The feeling had lasted several weeks.

Later that afternoon Harold and Maude Smith were scheduled to leave for Europe together. A couple in the twilight of their years enjoying a second honeymoon together. And Harold W. Smith had every intention of hating every minute of his time away.

For now, Smith had work to do. As the earliest streaks of dawn painted the sky, Harold Smith crawled through the silent streets of Rye to Folcroft.

5

When Claude Civray had first come to work at the old *deminage* depot in the town of Guise one hundred miles northeast of Paris, he was more than just a little ill at ease. After all, he knew the history of the depository for old mines.

The depot had originally been constructed on the banks of the Oise River. A foolish decision, it was later learned, as no one had taken into account the fact that water had a messy tendency to rust metal. If such a consideration had been entertained, the location would certainly have been changed because no one at the Guise facility wanted the metal casings of the old mines to deteriorate.

It had.

The French government only discovered the shoddiness of its planning when the original facility had blown itself to kingdom come after a particularly soggy spring.

Afterward the Guise depot had been moved far away from the river. It was an easy move. After the explosion, what was left of the base fit into the back of an old dairy farmer's truck.

The accident had occurred back in 1951. The French government was never certain what had caused the base to go up the way it had. It could have been a sudden jostling of stored materials. A guard might have tripped and fell.

Eventually the blame was placed on a single chain-smoking watchman and a carelessly discarded cigarette. However, this was mere speculation. The real truth of what had happened would never be learned. Fiery death had erased all traces.

Claude wasn't sure what had caused the accident, either. But one thing was certain. Given the possibility of even a kernel of truth to the rumor, Claude Civray never, *ever* smoked at work.

He toured the facility now, cigarettes tucked away inside his pocket, careful of where he stepped. Though it was night, there were small spotlights positioned at strategic points around the various yards and buildings.

Claude found that the lights helped very little. Several had been angled, it seemed, to blind a casual stroller. One misstep and it could be 1951 all over again.

Worse than 1951. There were many more bombs now.

They were everywhere. Even in the shadows cast by the uncertain spotlights, Claude could make out the rusted casings piled high in the open yards. It wouldn't take much to set them off.

France had had the unlucky fate of being a focal

point of the two major global conflicts of the modern era. For the French people, even after the armies had left, the wars were not over. By some estimates more than twelve million unexploded shells from World War I alone lay hidden in the fields and forests of Verdun.

The closer an area was to conflict, the more densely packed were the bombs that were left behind. And while Guise was certainly not Verdun, it had still seen its share of military action.

More than its share, if anyone had bothered to ask Claude Civray.

Claude was acutely aware that there were dozens of deaths or injuries every year directly attributed to shells that turned up in unexpected places. French farmers tilling their fields seemed to suffer casualties most frequently.

What was unearthed intact was brought here, to the depot at Guise and others like it. All around the acres of grounds that comprised the storage facility were piles upon piles of unexploded military ordnance.

The French government did try to safely detonate as many of the explosives as they could, but there were simply too many. All would be gotten to someday. In the meantime, they were stored away for that eventuality.

It was Claude's job to watch the bombs rust. And to hope that they didn't blow up in his face.

Claude made his way around the far end of the

depot. Back here were huge aerial bombs—five feet tall and so thick a man's arms could stretch around the corroded casing and still not meet on the other side. They sat upright on their fins—stranded birds with clipped wings.

Some of the ordnance had been at the depot so long that the earth was beginning to reclaim them. Mud had collected up around the bottommost shells. High weeds grew up around the stacks, partially obscuring them.

Civray rounded a cluster of rotting pallets laden with tons of unexploded 170 mm shells. This spot always made his stomach tingle. It was here that he was at the farthest point of his nightly circuit. He always imagined that this would be the place he would be when the depot went up in flames.

Holding his breath as he did every night, Civray quickened his pace. He stepped around the many stacks of huge shells and back out onto the road used by the *démineurs'* trucks. He moved swiftly away from the long 170 mm casings.

Only after he was a few yards distant did he release his breath. He had made it.

Claude wouldn't have to tour the yard for another two hours. Moving more briskly now, he made his way back to the main clapboard building near the barbed-wire-festooned gate of the large facility.

When Claude had hiked the quarter mile back to the front of the yard he was surprised to find the main gates open.

There were two large halogen lamps positioned on curving poles on either side of the gate. Insects fluttered crazily in the light.

Claude could make out a line of trucks sitting idle along the desolate dirt road leading into the depot.

This was more than just a little unusual. The *démineurs* never worked at night. It was dangerous enough to stumble around fields in broad daylight looking for eighty-year-old shells. To do so at night would be suicide.

It couldn't be a delivery.

So what was going on, then?

Maurice St. Jean, the second man on duty that night, had been working alone in the main office when Claude left on his rounds. Now there seemed to be several figures moving in the windows of the wooden building. Something was wrong.

Thoughts of 1951 immediately sprang up in Claude's mind.

Heart fluttering, he hurried over to the office.

CLAUDE FOUND several men inside. None was a *démineur*. St. Jean was nowhere to be seen. As one, the men inside turned to the door when Claude entered.

"What is wrong?" he demanded anxiously.

"You are Claude Civray?" one of the men asked.

The speaker was old. Perhaps seventy, perhaps older. Though his words were French, they were spoken clumsily. He was clearly a foreigner.

Claude became immediately suspicious. And haughty.

"This is a restricted facility," he said, pulling himself up proudly. "What is the meaning of this invasion?"

The foreigner carried a walking stick. He tapped it on the wooden floor.

"Curious choice of words," he said, casting a glance at the others in his party.

Some of the men laughed. The younger ones in particular. They guffawed loudly, slapping one another on their backs at the wit of the old man.

One man pulled off his winter hat. His head was shaved bald. Tattoos covered his bare scalp. Though the others didn't remove their hats, it was apparent from what could be glimpsed of their scalps that they were adorned like the first.

Civray had seen their kind before. Skinheads. Neo-Nazis. Though the young men laughed loudly and nervously, the leader of the group didn't even crack a smile.

The old man used his cane to point at Civray.

"Put him with the other one."

The skinheads pounced. Claude found himself being grabbed by the arms, by the legs. He was half dragged, half carried out the door and into the yard.

"Unhand me!" Civray cried, twisting in their hard grips. His pleas fell on deaf ears.

They carried the struggling guard back several

yards to an isolated spot off to the right near the side hurricane fencing.

Claude saw Maurice immediately. When he did, he stopped fighting. The other guard had been beaten to insensibility and tied to a wooden pallet beside a pyramid stack of 75 mm shells. For whatever reason Maurice must have foolishly opened the gate for these men. Civray would never find out why.

The skinheads didn't pause to give Claude the same treatment they had given his compatriot. They forced him down atop a neighboring pallet. They lashed him quickly and efficiently to the wood.

Even before he was tied down, the trucks began rolling through the gates.

There had been only the two of them assigned to guard the facility. Maurice must have told them that. With Claude out of the way, the intruders would meet no opposition.

An army of men swarmed from the backs of the trucks. They went to work immediately, gingerly collecting rusted shell casings and hauling them off as speedily as possible into the rear of the awaiting vehicles.

They worked for hours, carrying and loading. At one point one of the men working the truck nearest Claude dropped a case of "racket" German grenades. Claude was certain that it would go off.

It was a miracle that it didn't.

"Dummkopf!"

The skinhead was berated for his carelessness by

one of the supervisors of the operation. The grenades were carefully collected and the box was placed in the rear of the truck.

Eventually the trucks were packed to the point where they could hold no more. Only then did they begin turning slowly around. They headed in a long, careful convoy back out the gates of the Guise facility.

Claude couldn't see his watch, but he felt that it had to be somewhere near 3:00 a.m. The intruders had toiled for nearly four hours.

The last truck stopped in the inverted-V-shaped clearing made by the stacks of bombs that had been left near Claude and the still-unconscious Maurice.

The elderly man who had spoken to him in the main guard house stepped down from the passenger's side of the truck.

Several of the skinheads came running in from a point somewhere farther up the convoy. They each carried a large red metal can. The men shouted encouragement to one another in a language Claude was now certain was German.

Claude could hear liquid sloshing within the cans.

The young men began dumping the contents of the containers in a trail from the gate up to the bombs nearest Claude.

While the young ones worked, the old man strolled over to view Civray, trussed up like a lamb for slaughter. He tsked when he glanced at the stack of 75 mm shells.

"Very dangerous," he confided to Civray, tapping the column of bombs with his cane. It made a dull rapping noise. The bombs sounded as solid as an anvil.

Claude cringed, waiting for the shells to explode. They remained blessedly intact.

"I thank you for holding these for us. They are back in the hands of their rightful owners now."

One of the skinheads had come over next to the old man. He stood there patiently.

The wind suddenly shifted, bringing the sharp scent of gasoline to Claude Civray's sensitive nose. The rest of the men hurried away, out of sight.

In that moment Claude understood what these men had in mind for him. He shook his head dully.

"No," he begged. The word was a croak.

The old man ignored him.

"Soak them," he said to the skinhead. He turned and walked briskly back to the truck.

Grinning, the young man upended his container over the bodies of Claude Civray and Maurice St. Jean.

The gasoline poured out clear in the dull lamplight. The acrid smell cut into Civray's flaring nostrils.

As the gas soaked into his clothes and mottled his hair, the truck carrying the old man drove calmly away. The man did not even cast a glance in Claude's direction.

When the man had finished dousing him with gasoline, he laughed uproariously at the two helpless Frenchmen. Dropping the can onto Claude's legs, he ran from sight.

Maurice began to stir groggily. Claude prayed that his friend wouldn't awaken.

The minutes dragged on.

It seemed to take forever.

After a time Claude allowed the hope that the men had reconsidered.

As the night insects chirped in the grassland around the facility, Claude Civray heard something approaching. It was a soft whooshing noise. Like the sound of a distantly racing train or wind across an open field.

The wall of flame slipped into sight up the dirt path. It glowed malevolently, illuminating the sides of the guardshack in weird patterns, stabbing streaks of yellowy-orange into the black French sky.

It came slowly. Looping in from the main gate, it almost seemed as if it might pass him by. But like a dog on a scent the flames caught the path of gasoline poured in to the spot where the two guards lay.

Much faster now, the strip of fire raced toward Civray.

Bracing for the flames, Civray didn't have time to be surprised that he felt nothing at all.

He didn't feel the fire because before the flames had reached him they had already found an opening in one of the stacks of shells.

As the first shell detonated, the rest in the stack of

75 mm shells exploded, as well. The ground rocked as the huge pallets with their tons of ordnance blew apart in a massive eruption of fire and twisted metal.

In less than a single heartbeat, Claude Civray was shredded into hamburger. Torn to pieces by bombs that had been dropped on his country at a time when his grandfather had been a young man.

OUTSIDE THE DEPOT, Nils Schatz watched the initial eruption with satisfaction.

The other trucks were gone. His was all that was left.

The first explosions set off a chain reaction around the base. The blasts spread in violent white pockets across the length of the depot. Finally, in a concussive burst heard for miles around, the entire base exploded. In the sleepy French countryside it was as if the end of the world had come.

Schatz's truck swayed ever so slightly on its shocks.

Unmindful of the bombs in the rear of his own vehicle and the danger they posed, Nils Schatz watched the entire depot erupt into a single ball of glorious fiery orange.

The brilliant light danced across his weary eyes, and for a blessed, happy instant the old Nazi was certain he could see an army of jackbooted soldiers marching from out the flames of history.

For the first time in more than fifty years, Nils

Schatz smiled. Sitting back in his seat, he tapped his cane on the dashboard.

The truck drove off into the night.

THE SAME DRILL WAS completed simultaneously and without incident at three separate *deminage* facilities ranged around northeast France that night.

Of the many trucks laden with stolen ordnance, only one ran into trouble.

In the back of a truck parked the next day at an intersection in the busiest city in the country, a single bomb was accidentally dislodged from a stack. The resulting explosion took out half of the nearest building and most of the street.

Thirty-seven people were reported immediate casualties of the incident in Paris. Another seventy were severely wounded.

A sign had been blown from the column beside the gate of the building that had borne the brunt of the attack. It read simply United States Embassy.

"Morning, Smitty," Remo's voice said sullenly though I'd chucked the receiver left.

Smith arrived at Folcroft Sanitarium just before dawn and had been working at his computer for the better part of three hours. He wanted to get as much work done as possible before leaving for Europe. There would not be much of an opportunity to get anything accomplished with his wife around twenty-four hours a day.

Just the same, Smith planned to bring his laptop computer along on their trip.

His wife had told him the previous night that she would call him at noon to remind him of his flight. Mrs. Smith was well aware of her husband's ability to get lost for hours at a time in his work.

When the phone rang, he assumed it to be her. He glanced at the time display in the corner of the computer screen buried beneath the onyx surface of his high-tech desk. It was still midmorning. His wife wouldn't be calling for another three hours.

The call was on Remo's special line.

"Yes," Smith said, picking up the blue contact phone.

"Morning, Smitty," Remo's voice said. "Just thought I'd check in before you left."

"I take it by this morning's news reports that you had a busy night?" Smith asked dryly.

He had programmed his computers to pull up any suspicious deaths that might be attributable to Remo—who was CURE's special enforcement arm— or to Remo's mentor, Chiun, the Reigning Master of Sinanju. The body of Linus Pagget—with its knot of compressed skull—bore the unmistakable stamp of the ancient martial art of Sinanju.

"I told you I was antsy," Remo said.

"That was not a CURE assignment," Smith told him.

"It should have been."

"Nonetheless, I would appreciate it if you checked with me before engaging in these sorts of—" Smith searched for a word that would be appropriate when describing the gruesome condition in which the Nashua police had found Pagget's body "—*activities*," he finished.

"Next time. I promise. So, have you got anything else for me before you take off?"

"Nothing pressing," Smith admitted. "You and Master Chiun may enjoy the time off while I am away."

"You know I'd prefer to keep busy. C'mon, Smitty, there must be something."

Smith was surprised at Remo's eagerness to work.

It was not long before that he had been pushing for a vacation.

"Remo, if I had an assignment, I would use you. There is simply nothing large enough to warrant putting you into the field at the present time."

"I'm not a tractor, Smitty." His tone bordered on disgust.

Smith raised a thin eyebrow. "Is there something more to this than a simple desire to keep busy?"

Remo sighed. "You should be a shrink," he said glumly.

"I actually do hold a doctorate in clinical psychology," Smith noted.

"Yeah, right," Remo said absently. "It's just that there's always something more to do. One more creep determined to wreck the world for everybody else. Pagget left that nun barely breathing."

"She died this morning," Smith said tightly.

"I heard," Remo replied. His voice was laced with bitterness. "A fat lot of good I did her. I'm great at retribution, Smitty. What I stink at is getting there in the nick of time."

"Perhaps I am not the best person with whom to discuss this," Smith said, clearly uncomfortable. "Have you spoken to Chiun?"

"He thinks it's the same old story. Every year I get the blahs about the business. But it really isn't the same this time. I can't explain it. It's as if I know there's a lot of stuff that needs to be done, but I finally realize that I can't do it all. I mean *really* realize it.'' Remo exhaled loudly. "I don't know. Maybe it's time I finally packed it in.''

Smith had only been half listening while Remo spoke. Like Chiun, the CURE director had grown used to Remo's frequent bouts of melancholia. But when he raised the desire to abandon the dangerous life he was in, Smith took notice.

The CURE director frowned. "Remo, someone told you something a long time ago. He used to say the same thing to me. 'One man can make a difference.'''

He heard a pensive intake of breath on the other end of the line as Remo considered the words.

"I don't think I believe that anymore,'' Remo said after a long, thoughtful pause.

Smith pressed ahead. "It was true enough for him. Conrad MacCleary believed that his entire life. That was why he recruited you. He knew that you *could* make a difference.''

"MacCleary died more than twenty years ago,'' Remo countered. "He never lived in this America. He never saw anything as bad as what's going on out there today.''

Smith paused. How could he tell Remo of the shared horrors Smith and MacCleary had witnessed as members of the OSS during World War II? It was a time when darkness threatened to engulf the entire planet. Subsequent generations had never known such a struggle. It was already history before Remo was even born.

In the end Smith decided not to even try.

"I will try to find something for you," the CURE director promised.

"Thanks, Smitty," Remo said. The news appeared to do nothing to lift his spirits.

Smith hung up the phone, turning his attention back to his computer.

While he had been talking to Remo, a news story had come in from one of the wire services. Smith had failed to notice the interruption on his computer screen. The electronically reproduced story had waited patiently for his perusal.

Smith's lemony features grew more pinched as he read the details, sparse for now.

There had been several large explosions in the north of France during the night. All at *deminage* depots. The French government was attributing the nocturnal blasts to recent procedural changes in the storage of old war supplies. Unwise changes, it had turned out.

The interior minister, speaking on behalf of the president, had assured the public that in the future there would be no more such alterations in the handling of the dangerous items warehoused on the bases. In the meantime the military and police were conducting house-to-house searches in the towns around the blast sites. They stressed that they had no desire to alarm the public, but they admitted that there was a possibility that some of the unexploded mustard-gas shells that had been stored on the bases could have been corrupted in the blasts. The gas would have been released during the explosions. They wanted to be certain that everyone in the surrounding communities was all right.

Something about the report struck Smith as false. Of course the mustard-gas shells would have gone off along with everything else. Why would the French army be involved for so simple a matter as this? Surely the gas would have dissipated long before it reached a populated area.

Smith dumped the story from the screen and began typing swiftly at his special capacitor keyboard. In a moment he had accessed the private lines within the Paris headquarters of the Direction Générale de la Sécurité Extérieure, or DGSE.

Electronic mail inside France's premier spy organization was flying fast and furious. No one seemed to know precisely what was going on, but one thing was certain. The army was *not* conducting a door-to-door search for mustard-gas victims.

The explosions at the depots were not large enough, the resulting devastation not great enough, to account for all of the stored ordnance. According to reports, there were tire tracks leading away from every site.

All indications pointed to the fact that a massive amount of unstable surplus World War II explosives had been stolen. By whom and for what end had yet to be determined.

Smith was reading the most recent memos, dated

3:02 p.m. Paris time, when his computer beeped impatiently. His system had found something that warranted the CURE director's attention.

Smith quickly exited the DGSE network and returned to his own system. He found a fresh news report waiting for him.

The first stories were coming in of the bombing at the American Embassy in Paris. Smith read them with growing concern. Some members of the press were already connecting the Paris bombing with the explosions far north of the city.

When he had finished reading the news reports, Smith sat back in his creaking leather chair, considering. Through the one-way window behind him, Long Island Sound lapped lazily at the shore below Folcroft's rear lawn.

His plane took off from JFK International Airport at five that evening. It was a direct transatlantic flight to London's Heathrow Airport. His wife's itinerary wouldn't bring them to France for another two days.

If the situation there—whatever it might be— could be cleared up before then, there wasn't much of a chance he and Remo would run into one another.

It would also give Remo something to keep his mind off quitting the organization.

The decision was made.

Chair creaking as he leaned forward, Smith reached for the phone.

7

Helene Marie-Simone watched as the medical examiners pried the charred bodies from within the twisted remnants of the truck's cab. They cracked like crusted bread sticks.

There was practically nothing left. Black-smeared bones clutched a melted, U-shaped object that had once been a steering wheel. From the waist up, most of the soft tissue of the bodies had been burned completely away. Below, the skin had been turned to something resembling black leather. Clothing had been burned to ash.

Any attempt by the forensic scientists to do dental identification would be fruitless. If the doctors were able to find a single tooth, they would be lucky. The explosion had hit the men from behind. Their heads had been blown from here to Belgium.

"The lorry was rented from a place in Lille," a nearby police inspector informed Helene.

"Witnesses?" she asked sharply.

"*Non,*" the inspector replied. "It was not a first-rate establishment. The transaction was completed over the phone. Local police have informed us that the owner was involved marginally in drug trafficking. An envelope stuffed fat with franc notes, and he would not ask a question."

Her face was stern as she eyed her subordinate.

"Bring him here," she ordered.

In the blown-out shell of the truck a brittle femur snapped. Helene winced angrily.

"Are you *trying* to destroy evidence?" she demanded.

The MEs looked apologetic. With greater care they resumed their work.

"The rental agent is already on his way," the inspector cut in. He looked back to his notes. "That is all we have so far." He stood, pen poised over paper, awaiting Helene's next orders.

Helene didn't offer any. She looked back toward the building behind her, biting her cheek thoughtfully.

She was the kind of woman who inspired resentment among professional men. Beautiful, arrogant. Helene knew that she was both of these things and cared not that she was either.

Her long, thin brown hair was a perfect frame for her pale, classically chiseled features. The designer clothing she wore clung to her every curve in the exact way it was supposed to but never seemed to do on ordinary women. She had been approached more than once by talent agents from the modeling business. Helene had laughed them all away. With her sharp mind and fierce patriotism, she preferred her job as a spy for the French government.

Except on days like today.

The American Embassy lay in ruins. The entire front had been blown apart, exposing the interior to the street. The partially furnished rooms reminded Helene of a dollhouse she had had as a child.

Most of the outer portions of the floors in the multistoried building had collapsed after the blast, filling the courtyard with debris. Men in windbreakers were sifting carefully through the wreckage. Not one of them was French, Helene noted with agitation.

The Americans had flown in special investigative units that morning. Simultaneously an official offer had come from Washington to assist the French with their investigation of the bombing.

Of course, the French government had flatly refused the American offer. France was perfectly capable of handling the situation and had said so quite firmly. Stung, the Americans had left the local constabulary to clean up the aftermath in the street.

The French officials had begun to do just that. But when they expressed a desire to investigate the wreckage within the embassy courtyard, they were politely yet firmly rebuffed. The Americans had returned the rudeness of the French government in kind.

There was nothing that they could do about the embassy. Since it was officially United States soil, the government of France couldn't go in unless asked. The shortsightedness of Helene's superiors had effectively locked her out of a potentially vital aspect of this investigation.

Helene, an agent for France's DGSE, had been waiting impatiently on the street corner for the past three hours while the American men in their windbreaker jackets sifted through the charred ruins in the small embassy courtyard.

"If there is nothing else..." the inspector said leadingly.

Helene had been lost in thought.

She turned back to the man, perturbed.

"No," she sighed. "Nothing for now. Unfortunately." She indicated the blackened remains of the truck. "Go and tell those fools to be more careful with the bodies. There is little enough to work with as it is. They do not need to smash the skeletons any further."

Dutifully the inspector went off to comply with her orders.

As the man began arguing with the medical examiners, Helene stepped closer to the demolished embassy wall.

Chunks of brick lay strewed about the sidewalk and street. She picked her cautious way over these to the edge of where the embassy yard began. Yellow tape brought from America roped off the area. It fluttered and snapped in the stiff breeze.

Hopefully the Americans would soon come to

their senses and allow her inside. This inactivity was *killing* her.

She was peering in around a broken yet still upright section of wall when with her peripheral vision she caught sight of a pair of men stepping toward her across the rock- and metal-strewn street. They were nearly upon her when she turned.

"You may not go in there," Helene insisted, her tone official.

"By the looks of it, most of in there is out here," said one of the men. He was looking at the rubble on the sidewalk.

"Oh. You are American," Helene said with some distaste.

"As American as apple pie and Chevrolet," said Remo Williams proudly.

"I, on the other hand, demand an apology for your coarse greeting," said Chiun, Reigning Master of Sinanju.

The old Korean stood at Remo's elbow, long-nailed hands drumming impatiently atop the flapping sleeves of his fire-engine red brocade silk kimono.

He was five feet tall if he was an inch and had never seen the far side of one hundred pounds. Twin tufts of gossamer sprouted from a spot above each shell-like ear. The tan, taut flesh of his aged skull was otherwise bare. A wisp of beard adorned his wrinkled chin. Two young-appearing hazel orbs peered with bland malevolence from amid the knots of crumpled vellum that surrounded the old Asian's almond-shaped eyes.

Together the two men were an odd sight indeed. Helene was certain that these two were not associates of the Americans in windbreakers.

"I'd do it if I were you," Remo suggested knowingly to Helene.

"What?" Helene asked. She was genuinely confused.

"Apologize. It'll make things easier for all of us in the long run."

"Apologize?" Helene said. Her superior demeanor reasserted itself. "For what am I to apologize?"

"For a slur most base," Chiun sniffed.

"I said nothing to you," Helene insisted. "Much less insult you."

"She doesn't even know what she said, Little Father," Remo said.

"Typical for a Gallic wench. Their mouths are occupied in other depraved ways so much of the time, speech becomes secondary. Words of hate drip like poison from their weary tongues without even their knowledge." A single sharpened talon raised instructively. "Beware the daughters of Gaul, Remo. Their mouths are known for neither thoughtful consideration nor the ability to close when in the company of men, women or beasts of the field."

"I'll make a note of it," Remo said dryly. "Let's go."

Jumping, Helene barred them from entering the courtyard.

"Who are you? How did you get through the police cordon?" she demanded.

"Name's Remo. You just heard that. I'm with the State Department. I was supposed to be assigned here today." He looked at the bombed-out remains of the embassy building. "Guess I should have put in for that Bahamas assignment, huh, Chiun?"

The old man merely harrumphed, stuffing his hands inside the voluminous sleeves of his kimono. He stared at Helene.

"I demand to see some form of identification," Helene said officiously.

Remo shrugged. He pulled his and Chiun's dummy State Department ID from the pocket of his chinos.

Helene peered at the plastic-laminated cards for a full minute. At last she presented them back to Remo.

"These are in order. Though I am surprised that you would have come here today, considering what has happened," she added suspiciously.

"Diplomacy must go on." Remo smiled. He began stepping beneath the yellow tape.

"Wait," Helene said, struck with sudden inspiration.

"What?"

"Perhaps you could get me inside," she suggested, nodding to the embassy courtyard.

"There's really nothing to it," Remo said. "Look." He slipped beneath the tape, dropping it from his hand once he had reached the other side. "See?"

"You do not understand," she persisted. "There was an earlier misunderstanding between our respective teams. Your men have since stubbornly refused us entry."

"Perhaps you accused them of being American," Chiun offered, still on Helene's side of the flimsy barricade.

"They *are* American," Helene told him.

"Ah, but perhaps they do not like to be reminded of that fact," Chiun said sagely. Bending double, he joined Remo on the other side of the tape. The back of his kimono didn't even brush the tape.

"This is the point where you're supposed to figure out he wants you to say you're sorry for thinking he was American," Remo offered. "It's called the subtle approach."

Helene's eyes finally showed dawning understanding. She glanced at Chiun.

"I apologize," the French agent said. "Most sincerely. You are quite obviously *not* American." Her eyes narrowed, as if she were seeing the Master of Sinanju for the first time. "In fact, I would venture to guess that you are Korean, if I may be so bold."

Chiun's lined face brightened. "A woman of obvious good judgment," he said. "If somewhat delayed."

Helene knew at once that she had struck gold. She forged ahead.

"Forgive me, but sometimes my eyes are not so good," she lied. She nodded to Remo. "I saw this one and assumed you were both American. I see now that I was obviously in error."

Chiun studied her for a moment. "There is nothing wrong with your eyes," he concluded. Reaching out with a single curved fingernail—sharp as a titanium razor—he sliced through the yellow tape. The ends fluttered gently to the ground. "However, there is nothing a Frenchman does better than grovel." He indicated that Helene could join them within the courtyard.

Quickly she stepped over the split sections of tape.

"The FBI isn't going to like this," Remo warned.

"You will talk to them," Chiun sniffed indifferently. "After all, they are Americans and are therefore better dealt with by their own kind."

Chiun and Helene stepped in through the wreckage, leaving a grumbling Remo to deal with the officials from Washington.

REMO DID TALK to the investigators. Rather than get into a hassle explaining why a low-ranking State Department official was stumbling about the remnants of the most significant foreign bomb attack since the Marine barracks explosion in Lebanon, he showed the agent in charge a different badge, this one identifying him as a member of the National Security

Council. Chiun, Remo said, was with him. Helene was with Chiun.

There was surprisingly little said by the special agent within the cordon. He was far too busy directing his team of experts. His only warning was that Remo and his party should not destroy too much evidence in their pointless tour of the scene. A shot at the NSC. The harried agent had then gone back to work.

Remo found Chiun and Helene near the battered wall of the courtyard. The exploded truck was parked just on the other side. What was left of the men in the cab had at last been removed. The back of the truck was nothing more than a bare chassis. All around, the ground was charred black.

Helene was stooped down examining small fragments of debris on the ground. The Master of Sinanju was standing upright. His button nose was angled upward. He appeared to be doing some sort of deep-breathing exercises.

"We're okay with the Feds," Remo announced, coming up to them.

"Good," Helene said distractedly. Chiun ignored Remo altogether. He continued sniffing the air.

"What's your name, by the way?" Remo asked Helene.

She seemed peeved by the interruption.

"Helene Marie-Simone."

"Do you realize you have three first names?"

No reply. Helene had become so engrossed in her

meticulous search of the ground she no longer seemed to realize he was even there. Getting down on her hands and knees, she began brushing at the black grit that filled the spaces on the ground between the fallen embassy bricks.

Remo turned his attention back to Chiun.

The Master of Sinanju was still sniffing carefully at the air, drawing in delicate puffs of some distant scent.

"Okay, what is it?" Remo asked.

"I am not yet certain," Chiun responded. "But there is something here. Very faint. The boom devices have managed nearly to erase it." He turned ever so slowly in the direction of the battered truck, as if trying to sneak up on something long lost.

While they spoke, Remo caught Helene looking at them from the corner of her eye. When she thought that they were paying no attention to her, she pulled a small plastic bag from the pocket of her short leather jacket. Shielding her body from them, she quickly stuck something she had found from the ground in the bag and then hurriedly stuffed the whole bundle back into her pocket. Face flushed, she resumed her search.

"Back in a sec," Remo told Chiun. He wandered over to Helene. "What was that?" he asked, stopping above the kneeling agent.

She looked up at him, blandly innocent.

"What was what?" she asked dully.

"Can the innocent act, Madam Clouseau," Remo

droned, reaching down into her pocket and plucking out the small bag.

Helene jumped to her feet, eyes charged with horrified fury.

"That is evidence taken from the crime scene beyond the wall! It was collected on French soil!" She made a grab for the bag. Remo held it away from her grasping hands.

"I saw you pick it up from in here," he said. He held the bag up a few inches from his eyes.

Inside was a piece of jagged metal. It was a small fragment, no larger than a fingernail. It had survived the blast in surprisingly good condition, considering that corrosion had taken hold of it long before the explosives it had contained were detonated.

"Give me that this instant," Helene hissed. She snatched once more, missing again.

"Which world war is this from, do you think?" he asked aloud. He glanced over at her.

Helene's eyes immediately glazed over. It was a very deliberate affectation. She stopped jumping.

"What do you mean?" she asked blandly.

"It's obviously part of the munitions that were stolen from your depots last night. I'd say it was World War I. That metal has seen at least seventy years' worth of air and water eating away at it."

Helene's stomach knotted. The thefts were not yet public knowledge. As far as everyone was concerned, the bombing at the embassy was separate from the explosions that were still designated as accidents at the *deminage* depots.

Helene scrutinized Remo carefully, as if seeing him for the first time.

"*You* are with your State Department?" she asked finally.

Remo smiled. "I guess I'm really a Jacques of all trades."

"That may be, but here you are mistaken," she said flatly. "First there was no theft at our storage facilities. Second there is no evidence to connect the two events. My government has no intention of linking those accidents with this act of terrorism."

"Tell that to the DGSE," Remo said. "They seem pretty certain there's a connection. And they're also sure that a huge amount of stuff was stolen off the bases. Those explosions weren't accidents, but I'm willing to bet that this one was."

Helene refused to give in to incredulity. She forced calm into her voice. "Who *are* you?" she asked.

Remo brushed off the question as irrelevant.

"See where the truck is?" Remo instructed, waving the bag with the bomb fragment toward the street. "Stopped in traffic. It wasn't in a spot where it could have inflicted maximum damage. Look at the wrecked part of the embassy. Superficial on this side. They could have taken out a lot more of the place if they parked around the east wall. And here's the biggest proof. No one's taken credit for the explosion yet. Everyone knows the types of people who do this stuff on purpose love to see their names on page one.

"Nope, I'm willing to bet that one of the trucks with the stolen bombs just happened to be waiting here when one of the things went off by mistake." Remo waved the bag in her face. "One of *these* things," he mocked.

She made another desperate grab for the bag. This time he allowed her to snatch it away.

"Wild speculation," she snarled, stuffing the bag back into her jacket pocket. With sharp movements she fastened the flap with a metal snap.

"Call it what you like," Remo answered airily. "You're the ones with the problem. By now the metal casings on those things are so deteriorated a sneeze could set them off."

If Helene wanted to say something else, she didn't get the chance. The Master of Sinanju had completed his olfactory sweep of the area. He returned to Remo's side.

"What have you got?" Remo asked.

Chiun was frowning. "There is a hint of the gaseous condiment substance used by the barbarian Hun in the First Global Idiocy."

"Mustard gas," Remo said, nodding. "I thought I smelled it when we first showed up."

"No doubt there was some present on the vehicle when the booms went off. Though faint now, at first it interfered with my senses."

"But not anymore," Remo pressed.

Chiun shook his head. "I have isolated another scent. There is a definite odor of the Hun in this vicinity."

"From the bombs themselves," Remo suggested, though even he doubted the Master of Sinanju could smell traces of whoever had handled the rusted bomb casings some eighty-odd years ago.

"From the booms, yes," Chiun agreed. "But recently. The odor comes from the vehicle. The thieves were German."

"German?" Remo said with a frown.

"How could he know that?" Helene asked dubiously.

"Trust me, he knows," Remo informed her.

"But Germany and France are no longer enemies. We are in NATO together. We are both members of the European Union. What he says makes no sense."

"The Germans reek of the fermented grains they drink and the pork products they eat," Chiun said firmly. "They are the dastards responsible for this."

Helene's better instincts took over. She shook her head doubtfully.

"Your nose will no doubt forgive me if I investigate further?" Helene asked acidly. Stepping away from them, she resumed her search of the yard.

"There's nothing stronger to go on, Little Father?" Remo asked quietly once they were alone.

"I thought briefly there was, but the scent went away." The old man shook his head in frustration. "There are too many Frenchman fouling the area. If only a handful of them owned a washcloth and soap, it might be possible. As it is..." He threw up his hands, kimono sleeves snapping in annoyance like twin flicked towels. Irritated, he turned his attention away from the air and began examining the ground.

As the Master of Sinanju worked, Remo tried briefly to clear away the layers of odors filling the Paris street. It took a few minutes, but he finally got beyond the human and machinery scents. He found the distinctive German smell beneath the acrid odor of the burned-out truck.

Chiun was right. There was nothing more. The body odors made it impossible to go further.

With nothing more to do, he joined Chiun in his inspection of the grounds.

FORTUNATELY for the young man in the thick crowd of gawkers gathered on the other side of the French police line, the wind was blowing in the right direction. Had it not been, either Master of Sinanju would have easily been able to sniff out the beer-and-sausage lunch he had eaten not more than an hour before.

The man wore a black knit cap rolled down to cover the tattoos on his shaved scalp. A pair of khaki pants, a ripped black T-shirt and a denim jacket that advertised the name of an obscure German punk-rock band across the back and arms completed his ensemble.

The youth watched Remo and Chiun, as well as

Helene and the rest of the investigators, for a few minutes longer. Eventually he grew bored with observing the meticulous search of the embassy wreckage.

He left the scene.

The young man walked several blocks through the heavy pedestrian traffic. Some of the government workers were again on strike—this time calling for a two-day work week and eight months paid vacation. It was just another excuse for them not to work. And the strikers were not alone. It seemed as if everyone was taking advantage of the beautiful Parisian afternoon.

Taking an infrequently traveled side street, the young man walked down half a block to a narrow, cluttered alley. At the end of the dank passageway was a rusted metal fire escape. The man climbed the groaning steps to a third-story fire door.

Ducking inside the building, he found a closed door at the end of a dimly lit corridor. It was warped with age. He rapped sharply on the painted wood.

With a pained creak the door opened a crack, revealing a suspicious, bleary eye surrounded by a relief map of wrinkles. When the old man on the other side saw who it was, the door was opened just enough for him to pass inside.

The apartment was not large. There was a living room beyond the door. Other small rooms extended off this one. Men were crowded inside. Several—including the one who had answered the door—were veteran members of IV. The rest were young like the new arrival.

Nils Schatz sat imperiously in a plush chair that overlooked the rest of the room. A few of the older men sat in other, rattier chairs and on the nearby threadbare sofa.

The room was hot with the collected body warmth of dozens of nervous men.

Once inside, the young man quickly doffed his hat, revealing a bald head of large, unsightly tattoos. The Roman numerals "I" and "V" were stained in blue ink in the most prominent spot just above his pale forehead. Above them, etched below the surface in dull red, was the twisted image of a swastika.

At the sight of the new arrival, Nils Schatz's lips tightened, but he had to hide his true feelings.

Schatz was privately disgusted by the slovenliness of the young man. He and his kind would be the first that would be purged in the grand new order. But they were necessary. For now. The unkempt fools were loyal foot soldiers.

Schatz motioned the young man forward with a wave of his cane. A potentate granting an audience to an unworthy supplicant.

"What is happening?" the old Nazi demanded.

The young man shrugged. "Not much," he replied in a voice as dull as the light in his eyes. "The Americans have sent in some of their own people. The French are still everywhere."

Although none of this was fresh news, the repetition still seemed to upset Schatz.

"Are there any French government agents?" he demanded.

The young man shrugged. "Don't know. How can you tell?"

Schatz waved his cane wildly. "It is *obvious*," he spit, as if he had sent the man out to find the sky. "Were there any?"

"No, I don't think there were any agents," the boy answered cautiously.

There was fire in the old Nazi's eyes. He aimed his cane at the young man's chin.

"You do not think at all," Schatz threatened.

For a moment some of those gathered thought that this would be a repeat of the incident at the Banque de Richelieu. Before things got out of hand, one of the other men, a former Nazi lieutenant named Fritz Dunlitz, interjected.

"Anything strange at all, Rudi?" Fritz pressed. "We need to know if they have connected this to us in any way."

"There was nothing that has not already been on the news," Rudi replied. "It is like the American movies. The police are searching for little scraps of clues."

"Bah! He is stupid," Schatz stated firmly. He waved vaguely at the young man with the end of his walking stick. It was as if the boy wasn't even in the room. He dropped the blunt end of the cane to the floor.

"I do not believe we need to be concerned, Nils," Fritz assured Schatz. "The police are not yet cracking down on the city. Much of the plan is already in motion."

"There was an old man," Rudi offered suddenly.

Schatz and some of the other older men looked over at Rudi. The younger ones in the room were slower to follow suit, but eventually they, too, turned to the young skinhead.

"What?" Schatz asked tersely.

"At the American Embassy. An old Chinese man. He wore a long red robe. He came with another man. A younger man. They didn't look like police."

"An old Oriental," Schatz said flatly.

The other men from Schatz's generation were looking at one another and at their leader.

"How do you know he was Chinese?" Fritz demanded.

Rudi shrugged. "He was—I don't know...Chinese." He stuck his index fingers into the flesh at the corners of his eyes and drew them away from his face, causing his eyes to slant. "Chinese," he repeated.

Fritz spun back to Schatz.

"Is it possible?" he asked.

"Possible and probable," Schatz admitted thoughtfully. "The Master of Sinanju is still alive. At least he was several months ago. At that time IV learned that he was in the employ of the Americans. If it is he, they obviously sent him here to investigate the stupid, stupid accident at their embassy.''

"What about the other one?" asked somebody nervously.

Schatz waved his cane dismissively. "The young one is his protégé. We know of him, as well." His expression soured as he considered this new dimension to his plan.

After a time Fritz cleared his throat. Schatz looked up at him dully.

"It might be wise, Nils, to contact Kluge. He may have advice that—''

Schatz smashed his walking stick across the dusty surface of the wooden coffee table with a mighty crack.

"I know what his advice will be!" he snapped.

The skinheads were startled by the outburst. Even some of the old ones jumped at the noise.

"Kluge would have us sit like helpless invalids awaiting the undertaker," Schatz hissed furiously. "We will wait no longer. IV will wait no longer. What we need to do is to distract Sinanju."

As the cloud of startled dust played around his weathered features, Schatz settled back in his comfortable chair. He said no more.

For a time the others looked at him in silent concern. None dared speak.

"How?" Fritz asked, finally, a confused expression spreading across his face.

Nils Schatz didn't say. But his expression was obvious to the old men who knew him all too well. It was a look of disdainful confidence.

A plan was already under way.

8

Harold Smith had been in England less than one hour and was already wishing he were home.

The plane had been only one hour late leaving JFK but had somehow managed to arrive in London more than three hours overdue. How Royal Airlines had managed that piece of aviating trickery was beyond him. He imagined they had spent some of their time in the air flying backward.

Only one of his wife's bags had been lost in transit. The airline assured the Smiths that they would quickly locate the errant luggage and send it along to their hotel.

Maude Smith took the loss of the ancient bag in stride. She was so excited with the prospect of spending one full week alone with her husband that she accepted the inconvenience of one misplaced suitcase without so much as a single cross word.

His wife's lost bag was of little concern to Smith as well. After all, he carried his most important piece of luggage with him. Throughout the flight, the battered leather briefcase that carried his CURE laptop had been nestled carefully between his ankles.

However, if the missing suitcase was not returned by the end of their trip, Smith would use the CURE mainframes back at Folcroft to track it down. After all, the bag had been a wedding present from Maude's aunt and uncle, and Smith had no intention of replacing it this late in his life.

A too expensive cab brought them from Heathrow to their hotel, a disinterested desk clerk gave them their key and a bellboy who had learned his manners watching *Benny Hill* reruns escorted them to their room.

Once they were settled in, Smith mentioned that he wanted to do a little work on his computer. His wife—not hearing a word he said—was thrilled with the prospect of an afternoon of sight-seeing.

"Ooh, let's go to the Thames River, Harold," Maude Smith announced excitedly. She pronounced every letter in the word. Mrs. Smith beamed as she looked at the glossy picture in the brochure she had picked up in the hotel lobby.

"That's pronounced 'Tems,' dear," Smith said absently from his seated position on the edge of the hotel bed. He placed his briefcase on his lap.

Still, she didn't hear him. She was too excited.

"Oh, Hyde Park looks interesting. We could go there."

"Very well," said Smith. "Perhaps tomorrow afternoon."

He popped the special locks on his briefcase and

lifted the cracked leather lid, revealing the small portable computer within. The sounds drew a response.

"Harold." The voice of his wife was small. And sad.

Smith glanced up.

Maude Smith was looking down at the briefcase balanced atop Smith's bony knees. Her face was deeply hurt.

"This is our second honeymoon," she said softly. Already her eyes were welling up.

Smith hadn't seen his wife cry in many years. To witness such a display now came as a shock. She had always been a good wife. Undemanding. Dutiful. She had sacrificed her life for him and never had a complaint.

Something stirred deep in the rock-ribbed, unemotional core of Harold W. Smith. It was guilt. The same sensation that had compelled him to go on this trip in the first place. He found the emotion deeply unsettling.

Smith quietly shut the lid on the computer. He set the tamperproof locks on the briefcase and pushed it far under the bed. He stood up.

"Or we could go now," he offered, taking her hands gently in his.

Smith's rational mind knew that they had both changed. A great deal more than either of them had ever expected. But in that instant he was propelled back in time more than fifty years. The face he looked into was that of the shy young girl who had given him her youth.

A tight smile gripped his bloodless lips.

Maude Smith was so surprised by the sudden change in her husband that she wanted to burst out in tears of joy. But she knew Harold frowned on those sorts of emotional displays. When she cried, she generally cried alone. Ironically it was her aloneness that usually brought her to tears.

But she wasn't alone today.

She gripped her husband's gnarled fingers, sniffling slightly.

"I'll get the camera," Maude croaked feebly.

THEY FOUND several more rusted metal fragments from shattered bomb casings. Helene had even stopped denying that they were fragments of the ordnance stolen from the *deminage* bases. Her frown deepened at each discovery.

"So it was an accident," Remo mused. "But the stuff still got all the way down to Paris for some reason. Why?"

"There is only one reason to have booms," Chiun replied. He was watching the American investigators sift through the debris. They had found evidence of the *deminage* bombs, as well.

Remo nodded his agreement. "True. But we still don't know who has them. Any ideas, Helene?" he called over to the French agent.

She was talking into the cellular phone that she

periodically removed from the pocket of her jacket. She pitched her voice low, little realizing that Remo could have heard her even if she were on the other side of the building and locked away in an isolation tank. *Heard* but not understood. Remo had never bothered to learn French.

It hadn't been easy, but he had convinced the Master of Sinanju to quietly translate some of what she was saying. It was during the first of these calls that Remo learned she was an agent for the DGSE.

"I do not support your conjecture," she called back. She hunched farther into her phone.

"She's not very helpful, is she?" Remo said to Chiun.

"She is French." The Master of Sinanju shrugged, as if this explained everything.

Remo put his hands on his hips. Frowning unhappily, he surveyed the embassy wreckage.

"We've gone as far as we can here. I don't see anyone running up to tell us they did it."

"Perchance Smith might have new information," Chiun suggested.

"Chiun, I can't call Smith," Remo explained. "He's on the first vacation he's ever taken since I've known him. Besides, his wife is with him."

"Call Smith, do not call Smith. It matters not to me," Chiun said with a shrug of his birdlike shoulders.

Remo thought for a few more minutes. His frown deepened with each passing second.

"I think I'll call Smith," he said eventually.

He hopped over a pile of shattered wall debris and stepped up to Helene. When she noticed him coming toward her, she pulled more tightly into herself, whispering a torrent of French into the small phone in her hand.

Wordlessly Remo reached around her. Before she could issue a complaint, he plucked the phone from her clenched hand.

"She'll call you back," he announced into the receiver.

"Give me my phone!"

"Sorry, kitten. Official State Department business."

As Helene protested, Remo pressed the button that severed the connection. She continued complaining violently as Remo—humming all the while—punched in his personal access code for Folcroft. Smith had told him before he left that he could phone at any time in case of emergency. The call would be rerouted to wherever in the world the CURE director was staying.

"Give me that this instant," Helene insisted hotly, grabbing at the phone.

"When I'm through," Remo promised. He had finished dialing and, batting away Helene's grabbing hands, was waiting for the call to go through.

Eventually Helene gave up trying to get the phone back. Seething, she crossed her arms.

"You are a barbarian," she snarled.

"This from the people who brought you the guillotine," Remo said smilingly. He resumed humming a song from the musical *Gigi*. It was Maurice Chevalier's "Thank Heaven for Little Girls."

HAROLD SMITH HAD SEEN as much of London as he had ever wanted to see during World War II. And most of what he saw back then had been at night.

Large parts of his youth had been spent ducking shrapnel. As the air-raid whistles squawked their nightly preamble to horror, the streets emptied. Blackout shades were hastily drawn and Londoners huddled together in shelters awaiting the end of the Blitz.

That end had come decades ago.

The sirens were silent now.

The sandbags and antiaircraft guns were gone. As he strolled with his wife from Kensington Gardens and across the street into Hyde Park, Smith didn't see a single British soldier or military vehicle.

On their tour he noted that some of the buildings that had been damaged in the war had been repaired. Others had been torn down to make way for fresh architectural eyesores. It was as if World War II had never so much as brushed the shores of England.

To Maude Smith's eyes, *this* was London. She had never seen what Smith had seen, and so to her the images of the war had been restricted to the far-off unreality of newsreels and, in later years, the occasional advertisement for a PBS documentary. She never watched the programs themselves. They were too depressing.

Happily oblivious to the horrors that had nightly occurred on these very streets, Maude Smith clicked picture after picture on her old Browning camera. Smith thought it likely that she hadn't even loaded the film correctly. She had never been very good at it. Whatever the case, it didn't seem to matter to Mrs. Smith.

"Isn't it beautiful, Harold?" Maude Smith trilled. As she spoke, she clicked away at the pond in Hyde Park. It could have been any small duck-filled body of water in any city in the world.

"Yes, dear," Smith agreed.

"Aren't you having a wonderful time?" she asked. Her face was beaming. Briefly—through the rounder face, the slackness and other marks of age— a hint of the girl he had married peeked through once more.

"I am, dear," Smith said.

And the truth was, he meant it. Smith hated to admit it, but he actually was beginning to enjoy himself. He found her good humor to be infectious.

They crossed the street and were beginning to make their way up Piccadilly to Trafalgar Square when Smith felt an odd electronic hum at his waist.

"What was that?" Mrs. Smith asked.

Smith had already reached beneath his gray suit jacket to shut off the device. It was small and black—half the size of a deck of cards.

"I took the precaution of renting a pocket pager before we left home," he said, frowning.

"A pager?" she asked. "I didn't know one would work this far away."

"It is hooked in to a world satellite service," Smith explained. He glanced around for a phone.

"Harold," his wife said. It was an admonishing tone, but a mild one. Their day together had been too enjoyable so far to spoil it with nagging.

"It must be Mrs. Mikulka," Smith said. "I told her to contact me if there was a problem at Folcroft."

Mrs. Smith tsked. "Can't they run that place for a week without you?"

Smith spied a red phone box across the street.

"It is probably nothing," he said, forcing the tenseness from his tone. "But I should return the call."

"Oh, very well," Maude said in a mock-impatient tone. "I need some more film anyway. There was a small store near Hyde Park Corner, I think. Yes, there it is. Did you know they call their drugstores 'chemist' shops?" Maude Smith explained, proud of her erudition. Leaving Smith to dwell on this kernel of knowledge, she walked over to the door of the shop. Smith hurried across the street.

In the phone booth, Smith unclipped the pager from his belt and carefully entered the number on the small display strip. Remo answered immediately.

"Sorry to interrupt your vacation, Smitty."

"What is the problem?"

"Chiun and I have hit a dead end here. No one's taking credit for the bombing, and the French government hasn't been able to get much of anything from the truck or street, at least according to the DGSE."

There was a shout of surprised protest from the background. It was a female voice.

"Hey, it's not my fault you can't keep a secret," Remo called to the voice in the background. To Smith he said, "One thing we *have* been able to determine is that the bomb that went off outside the embassy probably wasn't really a truck bomb at all."

"Explain."

Remo went on to tell him about the metal fragments and his theory that the explosion had been accidental.

"Does Chiun concur with your hypothesis?"

"It is true, Emperor Smith," Chiun's squeaky voice called. "The attack on your Gallic outpost does not appear deliberate. And the parts of the boom devices we found were fifty or more years old."

"Did you get all that?" Remo asked.

"Yes."

"There's no doubt about it," Remo said. "The stuff that was stolen from the bases blew up the embassy."

"Only some of what was stolen," Smith clarified. "From what I learned, there was much, much more than a single truckload of explosives taken from the *deminage* facilities."

"That one truckload did a hell of a lot of damage," Remo said somberly.

"Yes," Smith replied, thinking. He was looking thoughtfully out one of the side glass windows of the phone booth. Across the street, he spotted his wife exiting the chemist's shop. "Remo, I will have to call you back. I do not have access to my laptop at present."

"You without a computer?" Remo said, surprised. "Isn't that part of your wardrobe? Like that itchy Brooks Brothers suit or that Dartmouth noose you wear around your neck? Better be careful, Smitty. If you keep going out like that in public, you're going to get nabbed for indecent exposure."

"At what number can I reach you?" Smith pressed wearily.

"This one'll do fine for now," Remo said.

"Very well. When I return to my hotel, I will uplink with the CURE mainframes and see what I can find." Smith hung up the phone before Remo could say anything more.

On the other side of the street, he found Maude Smith searching the sea of pale faces on the sidewalk. Her eyes lit up when she saw him.

"I thought you'd left me."

"I must return to the hotel," Smith said quickly.

Mrs. Smith seemed crestfallen. "What's wrong?"

"An emergency has come up concerning one of the sanitarium's patients," he lied.

She could see from the determined set of his jaw that there would be no arguing with him.

"I'll go with you," she said, unable to mask the disappointment in her voice.

"No," Smith said. "It should not take long." He checked his Timex. "I will meet you in front of the National Gallery at five o'clock."

When he looked back at his wife he could see that she was no longer paying attention to him. She was staring up in the sky. Along the sidewalk many other pedestrians were looking up, as well.

"What are those, Harold?" Maude aimed a curious finger in the air. Smith followed her line of sight.

The day was unusually sunny and mild for England. On a backdrop of thin, virtually transparent white clouds, he spotted several dark shapes flying ominously in from the western sky.

Smith's heart tripped.

As the small planes flew toward them, tiny objects began dropping from their bellies. A rumble—like distant thunder—rolled toward them in waves from the approaching aircraft.

They could *feel* the sound beneath their feet.

Moments after the first rumble began, a different noise filled the air above London. It was a pained electronic screech. The crowd around them became more agitated as the persistent scream continued to assault their eardrums.

"What is that?" Maude Smith asked, crinkling her

nose. She looked around for the source of the ungodly sound.

Smith was staring up at the sky, his haggard face clouded in disbelief and dread. When he spoke, his words were low.

"An air-raid siren," Harold Smith breathed.

And at that the first German bombs began dropping on London's Hyde Park.

9

Colonel E. C. T. Bexton of Her Majesty's Royal Air Force was single-handedly responsible for permitting the first planes of the modern London blitzkrieg to cross over England and drop their payloads unmolested. He allowed this horror to be perpetrated against one of history's most famous cities because he refused to believe the word of a simple potato farmer.

His precise words were: "I will not scramble one of Her Majesty's elite RAF squadrons because some obviously pissed-to-the-gills toothless old git sees cabbage crates flying in across the briny. Tell him to take an aspirin and have a lie down."

Hanging up the phone, Colonel Bexton attempted to resume his work on next week's flight schedules. He had barely brought pen back to paper before the phone resumed its persistent squawking. Placing the pen on his desk with exaggerated patience, he reached for the receiver.

"Colonel Bexton's office. Bexton here," he announced to the party on the other end.

"Listen to me, you fool! There are German bombers flying in an attack formation toward London."

Slender fingers tensed on the receiver.

"Who is this?" the colonel demanded. Though it was the same voice as before, he hadn't bothered to ask the clearly agitated man's name.

"I am Edmund Carter," the man explained with as much patience as time allowed. "I am a research scientist at the Jodrell Bank Experimental Station in Cheshire—"

"Jodrell Bank?" Bexton interrupted. "Aren't you supposed to be looking for little green men? I would have thought German warplanes would be a bit too terrestrial for your lot."

"We were alerted to this by a local farmer," the voice explained.

"Ah, yes," Bexton sympathized, "the poor old sot who still thinks he's seeing monkeys on the ceiling. You sound like a sensible chap, Carter. Surprised a man of science would be taken in by a boozer with one foot in the past and the other in the Boar's Head Tavern."

"*I saw them!*" Carter yelled. "My entire *team* saw them. We are tracking them as we speak."

"And what have *you* been drinking, Carter?" the colonel asked thinly.

"Let me talk to your superior officer."

"Oh, no," Bexton said, bristling. "You won't make me a laughingstock. Your old friend is merely reliving the war, Carter. Now I suggest that you and your colleagues over there in Cheshire spend more time in the heavens and less time in the pubs.''

He slapped the phone down in the cradle.

If this was meant as some sort of prank, that should put a stop to it once and for all.

When the phone rang a third time several minutes later, Colonel Bexton lost what little reserves of patience he had left.

"Bexton!" he snapped into the receiver.

His face grew pale as the nasal voice of his immediate superior outlined the situation. This time the instant he hung up the phone, Colonel E. C. T. Bexton was placing an emergency call down the defense chain of command.

Per Bexton's order, a squadron of eight British Aerospace Harriers took off from a base in the London suburb of Croydon less than six minutes later.

From what he later learned, it was already too late.

10

The first aerial bombs ripped through the neatly trimmed lawns of Hyde Park Gardens, spraying the cars and people on the streets and roadways with clods of rich black English soil.

The crowd on the sidewalk around Smith and his wife had panicked the instant they realized the significance of the high-pitched whistling sounds of the falling bombs, which were audible over the blare of the air-raid siren.

Crowds of people were running in every direction.

Smith pulled his wife into the relative safety of a stone overhang in the doorway of an old storefront.

"Harold!" Maude Smith shouted in terror.

He gripped her arm.

"We have to get to the Underground," Smith stressed, referring to the subway system beneath London.

It wouldn't be safe for them to try at the moment. The crowd was too unruly, the people too frantic. Smith watched for the initial mob of running men and women to thin.

As he waited, the bombers grew closer.

Smith was as surprised by the look of the planes as by the attack itself. They all appeared to be surplus World War I and II aircraft. By the looks of it, they were all in perfect working order. He had counted more than a dozen of the planes as they flew in. The aircraft remained clustered tightly together. Even with so few of them, the sky seemed thick with menacing shapes from his past.

Screaming down out of the midafternoon sky, one plane—Smith saw now that it was a Messerschmitt—buzzed the building across the street. It opened fire with a set of wing-mounted machine guns.

The staccato gunfire was deafening. Bullets ripped into the glass and brick of the building's uppermost stories. Shattered glass and chunks of brick and mortar exploded outward, falling like hail to the street below.

The plane looked as though its forward momentum would surely slam it into the side of the building. But at the last minute the pilot cut his angle sharply. With a whine of engines, the plane did a rolling maneuver away from the building back out over the street. It soared back up into the air, dropping a dozen screeching bombs as it did so.

They impacted in the street among the gnarl of small British cars. A BMW near Smith became an explosion of flame and metal, its hood flipping up as the shell struck its mark.

Mrs. Smith screamed.

They couldn't wait any longer. As the crowd continued to break around them, as the planes continued to disgorge bombs from their bellies, Smith hustled his wife from the protective archway.

Like leaves dropped into a raging spring river, they were immediately caught up in the stream of people flooding for the nearest entry to the London Underground.

Mrs Smith clung to her husband's arm both for support and in fear. Face hard, Smith did his best to keep her safe from the panicked, shoving masses as they moved along the sidewalk.

Fear rippled palpably through the crowd.

Someone had shut off the air-raid siren. The sounds of dropping bombs could be heard both nearby and from farther away. One struck very closely, pelting the crowd with bits of tar and dirt.

And something else.

Blood spattered the faces of some of the nearer pedestrians. Smith saw that he and his wife had been lucky. They were in the center of the crowd and were thus shielded from the heaviest flying shrapnel. Screams of agony erupted around them as the whine of the attacking plane's engine faded away.

As they ran, Smith saw one man with a streak of crimson flowing down the side of his head. A woman—presumably a wife or girlfriend—was trying to staunch the flow of blood with a strip of cloth as the crowd continued to race forward.

Some people had fallen, bloodied, to the pavement. The panicked mob trampled over them.

Smith saw the mouth of the Underground over the bobbing heads before him. They had only a few yards to go.

A new sound caught his attention. It was heavier than that of the other planes. The noise from the older aircraft was more of a whining complaint. This sound was a ferocious, thick rumble that rattled the buildings around them and shook the ground beneath their feet.

A huge shadow passed above them. Still moving, some, including Smith, cast wary glances at the sky.

There were more planes above London now. They had roared into view seemingly with the purpose of avenging angels. Smith saw that they were RAF Harriers.

Without hesitation, the newer planes opened fire on the German attackers.

The crowd had dragged the Smiths to the stairs leading down into the bowels of the British subway system. Smith guided his wife's hand to the metal railing. She hurried down the stairs away from him, so concerned with finding safety that she was oblivious to the fact that she was now alone. No matter. She would be safe.

Smith pushed flat against the wall of the subway stairwell, pausing briefly to look up at the dogfight above the skies of London. People jostled him as they bustled down the stone stairs.

A Harrier tore into sight from the east, leveling off after a fleeing Messerschmitt. As the newer aircraft banked over the string of sedate buildings, a long missile detached itself from the underside of the wing. For a moment it seemed as if this bomb would drop to the street, as well. But the tail quickly ignited and the missile was launched forward with a propulsive force greater than that of the Harrier itself.

The missile ate up the space between the two mismatched planes in an instant. The Messerschmitt took the full force of the explosion in a spot to the rear of its cockpit. The fragile explosives within the old plane detonated a split second after the fiery impact of the missile.

The plane erupted in a ball of flame, screaming down out of the sky in the direction of Hyde Park Corner. It hit earth a moment later.

Other Harriers roared in across the tall buildings.

The small planes were outdated and outmatched. They broke off the attack and headed away from the skies above Piccadilly. Some looped away from the others, streaking off in the direction of Buckingham Palace.

Two Harriers pursued the rogue planes; the rest gave chase to the largest group of fleeing aircraft.

It was over.

Not that it mattered to the terrified crowd.

Smith tried to move away from the wall in order to climb back up the stairs. He found it impossible to negotiate through the sea of running people.

Though the danger had passed, Smith was caught up in the rushing tide. Against his wishes he found himself being swept down into the subway along with the rest of the frightened crowd.

Though the money had passed, Smith was easy to un-
move. Having little American...dollar...could be found at
...it being spent hand-over-the...bulky...along with
the rest of the European...

Helene Marie-Simone had to be certain she had lost
Remo and Chiun before she could talk freely. She
had just received an urgent call from a most delicate
source and had been forced to put the matter off for
a few minutes until she was certain she was away
from prying ears. Somehow—impossibly—the two
men from America had been able to eavesdrop on
her private conversations with the DGSE.

After hissing to the caller that she would return
the call immediately, Helene had clicked off the cellular phone.

She shot a look at Remo and Chiun.

They didn't appear to notice. The old one was engrossed in the work of the American investigators.
The young one didn't seem very interested in anything that was going on at the scene. He was yawning
as he stared at the edge of the cordon.

Quickly she ducked out through a gap that the
truck explosion had created in the courtyard wall.
She headed down the street.

Helene didn't know who these men represented,
but she knew one thing for certain. They were *not*

with the American State Department. The men were obviously spies. Though for what agency she had no idea. They didn't seem like CIA. They were certainly not FBI. Probably they were with one of the more obscure American security agencies.

The Paris police had established a wide cordon around the bomb scene. Barricades had been constructed in the streets. Uniformed gendarmes kept the curious at bay.

Helene slipped between the wooden sawhorses and line of Paris policemen. Down the street a block she cut into a side boulevard near a florist shop.

She glanced back around the corner. There was no sign of the two men in the busy sidewalk traffic.

Good. She hadn't been followed.

Helene quickly tugged the phone from her pocket and stabbed out the direct country code for England.

"It's about bloody well time," a stodgy voice said by way of greeting.

Helene didn't appreciate the superior tone. But she was in no position to complain about it now.

"What has happened?" she asked furtively.

"A bit of a mess in London," the male voice enthused. "We've got bally Jerry kites strewn all over Park Lane and Piccadilly."

"Aside from the street names, I do not know what any of that means," Helene whispered impatiently.

"Kites. *Planes,*" the voice explained with a sigh. "Perfectly good English. Don't know what they teach you in those schools in Paris." He continued.

"German planes attacked London not fifteen minutes ago. The RAF scrambled a squadron too late to stop them cold. They got off a few good runs before we managed to send them nose over knickers. RAF's official word is that they had trouble with their ground crews. Bad weather slowed them up. Good chaps, ordinarily, but there's not a cloud in the sky."

"German planes?" Helene asked. "Why are you telling me this? Call the Germans."

"That's the thing," said the voice. "They're not exactly German defense-force planes. They're more or less Nazi era-ish."

"Nazi?"

"World War II and all that. Surplus planes."

Helene was trying to conjure up an image of airplanes fifty years out of date attacking modern London in broad daylight. She found it too out of her frame of reference to imagine.

"What about survivors among the pilots?" she asked.

"Not a bally one, I'm afraid," said the man on the phone. "Well, there was one. But the blighter went and blew the top of his head off with a Luger before we could get to him. Anyway, I was thinking that since you had a spot of trouble with your depots that you might be interested."

"Why would I?"

"I imagine it's more than coincidence that your surplus war bombs are stolen the day before London is bombed by surplus planes, don't you?"

Helene was so caught up in the incredible scenario that she failed to deny that the explosives were in fact stolen.

The voice pressed on. "Radar stations say the planes came down from the north, but local spotters saw them heading up from the south over the Irish Sea this morning."

"They went up and then down?"

"Most likely a trick to hide their true origin."

"Would they have enough fuel?"

"They could have been adapted to fly longer missions," the man said. "I'm really not sure what the range is on a Messerschmitt. However, if you're interested, after studying the possible origin of the flights we have traced them to only a couple of possible places. Mainland France or one of the Channel Islands. We have further learned that there were unusual shipments to Guernsey in the wee hours this morning."

"Why do you not investigate?"

"I've got quite enough to do here in London. And after all, they *are* your bombs. Therefore, they are *your* responsibility. Please do something about them, forthwith. There's a good girl."

The line went dead.

Helene clicked the small phone shut. She was frowning deeply.

Guernsey. In the English Channel. If the missing explosives had been shipped there, she would have to investigate at once.

Sticking the cellular phone in her pocket, she hurried back out onto the main street...

...and plowed straight into Remo.

He was leaning casually against the wall just around the corner from where Helene had been hiding.

"Hi." Remo smiled. "We missed you."

"Speak for yourself," said a squeaky voice.

Helene jumped at the sound of the old Asian's voice. Wheeling, she cast a glance at the spot where she had been standing. Somehow Chiun had gotten behind her. He stood on the sidewalk, arms tucked inside the broad sleeves of his kimono. His face was as unreadable as that of a cigar-store Indian.

"I have important work to do," Helene said officiously. She pushed past Remo and began marching down the street.

Remo kept pace with her. Chiun trailed behind.

"I heard. Mind if we tag along?" Remo said.

"Yes."

"Oh. Mind if we go anyway?"

"Yes."

"Too bad," Remo said with a grin.

Helene muttered a string of French phrases all the way to her official government car. Remo didn't bother to have Chiun interpret. Some things were universal.

HANS MICHTLER HAD BEEN a sergeant in the German army at the young age of nineteen. Back then his only brushes with the Luftwaffe had been unpleasant ones. He found the members of the German air force to be arrogant. "Bastards to a man," he was fond of saying.

It was ironic, then, that at the ripe old age of seventy-five he found himself in command of fully half of IV's new German air forces.

Michtler toured the tarmac on the tiny air base on the island of Guernsey.

The wind off the English Channel grabbed strips of steel gray hair, which had been carefully plastered across his bald pate, and flung them crazily across his face.

Around him were thirteen vintage aircraft. Ten of them were Messerschmitts, two were World War I Fokkers and the last—the lead plane—was a Gotha G.V.

"How soon?" Michtler demanded in German.

"Another five minutes," replied the mechanic who was in charge of seeing that the planes were airworthy. Michtler knew him only as Paul. He was forty-five years old with a thick neck and a face filled with burst capillaries. In private life he was an aviation buff. In an even more private life he was also a high-ranking member in Germany's underground skinhead movement.

Michtler scowled.

"They shot down the first wave," he snapped.

"Did you think they wouldn't?" Paul asked in surprise. He didn't look up from the fuel line he was attending to. It led into the hungry belly of the mint-condition World War I Gotha.

Michtler harrumphed impatiently.

Paul sensed the old man's anxiety.

"I have friends near Croydon," Paul said. He waved to the nearby tanker truck. A skinhead barely out of his teens began turning off the fuel. "Of course they have no idea who I am working for," Paul continued. "But they say over the computer that the Harriers have returned to their base. We will not have as easy a time of it this time, but it is possible."

"It had better be more than possible," Michtler threatened.

Paul smiled as he detached the fuel line from the plane. "Care to join us?" he asked. He knew full well Michtler's hatred of planes.

"Just speed it up," the old man growled. Spinning on his heel, he headed back to the small hangar at the end of the runway.

Still smiling, Paul climbed into his airplane. Clamping the dome—an added feature—down over his ruddy head, he began the start-up procedure. The other dozen planes arranged in a patient line on the tarmac nearby took this as a cue.

Thirteen plane engines coughed and smoked to life.

THEY HAD TAKEN a plane from Paris to Manche province. From there, a DGSE boat took them the thirty-five miles from Carteret to the cluster of England's Channel Islands.

They had already passed the small island of Sark. It seemed like little more than a speck as they raced by. Alderney was farther to the north, and the principal island of Jersey was to the south.

On the deck Remo watched, motionless, as the island of Guernsey rose up out of the sea before them.

Chiun stood beside him. The rocking of the large boat on the choppy waves had no effect on the Master of Sinanju. The wizened Asian appeared to be more firmly rooted in place than the rocky island they approached.

The two men had been silent a long time. Salty water broke across the prow of the boat and sprayed their stern faces. At long last Remo spoke.

"That phone call she got said that London had been attacked," he said. "You think Smith is okay?"

"I do not have a psychic connection to Emperor Smith," Chiun replied simply.

Remo glanced over his shoulder. Helene was on the bridge of the large boat. She wasn't paying them any heed.

Remo pitched his voice low.

"You recognize the guy on the phone?" Remo asked.

"I did," the Master of Sinanju replied.

"I'm surprised Source doesn't handle this themselves," Remo mused. "After all, these islands are British property."

"He was likely too involved with selecting the proper wardrobe to wear as his nation's capital burned," Chiun suggested.

"Good point. My luck, he pulled through and Smith got creamed."

"Smith is fine," Chiun insisted.

"How do you know?"

"Because that is *my* luck," the old man said. He aimed a finger to the sea. "Behold! Our destination draws near."

Guernsey had grown even larger.

The shore seemed totally inhospitable. It was comprised largely of sharp igneous rock, heaped and angled to form a natural barrier against intruders. Remo wondered why the original settlers hadn't just turned around and gone back to wherever they came from.

Instead of heading north to St. Peter Port—the island's chief town—the French boat headed south. Waves crashed over the bow as they cut in as close to the shore as the hidden underwater rocks would allow.

Helene joined them on the rolling deck.

"That end looks more hospitable," Remo said, pointing to the northern side of the island.

"I have been in contact with my government. They have used satellite information to confirm that the illegal shipments were sent to the south."

"So you're admitting the stuff was stolen now?" Remo asked slyly.

"Not at all. Something was sent here from France

during the night. I am merely here to find out what that something was.''

''You've got the patter down,'' Remo said, impressed. ''I'll give you that. You know, you remind me of another French agent I met a few years back. Remember Dominique Parillaud, Little Father?''

''Do not remind me of that dark time,'' Chiun sniffed.

They had met the French spy, whose code name was Arlequin, during an assignment that had taken them to the amusement park known as Euro Beasley. A weapon that used color to trigger heightened emotional reactions in its victims had caused both Masters of Sinanju to act in a less than heroic fashion. Neither man had been proud of his behavior during that crisis.

At the mention of the French spy's name, Helene's back stiffened.

''Looks like she knows her, huh, Chiun?''

''Knowing the proclivities of the French, it is no doubt in the biblical sense,'' the Master of Sinanju replied tightly.

''I do not know the person of whom you speak,'' Helene insisted.

''That's a load of crap,'' Remo said. ''I'm a student of body language. And you just screamed volumes.''

Helene bristled. ''I am *sure* I do not know her,'' she said haughtily.

''She got drummed out of the spy biz after she

failed to swipe the hypercolor laser, didn't she? Probably stuck doing full body-cavity searches at de Gaulle airport."

"And reveling in every depraved minute," Chiun chimed in.

"Poor Arlequin's persona non grata at DGSE HQ, isn't she?" Remo said sympathetically. "Better not screw up, Helene. She could be holding a seat for you."

"This is impossible!" the French agent announced, throwing her hands in the air. She marched a few yards away from the two men, dropping her hands on the slick boat railing. She kept her back to them.

"That was strangely unfulfilling," Remo said once Helene was out of earshot. In spite of the busy work at the American embassy and this unexpected side trip, he still found himself thinking about his earlier conversation with Smith. He and Chiun would track down a few stolen bombs and the world would continue to slide apace into the Abyss.

"You are still brooding," the Master of Sinanju said, nodding sagely.

Remo's mouth pulled into a tight smile. "I've managed to put on a happy face."

Chiun's own countenance was impassive. "Lamentably it appears to be the same as the ugly mask you always wear. The next time you change faces, you might try one with eyes of the proper shape. And the color is all wrong."

Remo sighed. "It was just a figure of speech," he grunted, dropping his knuckles to the railing.

"I would also trim the nose back by at least a foot." Chiun smirked.

THE SOUTH END of Guernsey rose three hundred feet to a rocky plateau. The small boat brought them into a harbor carved at the base of the foreboding wall of rock. A zigzagging staircase had been chiseled into the wall's craggy black face.

They found a dock that extended from a seawall of toppled stones. The boat moved in beside it, rocked all the while on the crashing waves. As soon as they were close enough, deckhands leaped out and began securing the boat to the dock.

The ship's pilot had barely cut the engines when Remo became aware of a collection of noises over the bluffs high above. There were thirteen distinct whines. Small engines.

He glanced at the Master of Sinanju. Chiun had heard the noise, as well.

The Master of Sinanju hopped from the deck of the rocking ship and onto the old wooden dock. He was running the instant his sandaled feet touched the pocked surface.

Remo jumped down after him.

"What is it?" Helene shouted from the deck.

"Planes!" Remo yelled back. "And by the sounds of it, they're ready for takeoff!"

PAUL NIEMLUR GAVE the young skinhead on the tarmac the thumbs-up sign. The youth pulled the canvas cord, wrenching free the oily wood chocks wedged beneath the wheels of the Gotha.

He ran over to the nearest Messerschmitt to repeat the procedure. Another skinhead was helping him, and between the two of them they quickly cleared the blocks away.

Paul began taxiing to the windswept runway.

The money that Nils Schatz had been skimming from IV accounts over the past several months had paid to construct this small runway on the site of a former Guernsey tomato farm.

It was somehow fitting that the attack against England should originate from here. After all, German forces had occupied the small island during World War II.

The runway was wide enough to accommodate two planes taking off at a time. The nearest Messerschmitt pulled in beside Niemlur. A second pair drew in behind.

Paul was certain to go slowly. The wind was heavy today. Ordinarily he wouldn't have risked taking off in gusts as strong as this. But this was different. The wind could go to blazes. After all, this was the dawn of the new reich. Anyway, once he was in the air it wouldn't be a problem.

For now he was concerned about the ancient bombs he was carrying. The Gotha had been designed to carry six one-hundred-pound bombs. He had that many aboard right now. They sat, rusted and beautiful, in the rear of the plane.

Paul pushed down on the throttle. The plane began to skim forward. The rocky scenery whipped past the Plexiglas dome he had installed aboard the aircraft.

For all he knew, some of the bombs he carried could have been dropped by this very plane over France more than eighty years ago. Back then they had been duds. There was no doubt about it this time, however. They were so fragile the slightest bump might set them off.

They would find their targets. And they would rain fiery death upon them.

As he picked up speed, this thought filled Paul with contentment while he carefully steered the plane toward the end of the runway. And into the jaws of history.

REMO AND CHIUN had attacked the first stone stairs with a ferocity of purpose. The staircases were like a stack of giant Zs carved into the solid cliff face.

Both men were buffeted by the cold ocean wind as they raced at top speed for the summit of the cliff.

The stairs ended abruptly at a rock-hewed landing. Here the rock tapered off and split in either direction. From this vantage they were able to see farther inland.

The runway was to their left. It cut off sharply toward the cliff face to the west. They could see the small tin hangar squatting in the scrub grass farther beyond the long asphalt strip.

More than a dozen planes were heading away from the hangar area. Though he had no idea what kind they were, Remo saw that they were from a different era.

Two had already picked up considerable speed and were racing for the edge of the bluffs. Others were moving obediently in behind them.

Remo and Chiun didn't stop when they reached the summit. Cutting west after the fleeing planes, they loped through the tall grass toward the runway.

They reached it in a few dozen quick strides.

"Should we try to stop these?" Remo shouted to Chiun over the roar of the planes and the wind. They had pulled abreast of the field of slower-moving planes.

Chiun shook his head. Wisps of hair flew wildly in the gale. "It is too dangerous. We will take those in the lead."

Remo knew what Chiun meant. The bombs the aircraft doubtless carried made this a tricky matter. They didn't want to jolt the planes and accidentally set them off. It would be an easier matter to stop them when airborne.

Although, Remo thought as he nodded his reluctant agreement, *easier* was a relative term.

The two men raced past the slower-moving aircraft toward the pair of planes that were even now preparing for takeoff.

Remo and Chiun were no longer running unnoticed. Radios aboard the planes squawked hurried questions in German.

A gunner opened fire as they raced past. A single bullet nicked the fuselage of one of the Fokkers. The old plane instantly exploded in a ball of bright orange flames and a spray of jagged metal fragments.

After that the other planes held their fire.

Legs and arms pumping madly, the two Masters of Sinanju left the edge of the runway and moved into the center behind the foremost planes.

The wheels of the Gotha had already left the ground. The Messerschmitt was outpacing it, but had not yet begun to skim the runway surface.

Chiun broke to the right, tearing off after the newer plane. Remo stayed on course, running at full speed for the tail of the fleeing Gotha.

Cold wind whipped against his face as he ran past the tail assembly. Wind caught the dorsal tail, fluttering it ferociously as he outpaced the rear of the plane.

A line of ragged grass sprouted up before them.

The end of the runway. Beyond that a three-hundred-yard drop to the rocks below.

And Remo was running full out. Even if he wanted to, he doubted he could stop on time.

There would only be one chance at this.

The Gotha was pulling up into the air. Legs pumping crazily, Remo forced a single burst of furious acceleration. He leaped from the surface of the runway and spread-eagled himself on the bottom left wing of the large biplane.

The plateau surface suddenly dropped out from beneath him. Far below, frothy waves crashed against basalt rock.

The plane was airborne.

The Gotha tilted slightly, attempting to right itself. The engine whined in protest as the aged aircraft soared off over the English Channel.

12

Unlike most people whose lives were fraught with doubt, Helene Marie-Simone was certain of almost everything. The most recent thing she found herself being certain of was the fact that she didn't trust Remo and Chiun.

But she had learned the hard way back in Paris that she should trust certain aspects of the two men. Their hearing, for one.

If they said that they heard planes taking off from the plateau high above the rocky shore, then she was certain that was exactly what they heard.

The minute the two men had broken for the stairs, Helene had climbed down from the boat and raced after them.

They were the most agile climbers she had seen this side of the monkey house at the Paris Zoo.

The two men quickly outdistanced her, leaving her to huff and puff her way up the many flights of stairs to the top of the cliffs. When she did finally reach the top, she was just in time to see Remo make a flying leap onto the wing of a departing Gotha G.V.

She thought she saw a streak of crimson that might

have been Chiun's kimono splayed across the wing of a fleeing Messerschmitt, but she couldn't be sure. Both aircraft dropped from the edge of the bluff and then ascended back up into sight farther out over the channel. They pulled into the sky in a whine of engines.

She could see neither man after that.

They had committed suicide. For however good their hearing might be, they would never survive perched like birds atop the wings of two ancient warplanes.

The rest of the planes were lining up for their turn in the air. Two more were about ready to tear off the edge of the cliff and soar into the pale blue sky.

They zipped past the burning ruins of a single plane.

The bouncing of the ancient ordnance aboard must have been the cause of its destruction, Helene surmised. Just as it had been in the truck back at the American Embassy in Paris.

And if a minor disturbance could destroy one plane, it could easily disable some of the others.

Helene pulled her handgun from her pocket. Her lungs were raw as she ran down to the field.

THE GOTHA WAS TEARING through the air at a speed in excess of one hundred miles per hour.

The wind pressed like a powerful fist against Remo's chest. His T-shirt fluttered crazily in the back. Short hair blew angrily around his head.

It was an old plane, but it had fallen into the hands of a tinkering hobbyist. Although it looked identical to the original model, structurally it had been greatly improved upon. Remo stood up on the aluminum lower wing. He held on to the hollow, lightweight metal support tubes that were strung between the upper and lower wings.

Mindless of the racing wind, he advanced on the cockpit.

Remo's presence on the plane hadn't gone unnoticed by the pilot. Paul Niemlur had been startled by the sudden shift of weight at the moment of takeoff.

Concerned that the unexpected imbalance might upset his sensitive cargo, he had quickly moved to right the plane. It was only after he had leveled off over the channel that he dared look out at his left wing.

He could not believe what he saw.

The thin stranger with the deep-set eyes and abnormally thick wrists was strolling over to Paul across the wing as casually as a friend might step across the road in Paul's native Dusseldorf. Except the expression Remo wore was not that of a friend. It was the face of Doom.

Ever mindful of the payload he carried, Paul slowly tipped the plane to the left.

Remo didn't budge.

Paul edged the plane farther over, trying to dislodge the man on the Gotha's wing.

All at once something heavy shifted in the back.

With a dangerous, instinctive quickness, Paul tugged the steering column level once more. He could feel the weight shift back to where it belonged.

He didn't have time for a sigh of relief.

Remo was at the cockpit dome.

Niemlur pulled at the authentic World War II Luger in its lovingly preserved leather combat holster at his hip. As he fumbled with the strap on the holster, he heard a horrid tearing sound all around him. He felt the sudden blast of cold air against his face. His eyes squinted and teared against the gale-force wind.

Turning away from the howling blast of air, he caught sight of the specially adapted bubble dome tumbling down the length of the fuselage. It bounced off the tail and disappeared into oblivion.

Even while this was going on, Paul had continued to fumble with his gun. The weapon was free by now.

He raised the Luger from beside his hip only to feel it being torn from his hand before he could even fire.

His fingers were numb. His wrist ached from the wrenching force that had ripped the gun away. Paul saw that the man on the wing was now holding his weapon.

"You won't be needing this!" Remo announced over the buffeting wind.

With a flick of his wrist, Remo tossed the Luger into the Gotha's slipstream. Paul saw the gun flying

backward, like the dome. It clunked off the rear of
the plane and fell to the sun-dappled water of the
English Channel some four hundred feet below.

"Time for twenty questions!" Remo was forced
to shout even though Paul was only a foot away.
"Let's start with who you work for!"

The German decided that politeness was the best
way to respond to this lunatic, particularly considering the capabilities he had so far displayed. Unfortunately, though he wanted to speak, he couldn't
bridge the language barrier.

"Entschuldigen Sie?" Paul said with a polite
shrug.

"Oh, crap," Remo griped. "Do you speak English?"

"Nein," Paul admitted with a helpless shrug. The
wind continued to howl against his exposed face. His
ruddy cheeks had grown bright red in the bitter gale.
He had turned his right ear against the wind. It ached.

"Great," Remo grumbled.

He peered over the cockpit and down the alley
created by the Gotha's long wingspan. Half a city
block away, the Master of Sinanju was climbing
along the fuselage of the Messerschmitt. As the old
man slid along the upper part of the plane, his crimson robe fluttered like a crazy flag in a hurricane.

Remo could kick himself sometimes for not trying
harder to learn some of these languages. Chiun understood German. The Master of Sinanju would have
to be the one to find out what was going on.

In the meantime the best Remo could do would be to turn this one plane back to Guernsey.

"Back," Remo ordered. He twirled his hand around in the air and pointed back in the direction of the Channel Island.

Paul seemed to get the idea. He nodded agreeably.

The Gotha's control panel looked pretty straightforward. Paul was drawing the U-shaped wheel to the left to begin his arc back to shore when there was a sudden, furious whine of engines from the south.

Both Remo and Paul turned in time to see a lone Bf-109F Messerschmitt tearing down towards them from an altitude of five hundred feet. Sunlight glinted off the plane's gleaming shell as the pilot opened fire from the wing-mounted machine guns.

Two dozen holes ripped through the nose of the Gotha from a spot just behind the propeller to an area a fraction ahead of the cockpit.

When the attacking plane opened fire, Remo immediately grabbed on to the lip of the open cockpit for support and vaulted over to the other side of the plane. With the sudden shift of weight, the Gotha angled downward on the right.

The movement shifted the hundred-pound bombs in their bays at the center of the plane.

Sweating in spite of the wind, Paul tugged at the steering column to straighten out the listing plane. As he did so, he scrambled for the radio microphone.

"*Nein! Nein!*" Niemlur screamed over the radio.

The pilot in the other plane wasn't listening. He

had torn over the wings and cut sharply back. Swooping around, he made another strafing run from the rear.

A hail of lead tore through the air around them. The old plane was peppered with fresh wounds, these near its tail. Miraculously none of the explosives in the back was detonated.

The Messerschmitt continued firing on the slower plane, stopping only as it buzzed over the upper wings of the Gotha.

Remo saw its gleaming underbelly as it soared above them. He glanced at the huge magazine case on the wing near him. There was another on the other side. Jutting out at the front of each of the upright boxes was a single machine-gun muzzle.

"How do you work them?" Remo asked, pointing at the guns.

Paul only shrugged, frightened and confused.

The Messerschmitt had broken off the attack for the moment. Spying Chiun sliding across the fuselage of the other plane, the pilot took a strafing run at that aircraft. The radio squawked with another panicked German voice as the Messerschmitt opened fire.

Chiun dodged the bullets by simply letting go of his grip. The wind grabbed his kimono and flung him back toward the tail section of the plane. He grabbed hold again as the shadow of the attacking warplane passed over the midsection of Chiun's plane.

The bullets had missed the explosives stored

aboard the aircraft, but they had caused damage nonetheless. Acrid smoke began pouring from the engine, filling the air behind it with a widening cloud of oily black.

With a pained hum the plane began losing altitude.

Like a shark smelling blood in the water, the attacking Messerschmitt swooped around for another pass.

Remo had no time to worry about the language barrier. He grabbed Paul by the back of the neck.

The pilot went as rigid as a board.

Remo manipulated the German's neck muscles expertly. Paul responded like a marionette. The pilot's hands gripped the half-moon steering wheel and tipped the Gotha into an angled dive.

One of the bombs broke free of its mooring in the rear of the plane. It tumbled forward into the bulkhead directly behind them with a crash. Somehow it failed to explode.

They were closing in on the attacking plane.

A stream of smoke continued to pour from the lead aircraft. Through the hazy black fog, Remo could no longer see the Master of Sinanju.

The pilot of the first Messerschmitt had cut back toward shore as his plane descended. The rock face of Guernsey's south shore rose up like a deadly stone barrier directly ahead of them.

They were within range of the attacking plane. Without help from the pilot, Remo would have to guess at what the firing mechanism was for the machine guns. Scanning the cockpit, he found what he was looking for. It was a single stick with a flat button embedded in the tip.

Delicately shifting the muscles in Paul Niemlur's neck, Remo had the German release one hand from the steering column. Helpless to do anything to stop Remo, Paul gripped the stick in his right hand. Remo had him stab down against the button with his thumb.

Nothing happened.

Up ahead the Messerschmitt seemed to take its cue from Remo's plane.

The instant Paul had depressed the firing button, the aircraft up ahead opened fire on the damaged and smoking lead plane. The bullets tore violently into the fuselage of the first plane.

One or more of the small leaden projectiles must have come into contact with the ordnance stored aboard the front plane. As Remo struggled to work the machine guns on his own plane, the lead aircraft erupted in a blinding ball of orange-white light.

Shattered bits of steel launched backward. Small shards pinged off the propeller of the Gotha.

Remo dodged the spray even as he searched the sky for bodies.

There was no sign of Chiun. What remained of the plane the Master of Sinanju had been atop belched fire and smoke as it raced down into the waters below.

It crashed atop the waves a moment later.

Furious, Remo glanced around the cockpit of the

Gotha. He found a small toggle switch on the dashboard marked in red. He reached over Paul and flipped the switch.

The attacking Messerschmitt had remained before them throughout the spectacular crash, but once the lead plane was down it began pulling up into the sky, exposing its back to them. Remo could see the pilot grinning victoriously in the cockpit.

Remo cranked a knot of muscles on Niemlur's neck.

The Gotha's huge wing-mounted machine guns with their stacks of ammunition burst to life.

The bullets caught the Messerschmitt square in the cockpit. The glass that didn't shatter was sprayed with the blood of the pilot as the projectiles ripped through the body of the plane.

The aircraft had been perched on its tail like a dolphin clearing the water. But now, with no one to guide it, gravity quickly took hold of it.

Spiraling out of control, it screamed back to earth. It crashed into the first cluster of rocks that stabbed out from Guernsey into the English Channel.

Remo was surprised that the island was so close.

He had little time left to work.

Paul seemed relieved that the ordeal was nearly over. That relief turned to shock as Remo turned his attention away from the crashed Messerschmitt back to the Gotha.

"Auf Wiedersehen," Remo said to Paul, summoning up what little German he knew.

He reached into the cockpit and ripped out a handful of wires. For good measure he wrenched at the steering column.

It came free like a half-loose tooth. Tendrils of wires still connected it to the rest of the plane.

Remo didn't have time to complete the job. The rock wall of Guernsey loomed larger before them.

Hoping he had done enough, he dropped the broken steering column onto the pilot's knees. Turning, he leaped backward, off the wing of the plane.

At the point when his feet left the wing, the aircraft was only about fifty feet above the channel. Remo sliced into the cold waters a few seconds later. Kicking sharply, he broke through the surface just in time to see the crippled Gotha crash directly into the cliff face of the island.

The impact propelled the payload of six hundred-pound bombs forward into the rear of the cockpit.

The explosion was massive. It blew up and back in a huge plume of fire and smoke. In slow motion the charred remnants of the aircraft broke away from the wall and fell to the sea. Minutes afterward huge slabs of loosened basalt rock continued to sheer away from the cliff wall, crashing down to the rocks below.

Bobbing in the cold water, Remo didn't exult in the scene. A sick feeling clenched his belly. Chiun was out there somewhere. In what condition, Remo had no idea. However, he couldn't help but think the worst.

He was about to head back out to sea to begin his

search for a body when a familiar squeaky voice called from the nearby rocks.

"Do you intend to splash about like a lazy walrus for the rest of the day?"

Remo turned his head in the direction of the voice. Relief had flooded his soul when he'd heard the first tones.

The Master of Sinanju stood on the strip of black rocks that jutted like a crooked finger from the unforgiving shore. The old Korean was dripping wet.

"You're okay!" Remo called over. His voice was a mixture of joy and relief.

"No thanks to you," Chiun clucked unhappily. "When I saw that you would be no help, I was forced to risk life and limb by jumping from that flying Hun contraption. First I made it so their aircraft would not gain altitude."

There was a hum of engines on the cliffs far above them.

Both men looked up.

Like angry wasps leaving their nest, a line of aircraft began launching into the air above the channel.

There were eight of them in all. The swarm of planes collected into a tight flight formation and took off across the channel toward the English mainland.

"It appears we were only partially successful," Chiun intoned gravely. "Hurry!"

As Remo swam to shore, the old Asian began picking his way across the uneven pile of rocks toward the main island.

WHILE REMO AND CHIUN were still clinging to their respective planes high above the English Channel, Helene Marie-Simone was racing on foot alongside the runway.

Her lungs burned from the long climb up the stairs. Though it was late summer, the air on the island was cold. Her throat was raw by the time she began gaining on the cluster of small airplanes.

Aside from a lone Fokker, the planes that remained were all Messerschmitt Me-262As. She recognized the early jet aircraft. Built during World War II, it could achieve a top speed of more than five hundred miles per hour. For these planes, it would be a short hop over the channel for London.

Helene couldn't allow that to happen.

The Fokker was much slower than the others. The runt of the litter, it lagged behind the rest of the pack, its engine humming with the manic intensity of a frantic puppy.

The bombs would be somewhere between the tail section and the cockpit. She was close enough now.

Dropping to one knee in the high grass, Helene lifted her pistol and began firing into the fuselage of the taxiing plane.

No sooner had the second bullet struck its target than the entire Fokker erupted in a ball of fire. The pilot threw himself out the door, his clothes ablaze. Helene caught the screaming skinhead in the forehead with a carefully placed round.

Burning, the old plane continued rolling forward down the small runway.

Helene heard shouting behind her. With the explosion, someone had radioed the other aircraft to stop. One did not heed the order. It launched itself out over the channel after Remo and Chiun's fleeing planes.

Helene saw several men running from the open mouth of the small hangar. One remained near the door. An old man, he screamed orders in German to the group of men.

They were coming toward her!

Helene dropped into the grass and began crawling toward the rest of the planes. They were close together, their engines idling. If she could take just one of them out, she might succeed in starting a chain reaction that would destroy all of the remaining planes.

A heavy footfall dropped nearby.

Helene rolled onto her back. She saw the young skinhead running into sight above her. A pair of Nazi swastikas had been etched in blue in the flesh at his temples.

The man jumped back, as if startled to be the one to find the object of their search lying in the grass before him.

In that split second of hesitation, Helene fired.

The bullet grabbed the young man in the throat, flinging him back into the grass in a violent spurt of blood.

The angry yelling increased.

She crawled faster now. With frantic purpose. But it was no use. She had given her position away. The next men to find her were not as timid as the first. They fell atop her from three different directions. A football tackle.

She tried to get off even a single shot, but a knee had dropped solidly onto her wrist. Something hard—perhaps a rock, perhaps a gun butt—slammed against her curled fingers. She dropped her weapon.

The group of skinheads dragged her roughly to her feet. Grabbing her arms and loose clothes, they hauled her back through the grass and onto the tarmac.

The lone figure was still waiting at the large door to the hangar. Even from this distance she could see that the old man's face was a mask of rage.

"Get her in here!" Hans Michtler screamed. Furious, he ducked back inside the hangar.

A minute later the engines of the planes whined back to life. The aircraft pulled farther down the runway in the direction of the building before wheeling back around. Two at a time, they began zipping once more down the strip of asphalt.

As Helene watched, the first pair launched out into the air over the channel.

The French spy felt the tingle of failure in her chest and stomach. She barely noticed the surrounding men as they dragged her into the hangar.

She had failed.

The next wave of bombers was on its way to London.

13

Nils Schatz accepted the news from Fritz with an angry tapping of his walking stick. When they had first set up shop in the small Parisian apartment, he had made a habit of striking the bronze cane tip against the bowed slats of the aged wood floor.

It was not long before the downstairs neighbors had complained.

After that he'd gone to great pains to muffle the sound by drumming the cane on the rug. It had been a supreme effort, but Schatz had no desire to call undue attention to himself in the early days of this great action.

Now he no longer cared. Now they were close to completion of his great plan.

Der Geist der stets verneint.

The words came to him now. Mocking him.

He banged the cane loudly against the wooden floor beside his straight-backed kitchen chair. There was a muffled shout of complaint from the apartment below.

"This is Michtler's fault," Schatz complained

hotly. "Is there no one in the SS that could have handled this assignment?"

Fritz shook his head. "There are few of us left, Nils," he apologized.

"Pah. How many planes were destroyed?"

"Two. Both Fokkers. The rest left the base unharmed. Although Michtler admits that he lost radio contact with three of them. There was some frantic talk of a dogfight."

Schatz closed his eyes. He was attempting to access stores of patience that he didn't possess.

As his thoughts roiled, he rammed his cane harder and harder in short, desperate jabs against the floor. A small section of the wood began to splinter, splitting away in long slivers at the force of the metal tip.

"Sinanju," he hissed.

"Surely they could not have survived," Fritz said. "They were atop the planes."

Schatz opened his eyes. He gave his assistant a glare that in his younger days had caused subordinates to release the contents of their bladders down the legs of their starched Nazi uniforms.

Fritz swallowed nervously.

Schatz pointed his cane at the man with whom he had grown old in that accursed South American village.

"You tell Michtler to be prepared."

"Yes, sir," Fritz snapped, clicking his heels. The movement came so naturally it was as if he had been magically transported back fifty years. "And what of the Frenchwoman?"

Schatz shrugged. "I do not care. Kill her." He began rapping his cane against the floor once more.

Fritz nodded his understanding. He started walking toward the living room, where the apartment phone was located. He hadn't gotten more than a few paces when the tapping of the cane stopped.

"Wait," Schatz called. His tone had grown considerably lighter. "I believe I have an idea."

His yellow teeth bared in an evil rictus of a smile.

HANS MICHTLER THOUGHT it was stupid to await the arrival of men who would never come.

The two fools who had leaped atop the planes as they soared off over the channel were dead.

The other aircraft had radioed back news of the wreckage moments after takeoff. Michtler had been late to the radio, so busy was he with capturing the French spy.

One plane had crashed into the bluffs just below the end of the runway. It had flown in too low for them to see from atop the rocky plateau. The other two were simply missing.

It was the bombs they had been carrying, Michtler concluded. They must have gone off prematurely. He had told this to Fritz in his second phone conversation with Paris, once it was learned why the planes had lost contact with the Guernsey base.

Their cargo was unstable. The pilots had simply

panicked when they found two fools clinging to the skins of their aircraft and somehow had shifted the dangerous cargo. Boom. It was that simple.

But it was only that simple for Hans Michtler. Schatz thought otherwise.

So, because of a couple of fools who had died twenty minutes before, Hans Michtler had to deal with this idiocy.

He was a good soldier. Always had been. He followed every order given him. Whether it was shooting at Russians, hurling grenades at Americans or marching his fellow countrymen into ovens. An order was an order. Hans Michtler couldn't be held accountable for the things his superiors had commanded him to do.

After the war he found that the world thought differently.

His zeal for his work in the Treblinka concentration camp had made him a target for the various Jew-sponsored groups whose job it was to persecute simple soldiers who were only following orders.

Michtler had been forced from his homeland to the small IV village in the mountains of Argentina.

When Nils Schatz had come to the other old Nazis with his bold proposal, Michtler had jumped at the chance to leave. The truth was, in life there were those who gave orders and there were those who executed those orders. Hans Michtler was one of the happy few who actually *enjoyed* following orders.

Until now.

"Your friends are dead. You know that, do you not, girlie?" Michtler sneered. He was a big, lummoxy thing. His hands were as large as small baseball gloves.

"They are not my friends," Helene replied evenly.

She was strapped to a chair in the middle of the hangar. There was a wooden floor beneath her, stained with oil. All around were stacked piles of ordnance stolen from the *deminage* depots. Helene had found some of what she was after, but was maddeningly unable to do anything about it.

Michtler curled his lip in disgust. He turned to the skinheads spread about the hangar. "Has the boat moved?"

"It is still docked below," one of the men enthused.

"No one aboard has made a move toward us?"

"There are only four aboard that we can see. They have remained on the boat."

Michtler nodded. "After we take care of her, we will kill them and scuttle their boat," he announced. He slapped his big hands together for warmth, glancing at the men. "For now we wait. Pointlessly."

There were about a dozen skinheads standing around the room. They each held a Schmeisser submachine gun. Michtler was so confident that the men they awaited were dead that he had left his own gun on a nearby table.

The man shot by Helene in the field beside the runway had been propped up next to a door that led into a small office. He sat wheezing and bleeding. Someone had given him a filthy cloth to hold over the gurgling wound in his neck. It was already drenched with blood. His complexion had grown waxy over the past several minutes. He appeared close to death.

Michtler glanced over to the open doorway. An oversize garage door, it was wide enough for two planes to roll in and out of the hangar.

Ordinarily there was room for four of the small aircraft inside at one time. But there were two partially dismantled Messerschmitts in the hangar now. They had been scavenged for parts for the working planes. These, along with the rusted shell casings, left little room for functioning planes.

When not being worked on, the IV air force had bided its time outside beneath heavy tarps and camouflage mesh.

Michtler looked out at the spot on the grassy field where the planes had sat idle for weeks. Two skinhead guards stood on either side of the open doorway.

Bored, he began to daydream.

He pictured the planes en route to England. His mind drifted to thoughts of London. Ablaze.

It was a beautiful sight.

REMO KNEW that their greatest challenge would be to keep the Germans from blowing them all sky-high.

When they had rounded the shore and gone back

up the stairs to the plateau airfield, the first thing he and Chiun had done was to sneak a peek inside the hangar from one of the side windows. They were disturbed to see explosives stacked everywhere.

Helene Marie-Simone sat strapped to a chair beside a doltish-looking, aging Nazi. The French agent was, in effect, seated in the middle of one gigantic bomb.

"That complicates things," Remo whispered to the Master of Sinanju. He was peering at the bound Helene.

"Why?" Chiun said blandly.

"For starters we've got to save Helene *and* one Nazi for interrogation without getting ourselves blown up."

"What need have we of the woman?"

"For one thing, I could use her phone."

"Save her phone, then," Chiun sniffed. "Allow fate to take charge of the daughter of Gaul."

Remo raised an eyebrow. "You're sounding more mercenary than usual."

"Sinanju has not found work from France for many years. Let the Bourbons worry about their own."

"Let's give them a freebie this time out, okay?" Remo replied deadpan. He looked back in the window. "Okay, here's the plan. We get the younger nasties out of the hangar. Less chance of their bullets setting off the bombs. Once we've thinned their

ranks, we can go in after Kaiser Baldy. Does that
sound good to you?''

"Everything save the part where we are to follow
a plan of your design,'' the Master of Sinanju replied.

"If you've got a better idea—'' Remo began.

But Chiun was no longer there. The diminutive
figure was already flouncing around to the front of
the hangar where the first of the skinhead guards
stood. Remo had to run to keep up.

STILL LOST in his own thoughts, Michtler had just
drawn up an image of the stodgy British parliament
building gutted by dancing flames when something
flashed across his line of sight.

It was a subtle movement. So small Hans Michtler
could not quite figure out what it was.

He blinked.

The hangar door was there. Open, as before. The
grass was still pressed down in the field beyond
where the planes had sat. The guards...

Hans Michtler started.

The two skinheads at the door were missing.

"Where did they go?'' Michtler roared.

"Who?'' one of the skinheads asked.

Michtler stabbed a pudgy finger at the door.
"Those two! Tell them to get back in here!''

With a sullen nod the young man went obediently
to the large entryway. Rifle in hand, he stuck his head
around the corner. In the next instant he was yanked
outside.

Michtler watched the young man's black boots disappear around the edge of the door frame.

"Impossible," he exhaled. Wheeling, he flung an open hand at the door. "Get them!" he snarled at his men.

As the remaining skinheads bounded obediently toward the door, Hans Michtler raced over to a desk against the wall. To collect his Luger.

SO FAR THE PLAN was working perfectly.

Chiun had taken the left, Remo the right. Already the Master of Sinanju had eliminated two of the guards. The old Korean flitted around the side of the building.

After Remo took out the man on the right of the door, he ducked around the side opposite Chiun.

Someone shouted inside. Although the order was in German, Remo guessed that it was a command to attack. The other men would be swarming out any minute.

There was a steel drum next to the corrugated-steel wall of the hangar. Remo vaulted atop it.

The toe of one loafer barely brushed the surface rim of the oily barrel before Remo was propelling himself farther upward. Twisting in midair, he landed on the back-angled roof with no more noise than that of a falling leaf.

Remo waited.

He didn't have to hold his position long.

The skinheads came barreling into sight. Outside

the door they split up. Some went right, while others moved to the left. Three of them tromped around the side of the building near Remo, waving their guns menacingly. One was farther ahead, and two were shoulder to shoulder taking up the rear.

All of them were anxious to fire. With the constant threat of detonating the war ordnance, their eagerness would make matters all the more tricky.

When the two in the back paused near the oil barrel, Remo dropped down from the roof, landing lightly behind the pair of skinheads.

They hadn't even become aware of his presence before his hands flashed out.

Years of diet and exercise had made Remo's fingers harder than titanium. The index and middle fingers of both hands struck off center in the backs of the skinheads. Splitting only a single rib in each body, the fingertips shot through the thoracic cavities, puncturing the rear walls of two nervously beating hearts.

Quick as a shot, Remo's fingers withdrew. They had gone in with the speed and precision of a surgical laser. So fast had Remo moved that not a single drop of blood showed on his fingertips.

The men grew rigid. The attack had come so quickly that they felt the pain and shock only when their hearts began spurting blood wildly throughout their chest cavities. That lasted only a second.

They dropped to the ground.

As the first fell, his gun dropped against the metal barrel. It made a loud clang.

The remaining skinhead was firing his submachine gun even before he wheeled on Remo.

Bullets pinged against the steel wall of the hangar. Remo twisted through the barrage, advancing on the shooter, all the while waiting for the building beside him to erupt in a ball of flame and fragmented metal. Luckily he reached the man in time.

Swatting the gun harmlessly into the nearby field with his left hand, Remo sent his right hand forward, palm flat. The skinhead's rib cage was crushed to jelly.

Remo waited a fraction of a second.

The only sound from within was an angry shout.

He heard more voices, these ones outside. They had heard the gunshots and were coming to investigate.

"I'm never going to live this down," he griped.

Leaving the three skinheads where they lay, Remo bounded back up atop the hangar roof.

As REMO DUCKED around one side of the building, Chiun was mirroring his pupil's movements in the opposite direction.

The old Asian found himself in a small, enclosed junkyard filled with discarded airplane parts. At the far end of the lot a chain-link fence capped with razor wire lent a prisoner-of-war-camp feel to the area.

There was too much junk between him and the

fence. And while Chiun could cross the space easily, his pursuers would have a much harder time of it.

Chiun had hoped to draw the men away from the building and the bombs within. He was angry at himself for not heading out across the tarmac and into the open fields.

Vowing that this would be the last time he would allow Remo to talk him into a plan, Chiun turned around and headed back in the direction from which he had come.

He hadn't gone more than two paces before a pair of skinheads marched around the corner of the hangar.

Seeing Chiun, they hastily raised their weapons to fire.

"Thank you, Remo the Plan Maker," the Master of Sinanju grumbled.

He couldn't allow them to get off a shot. Any one of the chunks of metal in the courtyard could cause a ricochet that would blow up the entire area.

His wizened face displaying his annoyance, Chiun quickly scooped up a pair of five-foot-long propellers that were leaning against a rusting engine nearby. Bringing the heavy blades back up over his shoulders, he snapped his hands down and forward, releasing the curving pieces of metal when they were at the farthest point from his body.

The propellers whizzed through the air at a speed faster than any aircraft engineer could have dreamed of.

In that fraction of an instant before the fingers of the skinheads pressed against the triggers of their machine guns, the props slammed against the extended gun barrels.

The propellers ripped through the metal barrels, bending them back like banana peels, embedding both curling ends into the chests of the two men. The propellers continued on their forward paths, pulling both men from the ground and launching them back into the steel wall of the hangar.

The side of the structure quivered like a beaten drum as the men slammed against it, chunks of gun and propeller jutting from their chests. An instant later they grew limp against the wall, their boots hanging slack a foot above the ground.

More voices.

There were other men coming in his direction. Chiun prepared himself for another assault.

There was a sudden short burst of gunfire on the other side of the hangar. The men coming toward him grew distracted, running back in the other direction toward the new sound. Muffled, wet thuds met them. Then all was silent.

In the next instant Chiun saw a flash of movement atop the hangar. When he looked up, he saw Remo crouching on the flat rooftop.

"Before you blame me, it wasn't my fault," Remo whispered.

"No," Chiun agreed, his expression stern. "It is *my* fault for being foolish enough to listen to you."

"Fine with me. As long as we've got the blame thing settled."

Chiun frowned with his entire face. "Get out of the way, General Patton."

As Remo ducked back, Chiun bounded up onto the roof next to him. Red kimono skirts settled around pipe-stem legs.

"How many did you get?" Remo said as they slid stealthily away from the edge of the roof.

"Two."

"Three for me. I took out a couple more from up here. Aside from Conrad Siegfried downstairs, that should be it."

Chiun stopped dead. "Siegfried? Who told you that was his name?" he demanded. The look in his hazel eyes was furiously intent.

Remo was taken aback by Chiun's jarring attitude change.

"No one," he said. "It was just a joke."

The old man eyed his pupil with suspicion. Detecting no visible deceit on Remo's part, he at last nodded.

"Very well."

Chiun began moving away across the roof. Remo hurried to keep up.

"What was that all about?"

"There is no time for idle conversation, O Plan King. In case you have forgotten, we are standing atop a giant boom device. We must find a way inside that does not result in our untimely arrival in the Void.''

As they slid along the steel roof, Remo spied what looked like a square hatch near the rear of the building. He touched Chiun on the sleeve.

''I have a plan,'' he said with a smile.

MICHTLER DIDN'T WANT to think about what was going on outside. He'd heard the gunfire to his right a few minutes before.

He immediately dropped to the wooden floor, covering his head in his meaty hands.

He didn't care how foolish he looked, nor did he consider the utter pointlessness of this gesture of self-preservation, given the amount of explosives that were stored around him.

The gunfire ended abruptly. It was proceeded by an even more frightening calm.

No one came to tell him that the two men were dead.

Michtler climbed unsteadily to his feet. He glanced up at the far rear wall of the hangar. A single red light shone down out of the darkness. Beyond it was the trapdoor to the roof.

Turning away from the light, he looked back toward the entrance.

Until the actual moment his Luger was ripped painfully from his huge hand, Michtler had no way of knowing that Remo and Chiun had slipped into the hangar through the office door during the split second he had turned away.

"I still say we should have used the roof door," Remo complained.

"Need I remind you that, had this pastry-fed Hun managed to fire a single shot, we would be having this argument in the company of my ancestors?" the Master of Sinanju declaimed, as if affronted by the mere idea.

It took the big German a moment to realize what was going on. Like a great lumbering dinosaur, Michtler turned on the intruders. He sent a huge fist toward Remo's head. There was a horrid sound of crunching bone. Again it was another moment before Michtler realized that the noise hadn't come from the skull of the man he thought he had just punched but rather from his own hand.

The German howled in pain as he stuffed the fist with its four shattered fingers into the safe haven beneath his left armpit. He dropped to his knees on the wooden floor. The boards creaked beneath him.

Hands tied tightly behind her, Helene watched the drama playing out before her in amazement.

"How——?" she gasped once Michtler was subdued.

"Clean living, baby. By the by, do you actually get paid for this spy stuff?" he asked as he tossed the German's gun out the hangar door. "You're really bad at it." He wrenched apart the ropes that bound her to the chair.

It was as if she hadn't heard him.

"There are not enough bombs here," Helene announced, standing. Her face was urgent.

"There's plenty for me," Remo replied.

"No. There was much more than this stolen from the bases," she insisted. "This is only a fraction of what is missing."

"You're admitting they were stolen now, hmm?" Remo said with a superior smile.

"We *must* get back to France at once," Helene insisted. She glanced from Remo to Chiun, hoping the men shared her sense of urgency.

When she looked at Chiun, she saw that the Master of Sinanju was peering up into the distant corner of the large room where the single red light glowed from the shadows.

"We are being observed," the old man said.

Remo glanced up at the stationary camera on the wall. He had felt the hum of electronic equipment upon entering the building but had been too preoccupied with Helene and Michtler to locate the source. The single red eye peered angrily at them.

Remo turned his attention back to Hans.

"Okay, Colonel Klink, who's running—?"

He never had a chance to complete the thought.

There was another hum of electronic equipment from somewhere beneath their feet. All four of them heard a single metallic click, followed by a steady hiss.

An oily yellow mist began seeping up through dozens of knotholes in the pitted wooden floorboards.

The short hairs on Remo's exposed forearms telegraphed the danger before the mist reached their small group.

"Mustard gas!" Remo snapped.

Chiun had sensed the hazard, as well.

"If you wish to save that one, you must hurry," he said sharply. With that the Master of Sinanju hauled Helene up off the floor. Dodging bursts of the deadly chemical agent, he raced toward the open hangar door.

The largest cloud had poured up through a hole near the kneeling Hans. His eyes bulged as he clawed at his constricting throat.

Remo was forced to reach in through the cloud to grab the big German. He immediately felt an intense burning sensation on the flesh of his bare forearm.

Pulling Hans free of the mist, Remo held him at arm's length as he raced out the door.

CHIUN WAS a hundred yards away from the hangar before he even began to slow down. When he sensed that they were free of the danger zone, he turned, depositing Helene on the grassy field. Remo ran across the tarmac to meet him.

As he ran, Remo's body worked double-time to slough the deadly toxin from his skin. By the time he reached the others, he was in no danger. Even so, the area where the chemical had touched flesh was a bright cherry color.

"You are well?" Chiun asked, concerned.

"I'll be okay," Remo said. "Which is more than I can say for him."

Hans Michtler was dead, his fat tongue jutting from between thick lips. Remo dropped the German's body to the grass.

"That is an unspeakable evil," Chiun intoned, nodding to the open door of the hangar. The mustard gas was seeping out in small dribbles, catching pockets of wind before swirling away across the grassy plains. "It interferes with breathing."

"That's putting it mildly, Little Father."

"My phone!" Helene said suddenly. "It is inside!" She made a move back toward the hangar.

Remo restrained her. "Are you insane?" he asked. "You'll have to wait for the gas to clear."

"But I *must* warn France," she insisted. "There are many more bombs still unaccounted for."

"Use the radio on the boat."

By the look on her face it was obvious that Helene had forgotten about the boat. Wordlessly she spun around and began racing back toward the cliff and its long, zigzagging staircase.

"And maybe you should call England while you're at it!" he shouted after her. To the Master of Sinanju he muttered, "They might want to know they're about to get bombed for tea."

14

Colonel E. C. T. Bexton was impressed at the civil tone the gentleman was taking—very proper, very British. Not like that frantic, shrieking scientist-type from Jodrell Bank. Probably a poofter, that one was.

But the colonel couldn't order the deployment of British planes over British soil on the say-so of one lone special agent. No matter how refined that one agent sounded.

"I am terribly sorry," Colonel Bexton drawled, "but the RAF cannot get involved in the matter at this time."

"I understand your situation," the gentleman argued.

"I am sorry, but I don't think you do. Did you see the morning tabs?" Bexton pulled one of London's tabloid newspapers from beneath a stack on his desk. He read the banner headline. "London Blitzed Whilst RAF Sits. We're getting positively murdered in the press."

"Perhaps you'll get a bit more ink on the positive side if you headed this squadron off before they actually reach the city."

"There *is* no other squadron," Bexton said patiently.

"Ah, there's where you're off, Bexton. I am assured by a very reliable source in the French intelligence community that a small attack force is winging its way Londonward even as we speak."

Bexton wanted to laugh in the man's ear. Somehow he restrained himself.

"There is no way a *snail* could fly out of Ireland, let alone a vintage Messerschmitt."

"Ireland?"

"Northern Ireland, to be specific," Bexton said smugly. "I gather you intelligence chappies don't know everything."

"You are monitoring Northern Ireland?"

"With everything we've got. The attack came in from over the Irish Sea. Makes sense, with all that's been going on there."

"But surely the planes flew north, *then* south."

"A ruse," Bexton said absently. He had pulled out another paper from the pile. The headline on this one read RAF-fing Stock! "Shameless. Honestly, these things sound more American every day." At that moment his private line lit up. That would be the wife to see if he was going out to his club later that evening. "Sorry, old man. Got to go. National emergency and all that. Wouldn't fret if I were you. Tah."

He hung up on the caller before the polite gentleman had a chance to inform him that snails do not fly.

15

The gas had cleared by the time Helene returned from the boat. Chiun opted to stay out in the fields beyond the small airstrip. Remo was inside the hangar.

He had already done a quick search outside of the camera's range before concluding that there was no triggering device connected to the bombs like the one that had been rigged up to the canisters of mustard gas in the floor. He was staring up at the remorseless red eye of the camera when Helene entered the building.

"I cannot get through to my government," Helene announced as she came through the door. "The boat radio is no good for direct communication."

She looked around the hangar for her phone. She found it in Remo's hand. When she tried to retrieve it, he twisted away from her.

"Business," he explained, cupping his reddish, burned hand over the receiver. "Hello, Smitty?" he said into the phone. "You've got a situation going on over there."

"Explain," Smith said.

Remo told him about the island airfield and the eight planes that had escaped.

"You need to let the English know what's coming," Remo said in conclusion.

"They already know," Helene volunteered.

"What?" Remo asked.

"Who was that?" Smith said at the same time.

"I don't know, Smitty," Remo muttered into the phone. "Some French spy we picked up. What do you mean they already know?" he asked Helene. "I thought the radio didn't work."

"I said I could not contact France. My source in England was easier to contact from here."

"You can relax on that end," Remo said to Smith. "Source knows what's coming."

"You know of Source?" Helene Marie-Simone asked, surprised.

"Helene, *everyone* knows about Source. It's England's funniest worst-kept secret next to Prince Philip."

The fact was, Remo had had several brushes with Britain's top spy organization in the past. Each time he found himself less impressed than the last.

"She was talking to Sir Guy Philliston earlier," Remo said to Smith. "He's the one that told her to come here to Guernsey. She also says that a lot more bombs were stolen than what's here. Maybe you ought to get through to DGSE and let them know they've still got a hot potato on their hands."

"He can do that?" Helene asked.

Remo nodded. "I'd keep on his good side. He can really screw with your credit rating."

He heard Smith begin typing on his portable computer. While he waited, Remo glanced around the interior of the hangar.

He was still out of camera range. As it was, he wasn't entirely certain that it was not an automated system. The camera hadn't made a move to pan over to him since he reentered the hanger. If someone was watching, he would take care of them after he was through on the phone.

The skinhead Helene had shot still lay inside the door. If he hadn't died from the gunshot wound, the mustard gas had finished him off. The body had toppled over and was lying in a pool of damp oil.

There was tattooing all around the top of the man's head. Most of the ink marks were small, but two were larger than the rest. One of the large tattoos was a swastika. Remo couldn't help but show a look of disgust when he scanned the symbol. Leaving the twisted symbol of hate, his eyes alighted on the second large image.

Remo tipped his head to read the numbers.

"Four," he mused aloud. Something about the number was strangely familiar.

"What?" Smith asked, still typing at his keyboard.

"Oh, nothing, Smitty," Remo replied. "It's just that some of these guys we've come up against have the Roman numeral IV tattooed on their scalps."

"On their scalps?"

"Yeah," Remo said. "They're skinheads or something. Didn't I mention that?"

Smith had stopped typing. "No, you didn't."

There was a pregnant pause on the line, broken only when Smith muttered a single word.

"Four," he said, softly. He was deep in thought.

"Is that an unlucky number for you or something?" Remo asked with a puzzled expression.

Smith's voice had grown troubled. "Remo, you no doubt remember the incident this past spring concerning PlattDeutsche America and that company's mind-controlling product, the Dynamic Interface System?"

"Remember it," Remo scoffed. "I'll never forget it. They had Chiun and me wired up like a couple of robots."

"You remember at the time the individuals involved in that scheme referred to something called IV."

"Yeah," Remo said. It was coming back to him. "That old Nazi scientist boxed up duplicates of mine and Chiun's brain patterns and was going to ship them off somewhere. We never found out where."

"Precisely," Smith said. "I assumed when I could not find a reference to a IV group in any of the neo-Nazi literature that it was a minor splinter group. Perhaps I was in error. It is possible that we are dealing with a much larger organization than I had anticipated."

"You mean there's more of those skunks around?"

"Look at the evidence thus far," Smith said excitedly. "German warplanes armed with stolen German bombs. A new blitz on London. And skinheads sporting a particular and otherwise unexplainable tattoo. I think it is more than possible. I think it is a high probability that IV is an organization of either former Nazis or like-minded individuals."

"The guy that was in charge here looked old enough to be from the World War II generation," Remo offered.

"He most likely was," Smith answered. "I will do further research into IV. With any luck we will be able to work our way down from the top."

"Well, whatever you do, do it quick, because going from the bottom up has gotten us squat so far." There was a sudden familiar whine in the background. At first Remo thought the planes were returning to Guernsey. It took him a moment to realize the noise was coming from the other end of the line. "Smitty, am I hearing what I think I'm hearing?"

Remo heard a rustling sound. Smith had gone to the window of the hotel, drawing back the drapes.

"It is starting again," the CURE director said flatly.

The first dull explosions from the aerial bombs began filtering over the line.

"Find cover," Remo said quickly.

Whatever Smith might have said next was lost forever. The connection to England was abruptly severed. Remo stared at the dead phone in his hand for a few long seconds.

"London is under attack," Remo said, turning to Helene.

"What?" she asked, shocked.

"I thought you told them they were coming," he pressed.

"I *did,*" she insisted.

Remo glanced up at the camera. It was still directed to the spot on the floor from which the mustard gas had emanated.

"I guess we made the same mistake England always makes. We put faith in British Intelligence."

Without turning in her direction, he handed the phone out to her. She accepted it. As a precaution, in case Remo's contact hadn't reached DGSE, she began punching in her direct line back to her Paris headquarters.

As Helene dialed, Remo walked over to the corner of the hangar. Avoiding a stack of shells, he drew an empty crate to a spot directly beneath the camera. He climbed atop the crate. For the first time since reentering the hangar he put his face in the camera's purview.

He stared coldly into the lens.

"I am going to kill you," Remo said. He exaggerated each word so that whoever might be on the other end would have no difficulty understanding him.

This accomplished, he held his hands out on either side of the camera. He brought them together with a sharp clap. The camera sprang apart in a million shards of plastic and metal.

16

I am going to kill you.

The camera had no audio capability, but that didn't matter. The words were plain enough.

Nils Schatz didn't even think to rap his cane on the floor as he watched Remo lift his hands up out of view of the camera. A moment later the extreme close-up of the young Sinanju master exploded in a spray of white-and-gray static.

As the snow-filled screen hissed mockingly at him, Schatz woodenly switched off the television monitor.

He stared at it for what seemed like hours.

A feeling of unease that he had not felt in many years had crept from the murkiest depths of his black soul.

It was Germany. April 1945.

Schatz was a young man then. He had been a colonel in the Geheime Staatspolizei, the Gestapo, under the notorious Adolf Eichmann. It was while he was working for the Gestapo's subsection four of the second section—which dealt with religion, and in particular the perceived Jewish threat to the glorious reich—that he had caught the attention of none other than Schutzstaffeln head Heinrich Himmler.

The leader of the SS was impressed by Schatz's unparalleled talent for brutally savage interrogation. Since the Gestapo had become part of the SS, no one protested when Himmler stole Schatz away to become his personal assistant.

Schatz was taken to the seat of Axis power.

Eventually Himmler had grown to rely on his young colonel. So much so that he one day brought him along to an important meeting in the chancellery in Berlin.

Schatz had never expected the führer to be at the gathering. He had thought it would be a collection of SS officials, as had been the case in many of the other meetings he had attended since joining the upper echelon of the secret state-police force.

His shock when Hitler entered the room was obvious—even humorous—to all gathered. Schatz was like a star-struck American teenager who had just run into Veronica Lake on a Hollywood sidewalk.

Hitler had laughed off the attention. The rest did, as well. The meeting was allowed to continue.

Schatz made a good show of getting himself under control. But the truth was he never got over that first thrill of seeing Germany's supreme warlord face-to-face.

It was not only Hitler.

That the man was charismatic was an understatement. He held a fascination for the German people that was misunderstood and forever mischaracterized by the outside world. They were like helpless moths drawn to an open flame.

But the führer was only part of the equation. It was what he represented that was even more important. Hitler had a vision for the future of Germany that had captured the hearts and the souls of millions of Germans.

The Third Reich. A thousand-year Teutonic empire.

Nils Schatz believed not only in Hitler—he believed passionately in the idea of the reich.

His wholehearted belief in the Third Reich remained strong up until one fateful morning only a few days before its spectacular collapse.

Things were already bleak when news was brought into the SS from a captain who was supposed to be stationed in Italy. For some reason the man had seen fit to abandon his post. He had traveled all the way back to Germany during some of the heaviest fighting of the war.

Schatz had intercepted the captain on his way to deliver a message to Heinrich Himmler. When pressed by Schatz, the man said simply that he brought word to those highest up in the modern Hun empire.

"Hun? That is insulting to your people," Schatz had sneered, his mien utterly disdainful.

"That is what the Master of Sinanju called us," the captain had responded.

"Who?" Nils Schatz had asked. With Berlin tumbling down around his ears, he had neither the time nor the inclination to deal with fools.

"The Master of Sinanju," the captain repeated, as if the name alone explained the man.

"Yes," said Schatz slowly. "And what is this message?"

"The Master wishes for me to tell the funny little man with the funny little mustache that death is on its way."

Nils Schatz grew pale. Not with fear—he had no idea at that time who this Master of Sinanju was and therefore had no reason to fear. No, the thing that drained the blood from the face of Nils Schatz was pure, unbridled rage.

While Allied bombs dropped on Berlin, Schatz had personally dragged the man down to an interrogation cell. For the captain's insolence in the manner in which he characterized the chancellor of Germany, Schatz delivered the beating of a lifetime. He asked repeatedly who this Master of Sinanju was and how he had managed to turn an officer of the SS so completely.

Schatz questioned the man for four hours. He used every method of torture he could think of, yet the man stubbornly refused to break. It was as if he had already experienced a pain so great that nothing Schatz could do to him could even come close to matching whatever force had sent him fleeing back to Germany.

Finally Schatz had given up. He signed the execution order personally and had returned, sweating from his labors, to his office. It was only in a later meeting with Himmler that he mentioned the captain and his strange message.

He never forgot the look that crossed the SS head's taciturn face when he mentioned the Master of Sinanju.

"When did you receive this message?" Himmler demanded.

"I am not sure," Schatz admitted. "Perhaps, nine, perhaps ten o'clock this morning."

"And what time is it now? Quickly, quickly!"

"Six o'clock, sir," Schatz had answered.

Himmler's normally bland face grew wild.

"We must see the chancellor," he hissed. He hurried from the conference room where they had been meeting. Confused, Schatz followed.

The streets were littered with debris. Bombs whistled endlessly around their speeding staff car as Schatz and Himmler raced to the führer's bunker beneath the bombed-out chancellery building.

The word among the Nazi elite was that the führer was even now planning his withdrawal from the city. It was well-known that he intended to flee to the south, where Field Marshal Schoerner's army group in Czechoslovakia and that of Field Marshal Kesselring were still intact. Hitler had every intention of joining them and using their collective forces to strike out anew against the accursed Allies.

Upon greeting Himmler and Schatz in the bunker, Hitler was vibrant and upbeat. Entirely unlike the accounts that would eventually surface detailing his last days.

The führer noticed Himmler's sickly expression instantly. At the SS leader's urging, the two men went into a private conference room.

Schatz never knew precisely what was said in that meeting, but he had a strong suspicion.

The meeting with Himmler took all of ten minutes.

When they again stepped out into the common room, Hitler was a drained man. His vitality was gone, his vision of a Nazi future all but destroyed.

Schatz and Himmler left the bunker together. When they parted company later that night, it was the last time Nils Schatz ever saw his mentor. A disguised Himmler was captured by Allied forces later that night while attempting to flee Germany.

Hitler lasted only another two days. A coward who was finally faced with a choice of death by his own hand or death at the hands of the Master of Sinanju, the führer chose the former. He committed suicide rather than suffer the wrath of the mysterious stranger.

The vaunted Third Reich was over. And with it, a young SS officer's dreams of glory. While Russian troops swarmed through Berlin, Nils Schatz slipped into the night.

Others escaped, as well. With the gold and price-less art treasures they had looted from all over Europe while the war had raged, these former Nazis set up a system to see that they and their kind would be safe from persecution. This band of fugitives founded what would eventually become known as IV.

While Schatz hadn't come up with the name, he wholeheartedly supported its purpose. To establish a new, true thousand-year German reich. The Fourth Reich.

But IV had not lived up to its purpose. The founding members were now retired. Most had died off. There were few around who understood the importance of their work. And of those who did not understand, Adolf Kluge was the worst offender.

Kluge had taken over IV more than ten years before. He was a young man. Barely in his forties. He didn't understand what IV represented to the men of Schatz's generation. No one who didn't live through those terrible times could understand.

No, Kluge—while a capable man and a dedicated fascist—was simply too young and inexperienced to appreciate that for which Schatz and his followers pined.

Nils Schatz understood.

And that was why Schatz had taken matters into his own hands. That was why he had stolen millions of dollars of IV money to finance this operation. And that was why he was sitting here now, in a Paris apartment, staring at a blank television screen.

He was an old man now. And for the first time in his life he finally understood the fear that had engulfed both Himmler and Hitler all those years ago. In another lifetime.

He heard the phone ring out in the living room of the apartment. Fritz answered it.

Schatz was too preoccupied to worry about who might be calling.

His thoughts were of the Master of Sinanju. The same man who had chased Himmler from Germany and frightened the führer to death. He was here. In Europe. Alive. And his protégé had just vowed to kill Schatz.

He was furious at himself for not having Michtler hook up a remote charge to the explosives. It would have been—what?—another fifty dollars in parts. Schatz had underestimated his opponent. He had assumed the mustard gas would be enough.

"Not again," he muttered to himself. Slowly he began tapping his cane against the floorboards. "Not again," he repeated, more firmly this time.

In the outer room Fritz hung up the phone. On reluctant feet he walked up to the small bedroom. He found Nils Schatz sitting in front of the television.

"Nils?"

"Not again!" Schatz screamed, wheeling on Fritz. He stabbed his cane like a fencer's sword.

Fritz recoiled in shock, grabbing at the door frame. The look of terror on his subordinate's face seemed to have a calming effect on Schatz. He dropped his cane tip to the floor, bracing his hands atop the blunt handle.

"Who was that?" he demanded.

Fritz seemed hesitant to speak. He took a few deep breaths to compose himself.

"Kluge," Fritz said at last. He waited for another outburst from Schatz. None came.

"What did our friend, Herr Kluge, want?" Schatz asked. He tipped his head, turning a lazy eye on Fritz.

"He has learned of the missing funds."

"Who told him?" Schatz asked flatly.

Fritz shrugged his bony shoulders. "I do not know. I am not certain anyone told him. He periodically reviews all IV accounts."

"Ah, yes. Kluge the accountant. Very brave. Very noble." Schatz wore a displeased expression. "How did he find me here?"

"IV still has resources in Europe. Contacts," Fritz added with a feeble shrug.

Schatz nodded. "When I have the time, I will learn the names of these contacts."

"Herr Kluge wishes for us all to return."

"No time," Schatz said, shaking his head. As if this reminded him of something, he smacked himself on the forehead. "Time! The planes surely have arrived by now. We are sitting here like old washerwomen while London burns."

He got up, leaving the closed-circuit television behind him. All thoughts of the Master of Sinanju and his protégé were banished from his mind.

It was fear that had done the others in. Even his

own mentor, Himmler, had succumbed. Nils Schatz wouldn't allow mindless fear to rule his destiny.

Leaving his fears behind him, he went out to the living room to watch the new blitzkrieg on the apartment's small black-and-white TV.

17

The bombings had turned London into a sight-seeing mecca.

Eager tourists—their suitcases bulging with camera equipment and extra rolls of film—had been taking every available flight into the city over the past two days hoping to get a glimpse of yet another bombing attack by the as yet unexplained German surplus aircraft.

Germany itself had disavowed any knowledge of the planes' origin and emphatically denied that the government of unified Germany was involved in any way. To show their good faith the Germans had offered a team of special government agents to assist in the investigation.

England had resisted the notion of accepting outside aid. The official statement from the government was that there was no difficulty that could not be defeated with a little British pluck.

Remo nearly choked with laughter when Helene Marie-Simone informed him of this.

"They didn't even send up planes until the Germans were nearly out of bombs,'' he said with a derisive snort.

They were touring Trafalgar Square. The Nelson Monument with its huge pedestal loomed two hundred feet above them. The imposing statue of Lord Nelson high above stared out over the bustling city.

The German bombs had knocked out London's phone lines. Remo hadn't heard from Smith since the day before, and so they had traveled to England in hopes of locating the CURE director. It would have helped if he had some idea of the hotel at which the Smiths were staying.

"It was thought in the RAF that the planes had originated in Northern Ireland," Helene explained. "All available technology and manpower was directed there."

Remo rubbed tears of mirth from his eyes, still chuckling lightly.

"This country is amazing," he sniffled.

The Master of Sinanju, walking between Remo and Helene, shook his head. "Not any longer," he intoned sadly. "During the reign of Henry the Benign this land knew greatness. Now it is a pale imitation of its former self."

"The benign?" Helene asked Remo.

"Henry VIII," Remo replied. "Chopped off his wives' heads, but he always paid on time."

"Prompt payment for services rendered must not be treated lightly," Chiun said, raising an instructive talon. "England in good King Henry's day treated us well."

The crowd through which they passed had grown thicker. Remo could see the tail of a downed plane jutting up at a right angle from the street. Swarms of people were gathered around it, snapping pictures. A gaggle of milling bobbies in blue uniforms and high police hats didn't attempt to hold the crowd back. They stood at attention, arms behind their backs, faces glancing intently around the square. What they were looking for, Remo could not begin to fathom.

"I am sorry," Helene pressed Chiun, "but are you claiming to have been an assassin to Henry the Eighth?"

Chiun fixed her with a baleful glare.

"Do I look to you, madam, to be five centuries old?"

Helene hesitated.

"Well—"

"Our family," Remo explained quickly, lest an insensitive answer from the French agent cause her head to suffer the same fate as that of Henry's wives. "An ancestor worked for Henry the Eighth."

With Remo in the lead, they had managed to push through the crowd. The aircraft around which the crush of people had assembled had been shot down by an RAF missile. Freed of its payload minutes before the final, fateful attack, the plane hadn't been destroyed wholly in midair. A piece of the tail section had been blown away, causing the plane to lurch forward and sail headlong into the hind end of a parked double-decker bus. Fortunately the bus had been unoccupied at the time.

The plane stood upright, enmeshed in the rear of the large red bus.

"Messerschmitt," Helene said with a knowing nod.

"It sure is," Remo agreed. "A big mess. What do you think, Little Father?" he said to Chiun. "I'll bet you thought you saw the last of these when you offed old Schicklgruber."

"Schicklgruber?" Helene asked, surprised. "Surely you do not mean Hitler?"

"You know any other Schicklgrubers?" Remo said blandly.

Helene looked at Chiun. He examined the downed plane, blithely indifferent to her gaze.

"Are you saying *he* killed Hitler?" she asked Remo.

Remo didn't want to get into an afternoon of Sinanju history lessons with the French spy.

"Indirectly," he admitted vaguely.

"The coward took poison and shot himself before I was able to carry out the deed," Chiun interjected. "A double death for a white-livered lunatic."

"It was totally self-serving," Remo explained. "You see, with wars people go out and hire local help. Who needs a professional assassin when you can slap a uniform on the grocery boy and send him off to fight for you?"

"No one," Chiun lamented.

"Which is why Chiun offered the Allied powers Hitler's head on a post. He figured he'd take out the guy who was causing all the trouble in the world gratis. After that everyone would line up for our services."

"But the little fool robbed me of my prize," Chiun said bitterly.

"I assume the plan did not work out as he envisioned it would?" Helene asked blandly.

"Let's just say that after the little jerk shot himself, the House of Sinanju entered a bit of a dry spell."

Helene was losing interest in Chiun and Remo's fanciful take on history. It was not that she did not entirely disbelieve them—after all, she had seen what these two were capable of. But France and now England were faced with a very real crisis. The plane before them was a part of that threat.

"Why would someone use these out-of-date planes now?" she mused. The question was aimed at no one in particular.

"Because so far they're working," Remo suggested dryly.

"But not any longer, my dear boy," a cheery voice said from behind them.

Remo knew that voice. It was the same one that had spoken to Helene on her cellular phone in Paris. Remo closed his eyes patiently. He didn't think he had the will to deal with this right now.

When he looked back at the speaker, the first thing he saw was that Helene Marie-Simone had grown dreamy eyed. Chiun's face held a look of utter disdain.

Before the three of them stood a man so handsome he made the average male model look as though his gene pool had been set on Puree. Remo knew him as Sir Guy Philliston. Head of the British intelligence agency known simply as Source. Their paths had crossed several times over the years. Remo had never been particularly impressed. The same, apparently, couldn't be said for Helene.

"Sir Guy," the French agent said in breathily accented English. Her face was flushed.

Remo frowned as he glanced at her. "Guy?" he asked. "I thought that was 'Gay.'"

"Quite," said Philliston. A look of minor displeasure sent the tiniest wrinkles up around his perfect aquiline nose. "Good to see you all again. Jolly good. Perhaps at your age you don't remember me, my old friend." He extended a perfectly manicured hand to Chiun. "Sir Guy Philliston," he said with a smile that flashed a row of flawlessly capped white teeth that had never seen the interior of a British dentist's office. The Phillistons imported their own personal D.D.S. from America.

Chiun looked first at the hand, then at Sir Guy. Spurning both, he looked over at the crashed plane.

"Yes, quite," droned Philliston, replacing his hand at his side with the gentlest of efforts. He had no desire to create a wrinkle in his impeccably tailored Savile Row suit. "Here to tour the scene of battle, eh?" he said to Remo and Helene. "Quite a matchup yesterday. Jolly good sport."

"Your team was a little late on the field," Remo said.

"Utter cock-up, that was," Philliston admitted. "It seems RAF and our boys were at cross-purposes. No bother. Everything is sorted out nicely now."

"Yes. Now that it's all over," said Remo.

"Rather," said Philliston affably. His expression as he sized up Remo bordered on a leer.

Remo glanced around. "Anyone know where there's a good bulletproof codpiece store around here?" he asked wearily.

SMITH HAD BEEN UNABLE to find out anything about IV. And that lack of knowledge frustrated him deeply.

As the night had worn on, he had become more and more convinced that he was dealing with a sinister shadow organization whose vile tendrils had its origins in the darkest days of the Nazi influence in Europe.

The clues were there when CURE had first encountered representatives of the group. The truth was, he had spent much of the night cursing himself for not seeing it before.

As his wife slept beside him, he had worked tirelessly, uplinking his portable computer with the

CURE database. All he had to show for a night's worth of work was a sore neck and blank computer screen.

Nothing.

There was nothing that suggested the existence of IV. If not for the physical evidence Remo had uncovered, he would have concluded precisely what he had concluded before: there was no larger menace.

It made him feel a little better to find out that he hadn't missed anything in his original search through neo-Nazi files. But not much.

Now Smith knew better.

When morning came, his wife had wanted to go out sight-seeing. Smith first made certain that the government of Great Britain was prepared to defend against a third attack. He learned through his computers that the British military was on high alert. Hoping that this meant a bit more than looking out an RAF window, Smith had sent her off on her own, promising to meet her at noon for lunch.

He continued working long after she had left.

When the bombs had dropped the day before and his line to Remo was severed, Smith and his wife had been forced to spend much of their time in the basement of the hotel. They had come through the attack unscathed. However, the phones still didn't work. It didn't matter. He had learned nothing that would aid Remo and Chiun's investigation.

At eleven-thirty Smith logged off his computer, storing it in his special briefcase. He closed the lid and carefully set the locks, sliding the case back under his bed.

He would resume work after lunch.

Leaving his work behind him, Smith left the hotel in order to meet his wife in Trafalgar Square.

HELENE MARIE-SIMONE continued to give Sir Guy Philliston the precise sort of look Sir Guy was giving to Remo.

"Have you any leads on who might be behind this?" she asked, sighing heavily.

"Not a bally one, I'm afraid," Guy replied, ignoring the lust in her eyes. "Every last man jack of the blighters was killed in the new Battle of Britain. Shame, really. No idea who could have sent these Boche monkeys to the shores of old Albion."

Remo raised a hand. "Excuse me, but could you please speak English?" he asked.

"Hear! Hear!" Chiun cheered. He was still watching the tail of the crashed plane.

"These were obviously German made," Guy said, indicating the plane. "But a lot of them are now in the hands of museums, private collectors. That sort of thing. We're looking into that angle."

"I saw where one of your papers this morning said they were dropped off by Martians from a UFO and are still fighting the war," Remo said flatly. "Maybe you should look into that."

"There isn't any need to bring the popular press

into this,'' Philliston said to Remo, as if mentioning the British tabloids were the height of rudeness.

Helene sneered condescendingly at Remo. ''He is like that,'' she confided in Sir Guy. ''I have found him to be very American.''

''Yes, very American,'' Philliston agreed. He licked his lips lightly as he eyed Remo's lean frame.

''Very, very American,'' Chiun piped in.

''Don't you start,'' Remo warned.

Sir Guy Philliston changed the direction of the conversation. ''Has your government any idea where the balance of explosives has gone off to?'' he asked Helene.

''They are investigating a minor explosion in a Paris Métro station,'' Helene replied. ''My government believes the incident to be related to the thefts.''

''Wait a damned minute,'' Remo interjected. ''When did you get this piece of news?''

''Last night.''

''And you didn't tell me?''

''Obviously not,'' she said in a superior tone.

She turned and smiled warmly at Sir Guy Philliston, happy to be sharing this information with him first. He had to tear his gaze away from Remo when he realized she was talking to him.

Remo rolled his eyes. ''He's gay as a parade, Helene,'' he sighed.

Helene became indignant. ''You say that because you find your masculinity threatened in the presence of a true man.'' Her words were flung out as a challenge.

"Whatever," Remo replied indifferently.

His tone made her even angrier.

"Well," Philliston said, clapping his hands together earnestly, "here we are. World War II renewed. The British and French along with their American cousins fighting the bally Jerry hordes.''

"Yes, except if this was really a replay, you'd be begging for our help and she'd be surrendering to anything with a spike on its helmet.''

As he spoke, Remo stared up at the pale blue London sky. Something wasn't right.

"I cannot imagine what it must be like to be American," Helene spit disdainfully.

"It's having drugstores with more than a hundred different kinds of deodorants," Remo said absently. "Do you hear that, Little Father?" he asked Chiun.

The Master of Sinanju had stopped watching the picture-taking crowds around the downed plane. He was staring up into the sky in the same direction as Remo.

"They are close," he said, nodding gravely. "This crowd should be dispersed at once.''

Remo spun on Philliston. "You've got to clear this street," he said, voice suddenly taut with urgency.

"Clear it?" Sir Guy laughed. "Why, in heaven's name?"

"There's another German squadron heading this way. At least thirty planes.''

"Thirty?" Philliston scoffed, stepping forward.

"Thirty-seven," the Master of Sinanju announced.

"I am sorry, my good boy, but nothing can get through the net we have established. The RAF has the shores of Old Blighty locked down tighter than the Queen Mum's bum."

"In that case I'd say it's about time to check the royal knickers," Remo suggested.

The first of the planes came into view, a mere speck against the distant clouds.

Helene stepped forward, mouth open in shock. The head of Source moved in beside her, eyes trained on the sky.

"Impossible," Philliston said, eyes wide.

"Get them out of here!" Remo snapped.

The tone jarred Philliston from his initial shock. He obediently charged over to a uniformed bobby who was posing for photographs beside the crippled plane.

"Have they gotten the phones working yet?" Remo asked, spinning to Helene. He was hoping that Smith might have some rapid way of contacting the RAF.

She fiddled with her cellular phone, stabbing out the number for London information. The line was dead.

"Not yet," she said, shaking her head.

By this time the planes were large enough to be seen for what they were. Some in the crowd began screaming and running for the Underground. Many more simply stood their ground, snapping endless pictures, as if they were participating in some sort of overblown amusement-park ride.

The air-raid sirens around London began sounding their relentless blare. The first dull thuds of distant impacting bombs reverberated through the pavement beneath their feet.

Sir Guy Philliston had convinced the bobbies that they should begin herding people to the Underground entrances. Those with cameras moved reluctantly.

"I vote we join them until this thing blows over, Little Father," Remo suggested.

"Agreed," said Chiun.

They had gone no more than a few paces toward the nearest Underground station when a familiar sound began emanating upward from the stairway. It was the pop-pop-pop of automatic-weapons fire.

There was a collective scream of panic from the mob. People began rolling back out of the staircase, stampeding directly toward Remo, Chiun and Helene.

Remo and Chiun easily avoided the crush of people. Helene wasn't so lucky. Though she tried to resist, she found herself helplessly swept along with the crowd as it surged back out into the blinding sunlight of Trafalgar Square.

By now the German warplanes were high above the square. They began dropping whistling bombs on the teeming throng in the square far below. Sections of pavement exploded upward, mixed with limp, bloodied bodies. A hail of shattered stones pebbled the ground for half a mile around.

At the Underground port, the sound of machine-gun fire had grown louder.

On the sidewalk Remo glanced from the black rectangular opening of the Underground to the carnage in the square.

"I'll take the square," he announced grimly.

The Master of Sinanju nodded his agreement.

"Have a care, my son."

As Remo ran into the thick of the bombing run, Chiun flew to the mouth of the subway station from which the gunfire had come.

FIVE MINUTES EARLIER Harold W. Smith was meeting his wife at a bus stop a few doors down from a small restaurant on Bond Street around the corner from Trafalgar Square.

"Oh, Harold," Maude Smith called. She smiled as he walked up the busy sidewalk toward her. Mrs. Smith actually seemed surprised to see her husband. "I wasn't sure you'd make it."

"Did we not agree we would meet at twelve?" Smith asked. He took the heavy paper bundles she held in her hands.

"Yes, but with your work and all..." She shrugged her round shoulders.

It wasn't an admonishment. Maude Smith would never complain that his work kept him away from her. She was merely stating an obvious truth about their life together. Nonetheless, Smith felt a twinge of too familiar guilt.

"Shall we have some lunch?" he said quickly, indicating the restaurant door with a bony elbow. The straps of the bags weighed heavily against his hands.

"Of course," Maude chimed. She talked excitedly as they walked. "I got some souvenirs today—not too expensive, I know. But since it's our last day in London I thought we should get something for Vickie. And Gert has been such a good friend."

Smith bit his tongue. He had no objection to buying a gift for their only daughter, but the prospect of wasting perfectly good money on a nosy neighbor was utterly distasteful to him.

Maude seemed to sense his mild displeasure. It was no secret to her that Harold didn't like Gert Higgins. But the fact that he didn't object to buying the woman a gift spoke volumes about her husband's patience. And—though he didn't like to show it—his love.

She was beaming when they reached the door to the restaurant. Maude opened it, Smith balanced the door with his elbow in order to allow her to pass.

He was about to step inside the hallway after her when he heard a familiar noise. Very distant.

Smith paused, half in, half out of the restaurant.

It could not be. Not a third time.

He cocked an ear.

"Harold?" His wife had come back out to him.

Boom…boom…boom…

It was like the footsteps of some remorseless movie monster, a celluloid beast come to devour them all.

"Maude, please step outside," Smith said calmly.

"What is it?"

"Please hurry," he pressed, a welling urgency in his tone.

Mrs. Smith obliged. At Smith's urging the two of them quickly made their way back up the sidewalk.

There was shouting coming from Trafalgar Square by the time they reached the Piccadilly entrance to London's Underground. Air-raid sirens sounded. Fingers and cameras were aimed at the squadron of incoming fighters.

Smith didn't dawdle. In another minute the crowd would become a mob. As it was, the first clusters of spectators were just beginning to herd themselves toward the safety of the subway as Smith and his wife climbed hurriedly down the stairs.

The stairway ended at a concrete landing that banked right into another staircase. This one was an illuminated tube with a metal railing running up either side.

Smith hurried down through the second enclosed staircase to the train platform below the city. He steered his wife to a spot near one of the largest support columns.

Already behind them the throngs of panicked people from the street were flooding down the stairs. Subway passengers soon got the message. They stopped heading for the exits, staying instead on the platform with the recent street arrivals. Anxious chatter rippled through the crowd.

The station began to quickly fill up.

"They said in the paper that this was over." Maude Smith's voice trembled.

"It is a mistake to trust the London press," Smith replied thinly. He was thinking of how wrong he had been for trusting the RAF.

The bombs hadn't yet begun to strike the streets above them. However, the crowd sensed it was only a matter of time. The smell of fear and sweat from hundreds of anxious people filled the long platform area.

Smith heard a sudden sharp series of noises.

It wasn't the German bombs. The sound hadn't come from outside. It was far too close.

It almost sounded like...

Again. The noise was more insistent. Screams followed.

The rattle of machine-gun fire grew worse. The crowd began to swell toward them. Pressing. Frantic. Behind the pillar Smith and his wife were safe. For now.

"What's happening?" Mrs. Smith begged.

Smith did not respond.

The sound of weapons fire ebbed momentarily. During the lull Smith took a chance to peer around the side of the column. He was just in time to see dozens of armed young men dressed in chillingly familiar uniforms. They were stomping up the staircase to the street.

He had to blink back his amazement. The men were dressed in the black-on-black uniforms of Germany's World War II SS. Their black boots clicked on the concrete stairs as they ran out of sight.

A moment later there was firing from the stairwell. Three bloodied bodies dropped into sight on the platform.

Smith wheeled on his wife.

"Stay here," he instructed, his face severe.

He started to go, but was stopped by a timid voice.

"Harold, I'm scared."

Smith stopped dead.

He looked down at his wife. A plump woman on the far side of middle age. There was alarm on her gentle features.

Smith touched her softly on the cheek.

"Everything will be fine, dear," he promised.

Maude blinked back tears. She nodded once, bravely.

The crowd had massed on the far end of the platform. There was no one between him and the stairs.

Leaving his wife huddled behind a pillar with her bags of souvenir statuettes of Big Ben and London, England T-shirts, Harold W. Smith ran to the blood-stained subway staircase after the fleeing band of neo-Nazis.

THE SMALL IV ARMY accomplished a feat that the Third Reich had never been able to achieve during the six long years of the war in Europe. They had placed an invasion force on the streets of London.

Neo-Nazi ground troops swelled up from the Underground stations, firing as they ran. Others joined them on the street, exiting from buildings and cars.

Bodies fell to the pavement as soldiers raced to find shelter in enclosures along the mob scene that was Trafalgar Square. A whistling bomb landed amid a group of three soldiers, tearing a mailbox-sized hole in the pavement and flinging the invaders through the smoke-clogged air.

The Master of Sinanju flew through the worst of the battle, a wraith in fiery red. Even as armed soldiers swarmed the square from hidden positions all around, Chiun ran into the mouth of the nearest subway station.

There was still shooting going on belowground. He would stop as many as he could before they were able to join their murderous fellows above.

The old Korean found himself in a steeply angled passageway. It veered off at a sharp bend far below. Footsteps clicked urgently against unseen concrete stairs.

Chiun raced down a half-dozen steps before flinging himself in the air toward the landing below.

The instant he was airborne, a crowd of black-suited men ran into view from the lower staircase.

The soldiers didn't have time to be shocked.

Chiun sailed in at an angle parallel to the stairs.

The heels of his sandaled feet caught the pair of men in the lead squarely in their chests. They flew backward from the pressure, slamming solidly against the wall of the stairwell. Their spines cracked audibly, bodies folding in half.

Some of the other men began firing. Flying lead pinged loudly in the cramped space. Bullets chipped holes in the sealed concrete walls around them.

Chiun swirled through the volley of projectiles, arriving at the far end unharmed.

His fists shot out in rapid-fire lunges, slamming against gun muzzles in the impossibly brief fraction of time between rounds. The weapons rocketed back with a force far greater than that of any launched bullet. The brittle crack of a dozen sternums collided into one single, horrific symphony of sound.

The men in the first line of storm troopers suddenly found their machine guns protruding from their chests. Blood spurted from around gun stocks as the men dropped to the staircase. They rolled downward, upending the next batch of soldiers who were even now racing up for the confrontation above.

Chiun leaped over the bodies, dropping into the middle of the next advancing throng.

His hands flashed forward.

The foreheads of a dozen men shattered under the force of unseen fists.

Chiun's elbows lashed back.

And the throats of another ten imploded, fonts of blood erupting from shocked mouths.

The Master of Sinanju became a blur of arms and legs. A twisting, hellish dervish. Knees cracked beneath heels; bodies dropped and were finished by lightning-fast toe kicks to the temple.

Some at the back tried to get off a few feeble shots. The nightmare blur in the bloodred kimono had already sliced through their lines with the power of a buzz saw and the speed of a lashing cobra. They were dead before the sounds of their weapons echoed up the stairwell.

It was over before it began.

Leaving the bodies to breathe their last, Chiun raced into the Underground, searching for any other modern-day SS troops that might be in hiding.

There were many wounded English civilians, but no more soldiers. He was about to head back upstairs when he caught sight of a familiar figure crouching beside a nearby pillar.

His black sandals made a skittering beeline to the column.

Chiun bowed. "Empress Smith."

Maude Smith looked up, surprised that someone here had recognized her. She saw the somewhat familiar face of the Master of Sinanju. She believed at one time that he had been a patient at Folcroft. He had also lived near the Smiths in Rye for a period several years ago.

"Oh, hello." She appeared shell-shocked, her voice distant.

"Is your regal husband near?" Chiun demanded.

"Harold?" she asked. "Why, no. No, he's—"
She pointed to the staircase up which Smith had vanished several moments before.

A red blur flashed across her field of vision. The next thing she knew, Chiun was flying up the distant staircase her Harold had taken.

Events had so rattled Maude Smith she didn't think to ask why the old man had called her "empress."

"CALL IN your frigging air force, for crying out loud!" Remo screamed. He was working through a group of neo-Nazi soldiers. As his palms drove like pile drivers into the faces of the swarming men, he twisted to face the head of Source.

Sir Guy Philliston was cowering behind the great pedestal that was the base of the statue of Lord Nelson. His handsome features had grown pale in the attack. He shook visibly.

"Can't do it, old chap," Philliston apologized. A glazed expression had taken hold of his aristocratic features. "Too frightened. Bad show, really."

The sky was thick with German bombers. Even though there were only about forty of them, they were flying so tightly together that the air appeared to be teeming with attacking aircraft.

One plane higher up than the rest dropped a payload to the square. The three dozen bombs screamed from the belly of the plane, sailing on ancient, rusted fins toward the mob of panicked people more than two hundred feet below.

The pilot was obviously inexperienced in bomb warfare. On their way down, a small pack of the shells impacted against the wing of a Messerschmitt flying at a lower level.

The struck plane exploded in a bright orange blast of flame and a horrifying tearing of metal. Shrapnel from the explosion tore into the fuselages of two nearby planes, causing an explosive chain reaction.

The trio of wrecked aircraft blasted toward the ground, striking the street in near unison, ripping up pavement and leaving a blazing gouge a hundred yards long.

Remo sent a foot into the groin of the last storm trooper nearby. The man's pelvis split in half from the force of the blow. He dropped, shrieking, to the ground. Remo finished him with a sharp toe to the temple.

Hopping over a carved lion at the slablike base of the Nelson statue, he grabbed Sir Guy by the lapels. He wrenched the Englishman to his feet, slamming him against the column.

Philliston was limp with fear. He put up no struggle against Remo. Indeed, he barely noticed the rough treatment. It was a shame, really, for it was what he generally enjoyed the most.

"Call them!" Remo snapped.

Guy Philliston merely looked at Remo with the dull gaze of lapsed reason.

"Oh, for pete's sake," Remo snarled.

He spun Sir Guy around like a top. Jamming his fingers against the base of the Source commander's spine, Remo kneaded a cluster of tangled muscles. There was a sudden intake of air from the Englishman. When he turned back around, it was as if Sir Guy had come out of a coma.

"You have exquisite hands," Sir Guy breathed dreamily.

"Tell me that when they're wrapped around your throat," Remo barked, reaching into Sir Guy's breast pocket. Pulling out a small cellular phone, he jammed it into Philliston's hand. "Call," he commanded.

Sir Guy took the phone obediently and began punching in the RAF number he had called the previous day. His attitude had changed completely from a moment before. He was now all business. As the line rang through, Philliston casually removed a Walther PPK from a shoulder holster and began firing at the nearest German soldiers.

Remo saw that there was nothing more he could do about getting air support.

There were still many people in the square. With the positions the troops had taken, there was no real place they could go. Until reinforcements arrived, they were sitting ducks to the German bombs and marksmen.

Remo was about to start working his way through the soldiers on the left of the huge open space when something enormous loomed into view over the southernmost buildings surrounding Trafalgar Square.

He looked up with a feeling of deep foreboding.

Another, larger, engine rumble had joined the insistent whine of the Messerschmitt Me-110s and 109Es. As he watched, the huge shape of a Heinkel He-111 bomber soared into view. The Messerschmitts zoomed around the larger plane like fawning attendants in a royal court.

Though unfamiliar with the model, he knew that a plane that size would certainly house an enormous payload.

Remo looked around.

Guy Philliston was on the phone. Helene Marie-Simone had vanished several minutes before. There was no sign of Chiun.

It was up to him. The only problem was, he had no idea what he could do to stop the enormous plane.

Remo abandoned all hope of quickly devising a plan.

He hopped atop a carved lion's head.

Hoping to improvise something on the way, Remo began scaling the large granite column of the Nelson Monument.

18

On the last day he would be serving in Her Majesty's Royal Air Force, Colonel E. C. T. Bexton received the urgent call from Sir Guy Philliston with intense skepticism.

"I am sorry, my dear boy, but that is utterly, utterly impossible. London cannot possibly be under attack."

"I am telling you, Colonel—despite RAF information—London is most definitely being bombed this very minute," Philliston shouted.

Why Sir Guy felt compelled to shout was beyond Colonel Bexton. There was a sudden, godawfully loud noise in the background.

"What is that?" Bexton asked, face pinched in displeasure.

"I believe it to be a Heinkel bombing the square," Philliston yelled.

"Heinkel? My good man, the Heinkel is an obsolete German number from the Second World War."

"Yes," Philliston said. "And at this precise moment it has begun a bombing run on the far side of

Trafalgar Square." Sir Guy suddenly seemed to be talking to someone nearby. "I say, what are you doing? Get down from there this instant!"

"Is there something wrong, Sir Guy?"

"Yes, there is. Aside from the German warplanes swooping around blowing up everything and his uncle, there is a crazed Yank agent climbing the statue of Lord Nelson."

Colonel Bexton pursed his lips as he considered this latest news.

"Sir Guy," the RAF man asked slowly, "have you been enjoying a few sundowners at your club this a.m.?"

"Listen to me," Philliston snapped. "There is a bombing raid going on against London this very minute. Do you intend to send in RAF planes or not?"

Colonel Bexton bristled. "*Not,* I'm afraid," he said haughtily. "You see, *Sir* Guy, after the success of the first run and the, um, miscalculation on my part during the second, Her Majesty's Royal Air Force has beefed up alertness to a point greater than any other time since the Falkland crisis. We have a web along our shores that cannot possibly be penetrated. There is absolutely no conceivable way an enemy plane could enter sovereign British airspace without my knowing it. Therefore, no matter what you may personally believe to be happening in the greater London area at this particular time, I assure you that it is *not* another bombing attack. Now, if there is nothing else, I have many duties to attend to, so you will please forgive me if I ask you to take your fanciful notions elsewhere and kindly piss off. Good day, sir.''

He hung up the phone, not realizing that his connection with Sir Guy had been severed midway through what he considered a well-deserved tirade.

Colonel Bexton did manage to do a little more light paperwork in the ensuing two minutes after Philliston's phone call. His peace was disrupted when an aide raced into the room with an urgent message from London. It had come not from RAF sources, but rather from the radio. The BBC World Service was reporting that London was, indeed, in the process of being heavily blitzed by hostile forces.

Colonel Bexton took the news with a choice of words that would be recalled for years to come among those aspiring to become officers of Her Majesty's Royal Air Force and who had no desire to follow the colonel's lead in reaction to a crisis.

"Oh, bloody hell," said the soon-to-be-retired Colonel E. C. T. Bexton.

19

Smith caught up to the last SS-uniformed soldier on the top few steps of the lower staircase.

The rest of the band had just rounded the corner and was heading up into the daylight. They weren't paying attention to their rear.

Smith flung himself at the legs of the escaping soldier, wrapping his arms around the man's knees. The man let out a startled yelp as he toppled forward against the stairs.

The heel of the young soldier kicked up as he ran, catching Smith in the jaw. The impact cut a small gash in the CURE director's jaw and shifted his rimless glasses. Smith barely noticed.

The image was ridiculous. A man in his seventies tackling a fit twenty-five-year-old man.

But Smith had not only the element of surprise on his side. He had training. These so-called soldiers, no matter their pretension of identifying themselves with the formidable Nazis of ages past, were exceedingly sloppy.

The man fell and turned, kicking at his still unseen attacker as he tried to grab for his machine gun. His hat dropped off, revealing a pale, tattoo-painted scalp.

Smith had already rolled away from the flailing legs. Grabbing the soldier by the belt, Smith dragged him down the stairs with a mighty tug.

The skinhead bounced roughly down the well-worn steps, the back of his shaved head slamming against the concrete. He had just located his gun. It slipped from his fingers, rattling down the stairs beyond Smith.

When the young man was within reach, Smith lashed out with his free hand—fingers curled, palm extended. His hand smashed into the bridge of the skinhead's nose with a sickeningly loud crunch.

Blood gushed from the man's nostrils. He wriggled woozily, trying to pull himself back away on elbows and heels.

Smith repeated the blow, more vicious this time. The crunch was louder, the effect lethal. The young skinhead's eyes rolled back in their sockets. His head lolled to one side. He didn't stir again.

Kneeling next to the body, Smith didn't take time to catch his breath. He scrambled down the stairs, snatching up the skinhead's dropped machine gun in his gnarled hands.

It was set to fire.

His bones creaked as he climbed to his feet. Ignoring the pain in his jaw, Smith ran up to the landing.

The group of SS-clad skinheads had no idea what

had just happened behind them. They were higher up the second landing, stuck in a bottleneck. The first men in line were waiting for a lull in the fighting at street level before racing into the smoke and flames in the road outside.

Not that there was much resistance from above. Even though some bobbies were allowed to carry guns in modern London, the police in the square were no match for the heavily armed IV troops. What the soldiers were avoiding were the bombs and occasional machine-gun bursts from their own attacking air force.

Smith braced his back against the wall as he stole a quick look up at the neo-Nazi troops.

Clustered together. An inviting target.

Smith twisted into the landing. His gray face a steel mask, he began firing carefully and methodically at the troops jammed tightly on the stairwell.

The gun rattled a relentless staccato in his steady hands. Bullet wounds erupted on the nearest startled troops. There were screams and shouts.

Caught off guard, the soldiers didn't know how to react. There were too many of them packed together to maneuver well. Those who did manage to wheel around succeeded only in firing on their own troops.

Bodies fell in crumpled masses, toppling atop one another in an avalanche of twisted limbs.

In a matter of seconds the subway staircase was transformed into a blood-drenched abattoir.

For several long moments Smith was forced to

duck and hide behind the wall. For short stints he would pop out and fire on the dwindling German forces.

Eventually all that was left in the staircase was Smith. And the bodies of the men he had killed.

He peeked around the corner.

The others had fled.

A rectangle of daylight that appeared to have been cut out of the concrete around him opened into the street. He could hear the angry pop-pop-pop of machine-gun fire echoing down the now silent stairwell.

Dropping the weapon in his hands, Smith scooped up two others from a pair of nearby corpses. Slinging one gun over his shoulder, he held the other firmly in his hands.

Ignoring the pains that screamed from every joint, Smith hurried up through the scattered dead to the street above.

THE CHAOS of Trafalgar Square was far below.

Remo had just reached the top of the nearly two-hundred-foot-tall granite pedestal. He was standing next to the legs of the sixteen-foot-tall statue of Lord Nelson, and he *still* didn't know what to do about the huge German bomber.

The Heinkel moved with a plodding remorselessness across the smoke-choked sky.

Remo saw that its bay doors were open. Briefly a broad face came into view. It disappeared into the cavernous interior of the large aircraft.

What could Remo do?

Remo patted his pockets. He had nothing but his phony ID, a few credit cards and a roll of cash.

Desperation.

There was nothing he could use. Nothing he—

The Heinkel was directly above him. It was like the Shadow of Death had passed over London.

All at once Remo became aware of something new in the air above him. Something small had fallen from the plane.

He looked up.

The bomb—the first of many, Remo was certain— was whistling angrily toward his head.

He glanced around frantically. He could rip one of the legs off Lord Nelson and use it to bat the bomb harmlessly away.

Bad plan. That wasn't how bombs worked. They waited until they hit something and then blew up. This wasn't a game of tag. He'd never win a contest with a bomb by striking it first.

It was closer now…twenty feet…ten feet…

There was not much choice. Remo steeled himself.

Five feet…

It would have been easier if the bomb hadn't been sitting in a French farmer's field for thirty-seven years and then in a *deminage* depot for another eighteen.

Two feet…

No choice.

One foot…

Remo slapped his hand out.

The whistling bomb was at chest level now. He caught the nose of the 75 mm shell with carefully cupped fingers.

Slow the descent. Turn the bomb around.

Remo felt the rough, corroded surface of the unexploded shell through every nerve ending in his hand.

Fingertips became suction cups. A variation of the technique that allowed him to climb sheer faces. Using the coarse bomb exterior for leverage, Remo whipped the explosive device back in the direction it had come.

The entire sequence took a split second to perform.

The shell soared back up through the open bay doors of the Heinkel just as the aircraft began to drop another small handful of bombs.

There was a muffled explosion deep within the belly of the plane. Another distant sound of a single detonating shell was followed by an eerie second of silence.

All at once the huge aircraft erupted in a massive ball of flame. Smoking metal fragments exploded in every direction as fire tore down the length of the fatally wounded plane.

Lord Nelson became a shield. Remo ducked behind the statue as it was pelted with hundreds of chunks of jagged steel.

The Heinkel tore out of the sky with a pained scream, crashing solidly against the seventh floor of a ten-story building on the far side of the square. The nose buckled; the wings snapped forward into the brick walls and then sheared loose. Another explosion followed, after which the Heinkel's tail section ripped away and plummeted in a flaming mass to the street below.

What remained of the plane jutted out above the square. A burning hulk.

''Now, *that* was a plan,'' Remo announced to Lord Nelson.

Brushing the rusted metal fragments from his hand, he climbed swiftly back down to the ground.

RAF JETS INTERCEPTED the German warplanes above London at 12:25, Greenwich mean time. By most estimates, that was precisely twenty-five minutes after the attack had begun.

Rockets blazed into the sides of the woefully outmatched IV air force. Crippled and burning planes flew nose first from the hazy afternoon sky.

Most buildings and tourist attractions from Oxford Street to Constitution Hill and from Shaftesbury Avenue to Park Lane had sustained some kind of damage.

Some police were on the scene in riot gear. More were arriving every minute. Sirens sounded in every direction.

Fires raged in several ravaged buildings as Remo made his way around the periphery of the neo-Nazi defenses.

Many of the skinheads he dispatched were clearly

in some altered state of mind. The bodies of their innocent victims lay everywhere around the smoke-filled square. For this reason alone, Remo continued to battle his way through the thinning troops.

A trio of men in an alley was firing against an unseen assailant near a burned-out car. Remo leaped into the middle of the dazed group of skinheads. His presence had barely registered to them before he was spinning on one heel.

With a triple crack, Remo brought both forearms and one knee against each man simultaneously.

They were dead before they hit the ground.

Remo slipped out of the alley.

Whoever had been firing on the three skinheads from behind the car had changed direction. The machine gun was now shooting at a group of men in SS uniforms fleeing for the nearest Tube entrance. Several of them dropped to the street, mortally wounded.

Remo assumed the shooter was with the police. He was trotting past the car when he was startled by something familiar about the figure crouching at its charred rear bumper. He stopped dead.

"Smitty?" Remo asked, shocked.

Harold Smith glanced once at Remo, his expression cross. Looking back to the fleeing German troops, Smith resumed firing.

At that moment the Master of Sinanju came racing into sight from the opposite direction. Seeing his pupil, he ran over to join him.

Chiun nodded. "You have found Emperor Smith."

"Sort of," Remo answered uncertainly. "Okay, Smitty, let me have it," he said gently.

Remo tugged the gun from Smith's hands, tossing it to the sidewalk. Smith immediately grabbed for the gun slung over his shoulder. Remo took that one, too.

"They're getting away!" Smith snapped. He started to give chase to the fleeing troops, but powerful hands restrained him. When he turned, he found the Master of Sinanju holding firmly on to his biceps.

"You are a valiant warrior, O Emperor. But the pinheads are undone."

"They're not getting away," Remo promised. "Not dressed like that. It's over."

Smith glanced from Remo to Chiun. All at once the fight seemed to drain out of him.

"Yes," he exhaled. "Yes, I suppose you're right."

Remo looked around the area. The street was a littered mess. Several bodies—both skinhead and civilian—lay about the roadway. Bullet holes riddled the walls. Shattered glass lay everywhere. Nearby, the wreckage of an Me-109E burned freely. Plumes of black smoke rose into the gray sky.

"Is this what it was like before?" Remo wondered aloud.

"No." Smith was in the midst of adjusting his tie. "It was far worse," he said tartly, brushing dirt from his sleeve.

"We've got to get these guys, Smitty," Remo said softly.

No one seemed to hear him. A thought had suddenly occurred to Smith.

"Maude! I left her in the Underground." He started across the street.

"I will accompany you," Chiun announced. He trailed Smith back to the subway entrance.

Remo stood for a few moments longer, staring at the wreckage around him. Smoke and fire raged, sirens wailed.

Before leaving home a few short days before, he had been struggling internally with his life as CURE's enforcement arm. It seemed like a lifetime ago.

Maybe he couldn't stamp out every last bit of evil in the world, but that didn't mean he should stop trying.

Smith was right. Conrad MacCleary had been right.

"One man *can* make a difference," Remo declared firmly. He resolved at that moment, looking at the grisly results of a reviled, decades-old evil, that—in this case—one man would do just that.

There was no way these people were going to get away with this. No way at all.

Face resolute, Remo walked back into the street. He headed back up the roadway in the direction of the battle-ravaged Nelson Monument.

20

While bombs rained down over London and historic buildings erupted in flame and collapsed into rubble, a lone van made its way up the Boulevard Invalides on the famous Left Bank in Paris.

It moved slowly in the afternoon traffic, traveling north toward the Seine.

The driver didn't wish to attract undue attention. To anyone who saw it, this should have been merely another government van. One of many.

It was an excellent cover. For this was Paris, where it seemed everyone had either a government job or was rudely interrupted on the way to real work by government employees whose duty it was to scowl at and deride those on whom they depended most. Namely the French taxpayers, of whom there was a dwindling force.

The van drove past the Musée Rodin on the right and the Musée de l'Armée on the left. It stopped short of the Quai D'Orsay, which ran parallel for a time with the Seine.

The driver cut the engine.

Four men climbed from the van—two from the

back, two from the front. The two in the rear carried with them a long, flat dolly, which they set on four well-oiled wheels. A retractable handle was drawn out from beneath the handcart and clicked into place at its side.

Three of the men went to work hauling heavy boxes out of the rear of the truck.

The fourth man looked on. Doubtless he was a supervisor of some sort. In a country with a per capita deficit greater than that of the United States, there were many government supervisors.

At the direction of the older man, the group pulled their handcart of boxes to the nearest Métro entrance. They used the wheelchair-access ramp to roll their supplies down into the Paris subway system.

A gendarme near the gate spied them immediately.

Instead of fleeing like men with something to hide, the group of four crossed directly over to the guard. They brought their cart with them.

"What is all this?" the policeman asked, indicating the boxes stacked on the wheeled conveyance.

"Traps. For the rats," said the oldest of the four men, in perfect French. Eyes at half-mast, he spoke as if it was an effort to talk. An unlit cigarette was pasted to his lower lip.

The officer sighed. "Finally. One ran across my shoe the other day," he said. He waved at the pointed tip of one polished black dress shoe. "Across the toe. When are they going to find a way to rid us of them?"

The man shrugged. "These are new. The company has guaranteed them to work."

"Humph," the police officer scoffed. "Give me the order," he said. He held out his hand for the paperwork.

The man reached into the pocket of his white coveralls and produced a few yellow and pink carbon copies. He handed them to the gendarme.

"Are you not past retirement?" asked the policeman as he peered at the papers.

The old man coughed up a ball of thick phlegm, which he swallowed with an audible gulp. "What am I going to do?" he said with an indifferent shrug. "Sit at home until I die?" He waved a lazy hand. "Eh, when they put me in a box, my son will get whatever there is left."

The gendarme was taking a little too long scanning the work forms. The old man had been assured by Nils Schatz's personal assistant that there would be no difficulties.

Schatz had procured the services of the finest forgers in all of France. The paperwork should have been impeccably crafted.

The gendarme finished up at the bottom of the third sheet of paper. He flipped them back together. According to the work invoices, these men were indeed subway custodians.

"Good luck," the gendarme said, handing the orders back. "I have heard stories of some that are more than a meter long." Like a fisherman telling

about the "one that got away," he held his hands
about three feet apart to indicate the size of the rats
in the Paris subways.

The old man again shrugged apathetically as he
replaced the paperwork in his pocket. Without another word he waved his men past the officer and
toward the cavernous black tunnel at the far end of
the raised platform.

Just before they disappeared on the chipped concrete catwalk above the dirty train tracks, the gendarme shouted at the backs of the men.

"Be certain you set the traps correctly!"

"I get paid whether they work or not," said the
old man who, fifty-five years before, had personally
put to death seven French Résistance fighters and had
ordered the deaths of many others. With his handcart
laden with explosives, he and his trio of skinhead
assistants vanished in the shadows of the long tunnel.

OVER THE COURSE of several days, while the eyes of
the world were on England, the same drama played
out in hundreds of locales around Paris.

At the Bibliothèque Nationale three deliverymen
brought sealed crates of what were supposed to be
books into a basement storage area. Instead of leaving them where they were instructed, they brought
them to a dusty room where they wouldn't be discovered for days. By that time it would be too late.

Unexpected shipments of historical artifacts and
artwork showed up at several museums around the

city. The Musée des Arts Décoratifs, the Musée National d'Art Moderne and the Musée de l'Histoire de France all received truckloads of crates. The Palais du Louvre received the most. Invoices accompanying the shipments stressed that the artifacts had to be opened under precise conditions, but didn't specify what those conditions were. Fearful of damaging the precious contents, the staff left the boxes untouched.

Invoices stolen from various museums gained the skinheads access to government buildings. Shipments of "art" were delivered with the same precautions given at the museums. Bureaucrats and government workers at the Palais de l'Élysée and other such buildings were even less likely to toy with the crates than the museum curators. The boxes were stored quietly away.

The Aéroport Charles de Gaulle and the Forum des Halles were easier by far to deal with than anywhere else. At the bustling airport and the large underground shopping center, vans were strategically parked and then abandoned.

By the beginning of the third day, all of the careful planning had finally paid off. Everything was in place.

In the little living room of his dingy, out-of-the-way apartment building, Nils Schatz accepted the news of the deliveries with growing excitement.

A detailed map of Paris was spread out on the scratched coffee table before him. Each time a call came in to inform them of a successfully completed mission, a small red mark was made in ink at the spot where the bombs had been placed.

The map was covered with such marks.

Fritz was on the phone, receiving another update.

"The Malesherbes bundle is in position," he said to Nils Schatz. Nodding, Schatz used his special red pen to make a mark on the map. "What about Avenue de Villiers?" Fritz said into the phone. As the party on the other end spoke, he glanced at a sheet of paper in his hand. "Oh, yes. Yes, I have it. Excellent, Klaus. Assemble your men. Call back when you are ready."

He hung up the phone, making a mark through "Avenue de Villiers" on the paper. He had missed it the first time, underlining the words instead of crossing them out.

"The last of the Métro packages are in place," Fritz announced, sitting down across from Schatz. He sighed heavily, as if he had personally hauled the hundreds of crates around Paris.

"I know," Schatz said. He didn't raise his eyes. He stared at the map reverently, like a nun entranced with the cross dangling from a set of rosary beads. "Have there been any reports of the Master of Sinanju?"

"None in France," Fritz hedged.

Schatz looked up. "Where?"

"London. As instructed, some of our ground troops stayed above the fray. They telephoned in as soon as the London phone system became operational. He and his protégé were on the scene during the blitz.''

"Why was I not informed?''

"I did not wish to upset you, Herr Schatz.''

Schatz looked back down at the map, jaw clenched. "In future, Fritz, do not concern yourself with my state of mind,'' he said icily.

"Yes, Herr Schatz.''

"Our men in Paris,'' Schatz continued. "Do they understand what they are to do next?''

Fritz nodded. "Klaus will lead them.''

"Klaus is a good soldier.'' He looked up at Fritz. "There are few of us left.'' His upper lip drew tightly across his yellowed teeth. The unaccustomed smile dropped so quickly, Fritz was surprised there wasn't a thud.

It was a rare display of goodwill. Fritz decided not to squander it.

"I am concerned about Herr Kluge,'' Fritz ventured.

"Pah,'' Schatz spit, waving his hand. He was still staring at the map of Paris. *His* Paris.

"I share your disapproval of his leadership, Nils. But Kluge is strong. My contacts at the village tell me that he is livid at our offensive against the English.''

Schatz looked up. His bleary old eyes gleamed with a distant brightness. They were embers stoked from the very heart of Hell.

His voice was disarmingly soft, frighteningly

cheerful. "If that is the case, tonight he will be very, *very* upset."

His evil face serene, the old Nazi turned his attention back to the Paris map.

21

In order to keep the enemy guessing, the secret head-quarters of the British counterintelligence agency known as Source had been moved several times throughout its history. Somehow the enemy—for most of its history, the Soviet Union—had managed to find the new location every time. And each time that happened, Source moved.

With the dissolution of the Soviet empire and the takeover at Number 10 Downing Street by the anti-intelligence Labour Party, Source was sent back to its roots. It now occupied the same modest digs it had at its inception. A few simple floors in a building above Trafalgar Square. An apothecary shop that faced out on the wrecked street marked the secret entrance to the spy organization.

For privacy, Remo Williams had come downstairs from the Source offices. He had left the false wall panel with its hidden staircase open wide behind him. At the moment he was talking to Smith on the phone in the back office of the dummy store.

"I was forced to cast out a rather wide web," Smith was saying. "But I think I may have a lead on IV. There is a man in Germany named Gus Holloway."

"That doesn't sound German," Remo commented.

"It is not. Holloway is American. The man is a neo-Nazi who has spoken a few times about a coming Fourth Reich."

"Him and about a billion other fascist wannabes," Remo said bitterly. As he talked, he waved his burned arm before his face. The reddish coloring the mustard gas had given it had faded to a light pink.

"Precisely why we need more information. Remember, Remo, with nothing more concrete to go on, this is all speculation at this time. I will continue to look into Holloway, as well as other potential sources of information."

"Speaking of Source," Remo said, "these guys haven't been much help. They got hold of some of the troops that were captured after yesterday's raid and came up dry."

"Perhaps you could persuade them," Smith suggested.

"No good," Remo said, shaking his head. "Chiun and I worked some of them over. They were just a bunch of stupid Nazi skinheads doing what they were told. No one who survived knows who's behind this. Somebody just aimed them at London and pushed them out of the nest."

"I am still puzzled as to how they were able to

penetrate the air defenses around Great Britain,'' Smith said.

"You didn't hear?" Remo asked, surprised. "They didn't come from outside England. The planes were here the whole time."

"How is that possible?" Smith asked. "You were at the air base on Guernsey."

"I was at *an* air base on Guernsey. The last attack came from a hidden airfield on a sheep farm in Shropshire. They took off from the middle of merry old England. I guess it never occurred to these royal doofuses to look inside the yard once they built their fence."

"Hmm," Smith said thoughtfully.

"I need something a little more concrete than that to go on, Smitty," Remo countered dryly.

"I am afraid I have nothing to offer at present," Smith admitted.

"Whoever these people are, they're well financed," Remo suggested. "Maybe you can get to them that way."

"How?" Smith asked.

"I don't know," Remo said, exasperated. "You're the one who's supposed to be the brains of this outfit. See if anyone's been out there buying up a lot of antique planes lately. Maybe you can use their credit-card records or something to trace them." Remo snapped his fingers. "Hey, that's not a bad idea."

"Remo, it seems unlikely that a neo-Nazi group that has been careful enough to cover its tracks so effectively would purchase their air force with a credit card.''

Remo had been very proud of his sudden burst of inspiration. His shoulders sunk visibly as the truth of Smith's words sunk in.

"I guess you're right," he grumbled.

"Nonetheless, there might be other ways to track them using the planes. I have already initiated a computer search to that end. I must inform you, from what I have seen thus far, it is not encouraging."

"Nothing has been lately," Remo groused.

There was a brief pause over the line, as if Smith found his next words difficult to say.

"How are you feeling, Remo?" he asked.

"Since when are you concerned?" Remo asked.

"I am concerned with everything that might affect the efficiency of the organization."

"You're a real sweetheart, you know that, Smitty? I'm not quitting, if that's what you mean. Not until we get rid of these scumbags, anyway."

Smith seemed bolstered by this news. "I am glad to hear that," he said. "I might not have even sent you over here if you were not despondent at home. At least one small part of these events has been fortuitous."

"Yeah, good fortune smiles on us all," Remo said lightly. "And don't talk to me about being despondent. You're the one who should be getting counseling. What was that Rambo act you pulled yesterday afternoon?"

"Er, yes," Smith said uncomfortably. "There were no police present when the troops attacked. I merely saw an opening to assist. It was the proper thing to do, given the circumstances."

"Bullshit," Remo said. "I saw the look on your face. You were reliving your glory days. Smith versus the Axis powers. You could have gotten yourself killed."

Smith refused to be drawn in.

"I will be leaving England within the hour. I will try to find some information for you to go on before that, but it seems unlikely that any will be forthcoming. I suggest you stay close to Source headquarters. They will be the first to learn if there are any new attacks against England."

"I like to *act*," Remo muttered. "Not react."

"That is all we can do until we locate the shadow organization behind all this. By the way, is the French agent nearby?"

"Helene?" Remo asked. "She's upstairs. Why?"

"I will call you on her phone if I learn anything. If you need to make contact, you may page me."

That said, Smith hung up the phone. It was always the same way with the CURE director. The simple courtesy of a goodbye was a waste of valuable time.

Remo dropped the old phone in its cradle. Leaving the dusty apothecary shop behind him, he trudged up the stairs to Source headquarters.

REMO FOUND Helene Marie-Simone seated at a desk, talking in angry French into her cellular phone.

The Master of Sinanju stood near her. The old Korean had changed into a pale blue kimono. He was staring out one of the large tinted-glass windows that looked out over Trafalgar Square.

All of the fires had been extinguished. The crashed airplanes had been hauled away. Small remnants of shattered planes, piles of brick and gaping craters signaled some of the worst physical damage.

The bodies of those who perished in the attack were gone from the square. A total of 687 had died.

The streets of London were empty. Martial law had been declared, and an eerie stillness had settled over all the British Isles.

The main office of Source looked like the sterile city room of a midsize newspaper. Neat desks were lined up in two rows. Except for the one Helene occupied, the desks were empty.

Sir Guy Philliston had left the building a few minutes before on an important mission. Source HQ was completely out of tea. He had vowed to remedy the problem or die in the attempt. Remo was hoping for the latter.

For now Remo sidled up to the Master of Sinanju. "Anything new?" he asked, nodding to Helene.

Chiun shook his head.

"In the time you have been gone, she has placed seven telephone calls. Four were to her government, and three were of a disgusting personal nature."

"And?" Remo asked leadingly.

"And the French appetite for perversion and licentiousness is bottomless."

"And their beaches are topless," Remo said dismissively. "What about the calls to DGSE?"

"They know nothing," Chiun declared.

Remo exhaled loudly. "Great."

"Except..." Chiun began.

"Yeah?" Remo said, brightening.

"One of their politicians vanished during the night. Doubtless the victim of his own libido. Or of the lack of an alarm clock. The French do not know which."

"Oh," Remo said dejectedly.

"And," Chiun began again, raising an instructive finger.

"Yes?" Remo asked skeptically.

Chiun lowered his hand. "Nothing. That was all." He went back to staring out the window, a tiny smile playing at the corners of his thin lips.

Helene shouted a string of rapid-fire French before hanging up the phone. She growled in exasperation. When she glanced up, she saw Remo looking at her.

"That man is—how do you say?—impossible."

"I've got a boss like that, too," Remo commiserated.

"What?" she snapped impatiently. She shook her head in sudden understanding. "No, that was not my boss. It was my lover. He is upset that I am not home."

Remo tried to be understanding. "Yeah, this job has rotten hours. Have you two lived together long?"

"What are you talking about?" Helene asked. "He lives with his wife. And what do you know of this job? Or have you abandoned posing as a State Department official?"

Remo decided that being understanding was for nitwits.

"I keep forgetting to ask you," he said, "where did you run off to when the fighting broke out yesterday?"

Helene waved to the statue of Nelson beyond the window. It was pitted with bullet holes.

"While you were scurrying up that statue like a monkey, I was on the phone."

Behind Remo, Chiun chortled loudly. "Like a monkey. Heh-heh-heh."

"Oh?" Remo asked, annoyed with both Helene and Chiun. "Make a date with an English soccer team? Better make sure they're all married first."

"There was another explosion in a Métro station in Paris yesterday afternoon," she snapped. "Since you listen in on all of my phone conversations, I am surprised you didn't hear that one."

"I was too busy not hiding," Remo said. "Hey, want to see the French army on maneuvers?" He threw both hands high into the air in the classic gesture of surrender.

"Arrgghh!" Helene snarled, pushing away from

the desk in helpless exasperation. "I cannot take this!"

She stormed from the office.

"That went well." Remo smiled at Chiun. He felt cheerier than he had in several days.

"Like a monkey," Chiun said. "Heh-heh."

Remo felt his good mood fade as quickly as it had come.

"You're a real comfort, you know that, Chiun?"

"Ooo-ooo-ooo," said the Master of Sinanju with a distinctly simian sound.

HELENE BUMPED into Guy Philliston in the apothecary shop downstairs. He was hustling through the soot-smudged front door with a tin of East Indian tea he had liberated from the window display of a closed shop down the road.

"Ah," Philliston said, "leaving, are we?"

"I am going for a walk."

"Wouldn't go if I were you," Sir Guy warned. "Military rule and all that. They're supposed to shoot anyone on sight caught in the street. Questions later. Bad show all around."

"You seem fine."

Philliston straightened his spine proudly. "Yes, but *I* am British." This said, Sir Guy went into the back of the store, where the secret Source staircase was hidden.

Helene walked out into the empty square.

She hadn't gone more than a few yards before her cellular phone rang.

"Oui," Helene said, answering the powerful small phone.

Her face grew more and more shocked as the frantic voice on the other end of the line spit out a string of rapid-fire French.

"I will return immediately," she promised after the caller was finished. She pressed the button that disconnected the line and returned the device to the pocket of her leather jacket.

She glanced up once at the tinted Source windows two stories above. This was one phone call that the American agents didn't overhear.

Briefly Helene entertained the notion of going up and requesting Remo's help. After all, she had seen him do some amazing things over the past few days.

No, she finally decided. This was a French problem. It was best handled by Frenchmen.

She would deal with it herself.

A determined expression on her chiseled face, Helene hurried down the bombed-out street.

22

The president of France arrived at the Palais de l'Élysée by limousine in the wee hours of the morning.

It was the day after the third aerial attack against London, and the president had political concerns that extended beyond the shores of his native land. France's neighbor across La Manche—the body of water the rest of the world stubbornly insisted on calling the English Channel—had been receiving a beating in her most famous city. Ordinarily this would have been a matter of indifference to France.

Not this time.

There had been much bad blood between the two countries for many years. The president was acutely aware of the running feud between France and Great Britain, and he didn't wish to stir the embers by sleeping late after the worst of the three attacks against London. For this reason he came to the palace from the apartment of his mistress at a little after 6:30 a.m.

The limousine brought him through the high gates

and around to his personal entrance. It stopped in the great shadow cast by the historic old building.

He was a man who liked to project a public image of independence. This streak of stubbornness was regularly demonstrated by his insistence that he open his own car door himself.

This morning, like every other morning since assuming office, his driver jumped out of the front seat and raced around the rear of the car to open the door. It was a daily race that the president invariably won.

The president pulled at the door handle.

Odd...

In his eagerness to serve, after popping like a cork from the front seat, his driver generally pulled the door away from the president from the outside. Today there was no such pressure from the other side of the door. In fact, when the president looked more closely, he noticed through the window that there was no sign of his driver at all.

Not only that, when he tried to push the door open, he felt an opposite pressure. As if something was holding the door closed.

He pushed harder.

The obstruction moved. As it did so, an arm flopped into view beneath the half-open car door. The hand was covered in a sheen of bright red. Blood.

The president immediately yanked the door back. This was a security limousine. He would be safe inside.

The door was just inches from being shut when a black boot jammed into the opening between the door and the frame.

The president pulled harder, now with both hands. His knuckles grew white from the force he exerted.

Shouts came from outside. He recognized the language immediately. German.

Scuffling. He could see them now. Their angry faces outside the window. He pulled more furiously.

Hands curled in around the door frame, prying the door open. Though he struggled hard, there were too many of them. The president felt the handle being tugged away from him with a sudden wrench. The door sprang open wide.

His chauffeur was sprawled, dead, on the ground beside the car, still bleeding from the chest. His eyes were open wide, his face a macabre mask of shock.

The men outside the car reached in and grabbed the president of France roughly by the arms. They dragged him out into the cool morning air.

There were dozens of them. They wore the drab green German army uniforms of World War II. Each of them had a familiar old-fashioned curving helmet atop his bald head. Leather straps held the helmets in place.

On their arms were the chillingly familiar bands of Nazi soldiers. The black swastika—circled in white—on a red background.

There was no sign of the French troop on guard

detail within the protected walls of the palace. These silent soldiers apparently had free rein.

The president was held fast beside his limousine.

"I demand to know the meaning of this!" he sputtered indignantly.

The uniformed soldiers didn't react to his shouted words. They seemed unconcerned that his voice might bring assistance.

But his shout did have a reaction.

A lone man stepped from the doors that led into the interior of the palace—into the very heart of the French elected government.

Older than the rest, he wore a uniform slightly different than the others. He had the high-peaked cloth cap of a Nazi officer. A silver eagle perched atop the front of the mint-condition antique headgear. He came down the ornate outdoor staircase to the president's car.

"I apologize that we must meet under these conditions, Mr. President. Allow me to introduce myself. I am Field Marshal Fritz Dunlitz." He clicked his boots together in a gesture that rattled the black iron cross at his tightly buttoned uniform collar. "Please accompany me inside." He spread his hand toward the door to the palace.

"Unhand me!" the president insisted, twisting wildly.

Fritz nodded to the men. Obediently the soldiers released him.

"I demand that you—"

Fritz raised a black-gloved hand. He did it with such fury that the president halted his protestations.

When the leader of France grew silent, a brittle smile broke across the face of the gaunt old German. Again he motioned to the door to the Palais de l'Élysée.

His next words gave the president of France an involuntary chill.

"The führer wishes to meet you."

THEY HAD BEEN KIDNAPPED during the night and in the early hours of the morning. Each abduction was accomplished quietly, expertly. It was amazing even to Nils Schatz, considering the men with whom he had been forced to work.

But his army of skinheads with their aged Nazi leaders had proved their mettle in the most secret part of this shadow campaign.

On the floor of the small auditorium sat the mayors of the twenty arrondissements of Paris. With them was the prefect of the Seine and as many members of the senate and national assembly as could be found.

Those men in the room elected to national office were not as important to him as the others. They were, as the Americans said, gravy.

The mayors were the elected representatives of each division of France's most important city. They were the ones who separately controlled each small portion of Paris.

During the darkest hours of the morning, Schatz had persuaded all of them to sign an official document he had personally prepared. In order to do this, he had torn a page out of his own past history as Himmler's favorite torturer. Indeed, many of the men around him still tended the wounds he had inflicted upon them.

Schatz had enjoyed convincing them to see the wisdom of his position. The truth was, as he watched each man sign the important-looking scrap of paper, he had felt more alive than he had in years.

The document itself was only a few dozen lines, written both in German and in French. In effect it turned the city of Paris over to Nils Schatz. Now the führer.

Schatz was sitting on a small dais at the front of the auditorium when the president of France and his Nazi entourage entered the room.

The new führer placed onto the long table before him the document that relinquished control of the city to his army of skinheads. He rose politely as the French president was brought up onto the stage with him.

"Mr. President," Nils Schatz announced, clicking his heels formally.

"What is this outrage?" the president demanded. He noted the bruised and bloodied men and women seated near the far wall of the room. Guards sporting red-and-black-swastika armbands were posted all around them.

Schatz ignored the question. Instead, he continued speaking as if the French president were a silent guest.

"I thought that it would be more appropriate for us to meet in the railroad car of Marshal Foch," Schatz said. He shrugged helplessly. "However, there are still security issues for us."

"Foch?" the president echoed.

A national hero, Marshal Foch had received the surrender of the Germans in a railroad car at the end of World War I. Hitler had commandeered the car during World War II after the fall of Paris.

Schatz nodded. "Yes. His statue will, of course, be taken down at our earliest opportunity. For now I have a simple request. One your people have mastered over your long and—" distaste filled his face "—*distinguished* history. Please sign here."

Schatz drew the document toward the president. At the same time he offered the leader of France a gold pen.

The president quickly scanned the words on the large sheet of paper. He saw the signatories at the bottom. All of the highest authorities in the city. While Paris would certainly survive without them, their easy capitulation would be a major propaganda tool.

"*Non,*" the president of France said, proud chin jutting forward. "I will not sign this."

Schatz nodded, as if his refusal wasn't unexpected.

"Technology is marvelous, would you not agree, Mr. President?" Schatz asked.

The president was baffled by this sudden change of topic. He remained silent.

Schatz continued. "I confess to being completely baffled by all of these new inventions. Satellites, cameras. Even television."

There was a large TV on a metal chassis at the end of the conference table. At a sign from Fritz, an armed skinhead switched the set on. The screen was filled with an image of the famous Paris Opera House. Still a relatively new addition to the city, it had been constructed during the tenure of the president's predecessor.

It was a huge, curving semicircle of glass and metal. The facade of the building arced up from its cold concrete foundation and swung high into the air, stabbing back down sharply on the far side.

To many the building was an ugly blot on the city landscape. The current president of France shared this view.

On the television screen, early-morning sunlight glinted off its many panes of glass. They were seeing the Paris Opera House as it looked right now. There were three trucks parked in close to the front of the building. They appeared to be unoccupied.

"We have taken control of your television stations," Schatz said, as if this were so obvious that the mere mention of the fact was superfluous.

Schatz nodded to the back of the room. In the rear

yet another old Nazi bowed his understanding. He spoke furtively into a telephone in his gloved hand.

Schatz turned his attention to the screen. Fritz and the other troops watched expectantly, sparks of eager anticipation in their eyes.

The president of France looked on with dread.

For a long moment nothing happened.

Perhaps it will not happen, the president of France thought. Perhaps sheer will can keep this evil—

There was a sudden flash, so huge, so shocking that all watching—with the exception of Nils Schatz—blinked their eyes in surprise.

The trucks with their stolen surplus ordnance exploded upward and backward. The face of the ugly glass building burst apart in a blinding, sparkling flash of fire and smoke.

In an instant the building seemed to hang in the air like a pointillist painting, then collapsed in on itself, filling the square before it with huge plumes of smoke and dust. Tiny sparkling glass crystals danced on the choking dust cloud as it raced forward like an angry gray fog. In seconds it had enveloped the stationary camera.

Schatz let the frozen French president dwell on the image for more than a minute. At last he switched the television off.

"You have seen the DGSE reports," Schatz said with a patient nod. "You know how much of our materials we have reclaimed. I need you to believe me when I say that I possess the capability to destroy major strategic and cultural portions of this city. You alone can stop me from doing this. You alone can save your people a great deal of pain and anguish.'' He again offered the gold pen to the president. ''It will make my work so much easier,'' he added.

The president considered his options. He found he had none.

There was no telling where the bombs might be. And there were many. That the president knew beyond a doubt. They could be everywhere. Even in the palace.

Schatz had already demonstrated his might and his willingness to use it. His troops had commandeered French broadcasting. He had proved his seriousness in the destruction of the opera house. He had even taken over the palace of the president himself.

He was ruthless and efficient. With a small army at his disposal.

There was no other choice.

The president's hand shook with impotent rage. Without a word, he took the offered pen from the new führer.

23

Remo moped around the headquarters of Source until late in the afternoon.

Helene was gone. Apparently her fight with Remo had sent her back to France. Or perhaps she was elsewhere in England. For most of the day, he didn't care where.

He only became upset at around two o'clock when he realized that she had taken her phone with her. Without the phone Smith would have no way of contacting him.

Remo wished for a brief time that he had his own cellular phone. It seemed like everyone else had one. Helene. Guy Philliston. Even Smith had a pager.

However, he had never been very good at keeping track of gadgets. Smith had once given him an expensive two-way satellite communications device. Remo had broken it the first time he used it. After that Smith had relied on the telephone system.

It had always worked in the past. Until now.

Remo paced back and forth before the windows along the Trafalgar Square side of the office. He rotated his thick wrists absently as he walked.

"You are making me dizzy," the Master of Sin-anju complained. He was sitting cross-legged atop one of the empty desks. A bone-china cup filled with steaming tea sat in a gilded saucer. A delicate rose pattern adorned both cup and saucer.

"I can't just sit here," Remo grumbled.

"Why not?" Chiun asked, tipping his aged head. "Have you forgotten how?"

He picked up the teacup in his bony hand and brought it to his parchment lips. He sipped delicately.

Remo stopped pacing.

He looked once more at the empty square and then back at the Master of Sinanju. After a moment's pause he walked over to the desk next to Chiun. Climbing atop it, he dropped into a lotus position on the desk's barren surface.

"You see," Chiun intoned sagely, "it is not as difficult as you might have remembered."

Once Remo was settled on the desk, Chiun clapped his hands two times, sharply.

Like a genie summoned from a lamp, Sir Guy Philliston appeared from a small office that was off to the side of the main Source information center. He carried with him a sterling-silver tea set.

Chiun had sent Sir Guy out for some proper herbal tea after the Englishman had returned that morning with the inferior, stimulant-laced East India blend. It took little effort for him to convince the Source commander to serve the tea when beckoned.

The objects on the tray rattled like a curio cabinet

in an earthquake as Guy Philliston stepped nervously over to the Master of Sinanju.

"For my son," Chiun ordered.

Sir Guy gathered up the teapot and obediently filled a cup from the serving tray with the steaming greenish liquid. He handed it to Remo.

"The English make wonderful servants," Chiun commented. "I once had a British butler. He was a superb lickspittle."

"He tried to poison us," Remo reminded him, accepting the tea from Sir Guy.

"Yes, but he was polite about it," Chiun replied.

Sir Guy looked anxiously from one man to the other. "Does sir require anything further?" he asked.

Chiun waved a dismissive hand. "That is all, dogsbody."

Relieved, Sir Guy gathered up his serving set. He moved swiftly back inside the side office.

After he was gone, Remo sipped quietly at the tea. He stared out the window thoughtfully.

The Master of Sinanju watched his pupil looking vacantly off into space. A frown crossed his face.

"You are troubled," Chiun said.

Remo glanced at him. "Shouldn't I be?"

"No. You should not."

Remo looked back out the window. "Sue me," he said softly.

"What is it that you find so distressing?"

Remo snorted, almost spilling his tea. "Haven't you been paying attention to what's going on?" He set the cup down at his knees. "We've got World War III threatening to erupt in Europe. Or at least a second installment of World War II. According to Philliston's latest intelligence reports out of Germany, every skinhead or skinhead buddy is lining up to march on England. We've got one of the sickest times in modern history resurfacing right before our eyes." Remo exhaled loudly. "*That's* what's bothering me."

"Ah, yes," Chiun observed, "but were you not also troubled before leaving America?"

"That was different. I was ticked at that incident in New Hampshire. I didn't think I was making a difference back home. I'm over that now. This is a big deal."

Chiun nodded. "If you had been able to save the life of that woman who summoned images of your troubled youth, would you have been pleased?"

Remo shrugged. "Yeah. I guess so."

"You will never change, Remo Williams." Chiun smiled sadly. "Though I have labored lo these many years to alter your narrow perception of the world, my efforts have come to naught. The image you have of yourself is that of a fat sowboy in a white hat riding your trusty steed hither and thither in the defense of justice. I tell you this now, Remo. You are not here to root out injustice. You are here at the request of your emperor. The job of an assassin is a simple one. It is you who make it complex."

"I don't know," Remo said sullenly. "Maybe."

"It is fact," Chiun stated simply. "You were angry before coming here. Now you are no longer angry about the thing you were fleeing—you are angry at something new. When our work here is finished, you will find something even newer to be angry about. You are like a child flitting from one shiny toy to the next, never satisfied with what he has."

Remo knew that there was a great deal of truth in what Chiun was saying. He nodded reluctantly.

"So what should I do?" he asked.

"Learn from my example," Chiun said. "See what we do as the business it is. And never take your work home with you."

Remo wanted to laugh. Chiun was talking about assassination like a bookkeeper talked about the company's accounting ledger.

"I'll try," Remo promised, shaking his head.

"You will find that such an outlook lessens the complications in life greatly," Chiun offered. He lifted his teacup and took a thoughtful sip.

Remo glanced back to the office where Guy Philliston was hiding with his tea set.

"Tell me the truth," Remo asked, pitching his voice low. "Wasn't there a little part of you that wanted to zap Hitler all those years ago just for the satisfaction?"

"Absolutely," Chiun replied. "For the satisfaction of a job well done. The little Hun's head on a post outside my village would have brought much work to our House. Lamentably it was not so."

Remo shook his head. "You'll never convince me that you didn't want to bump him off for the sheer pleasure of it."

Chiun's sad smile deepened.

"That is where we will forever differ, my son," the old Korean said.

There was a sudden stomping on the staircase from the apothecary shop. Both Masters of Sinanju grew silent as a young Source agent came running into the main office area. Ignoring the men on the desks, he went racing into the side office of Sir Guy Philliston.

"Jilted boyfriend?" Remo asked, with a nod to the glass office door.

"I do not wish to think about it," Chiun sniffed.

A moment later Sir Guy appeared from the room, the young man following obediently in his wake. He marched over to a large television set in the corner of the room.

"This had better be important," Philliston complained. He shot a nervous glance at Remo and Chiun. "The lad is worked up about something on the telly," he explained. He scanned the front of the set. "How does one activate this box thingie?" he asked his underling.

The young assistant turned the TV on. The audio came on before the picture. The stentorian voice of a Thames television announcer blared across the room.

"...the scene in Paris this afternoon is a page torn from the history books. A document of surrender that has been authentically verified as being signed by the president of France himself was released to the world press not half an hour ago. In it control of Paris is ceded to the invasion force you see behind me now...."

The picture slowly congealed into recognizable shapes.

Remo blinked in disbelief as the camera image settled on a column of marching soldiers led by a single man on horseback.

He had seen the footage before. But always in the grainy black-and-white of decades-old newsreels. This was in full, glorious color and surround sound.

The Arc de Triomphe stood in the background, surmounting the hill of Chaillot in Paris. Before it, the soldiers marched proudly through the street, black boots kicking high in the familiar Nazi goose step. Red-and-black armbands were the single spots of brightness on their drab uniforms.

It was an image of historical déjà vu.

"Is this supposed to be some kind of joke?" Remo asked angrily.

"I'm sure I don't know," Philliston said nervously. He quickly turned to his underling. "Is this some sort of Gallic prank?" he demanded.

The young man shook his head. "No, Sir Guy. It's everywhere on the radio and telly. The World Service, ITN, BBC television, Thames. It became official at noon today. The French have surrendered Paris completely."

The column of men—Remo could see there were only about two hundred of them in all—turned in a wide arc as they passed by the camera. The long white tail of the lone horse in the lead waved merrily in the late-summer air.

"Thought they would have learned their lesson last time out," Sir Guy Philliston commented.

The television report next cut to a scene of raucous cheering near the Brandenburg Gate in Germany. The joy and optimism that had been displayed by the German people at the fall of communism on this very site was replaced by a dance of sheer blood lust by a huge crowd of skinheads.

The television announcer droned on. "This was the scene in Germany just minutes after the announcement of French surrender came. Obviously word of the impending bloodless coup had been deliberately leaked to fascist groups throughout the republic of Germany. Men who had until yesterday planned to join forces with the attack on London, have since switched their allegiance to the group that now controls Paris. The new regime has welcomed them with open arms. However, it remains to be seen whether they will encounter resistance upon reaching the French border."

Remo hopped down from the desk.

"I think we can guarantee them that," he said somberly.

Chiun had alighted to the floor also in a flutter of silk. Together they headed for the door.

"The two of you are going in alone?" Philliston's youthful aide asked, surprised. He turned to his commander. "Might that not be just a touch dangerous, sir?"

Remo and Chiun were just sliding out into the hallway. They vanished down the staircase.

As they were leaving, Sir Guy had taken a long-stemmed meerschaum pipe from his pocket. It was carved in the shape of Anne Boleyn's head. Tiny fissures indicated where the pipe had once been cracked and glued back together. Guy stuck the pipe between his lips and lit the already stuffed bowl with a single wooden match. He blew a thoughtful puff of smoke at the ceiling as he shook the flame off the match with a gentle back-and-forth movement.

"Yes," Sir Guy said finally, nodding. "For the Nazis."

THE IMAGE of the marching neo-Nazi forces was beamed via satellite to a small television set in a neat little office in the ancient stone fortress that perched on a small South American mountain peak separate from the rest of the IV village.

The bright blue eyes of Adolf Kluge turned a flinty gray as the line of goose-stepping soldiers marched beyond the camera's range.

Hands clenched in bloodless white knuckles, Kluge rose slowly from behind his large desk. Wordlessly he stepped from the office into the huge stone corridor.

He did not turn the television off.

24

Harold Smith pushed aside the heavy drapes in his hotel room, revealing an inch-wide strip of dirty glass.

His vantage point afforded him a fairly unobstructed view of the street three stories below. Occasionally a rental truck whose sides had been repainted red and emblazoned with an enormous black swastika would drive slowly down the road, turning off on a distant side street.

They were making their presence known. A lazy victory lap for the mighty conquerors.

At the moment two sets of armed guards had converged before the hotel. They stood on the quaint cobbled road, chatting and laughing. Three of them smoked cigarettes, casually flicking ash, like students sitting in some fashionable French sidewalk café.

Their Nazi uniforms propelled Smith backward in time. Unlike yesterday, he didn't feel an overwhelming compulsion to race out and fight the men. In fact, he admitted now that he had taken leave of his good senses in the London Underground the day before.

No, what Smith was feeling now was the old sense

of cold moral outrage he had experienced in his youth as a member of the OSS.

He hadn't realized that time had dulled his ability to be viscerally offended. He supposed his duties as CURE director were to blame. After seeing so much of the vile underbelly of American society, it was difficult to work up a stomachful of bile over anything. It had taken neo-Nazi storm troopers on the streets of Paris to rekindle the flames of revulsion that had burned away in youth.

"Is it safe, Harold?" his wife's timid voice asked from behind him. She sat in a chair next to the bed. Her face was filled with confusion and tension.

"No," Smith said simply.

The neo-Nazis on the street laughed once loudly and then parted company. A group of four walked down the street; the other three headed into the hotel. Smith watched them disappear beneath the windowsill.

He couldn't allow his emotions to dictate his next few steps. If they were to get out of this alive, he had to approach the situation rationally.

"Maude, please go in the bathroom," he instructed.

She didn't object. She didn't question why. Maude Smith merely stood dutifully and walked into the small room to one side of the bed. The door shut a moment later.

Smith looked at the night table. The cheap phone sat on the varnished wood surface. It was useless.

The invaders had disrupted Paris phone service during the night. He wouldn't be able to contact Remo.

Smith crouched down beside the bed. His legs and back ached as he reached beneath the dangling edge of the dust ruffle. He slid his briefcase out onto the worn rug.

Standing, Smith placed the briefcase on the neatly made bed. This accomplished, he sat down in the overstuffed easy chair his wife had vacated moments before.

Smith patiently stared at the cracked painted surface of the old wooden door.

Alone in the room, he waited.

PIERRE LePOTAGE'S grandfather had bought the small hotel for a modest sum in the early part of the twentieth century. Since that time it had been a tradition for all members of Pierre's family to work there.

Young Pierre had gotten his start in the kitchen during World War II. Back then, the LePotage family had been forced to make the best of a bad situation.

During the Occupation, his grandfather had retired to doing light duty around the hotel. Pierre's father had taken charge behind the desk. And in the kitchen young Pierre had the awesome duty of personally spitting in every meal prepared for the occupying German force. By the end of a busy day, his mouth would be as dry as the North African desert.

Both father and grandfather were long-since dead.

Pierre had many years ago assumed the vaunted family position of desk clerk for Hôtel de LePotage. So much time had passed since his youth that he had assumed his days of spitting into diners' meals were far behind him.

Pierre was surprised, therefore, when he felt a welling need to expectorate. It came to him the moment the three German soldiers came through the front door of his small family-owned hotel.

"We are under orders to search every building," the leader snarled in crude French as the trio approached the desk.

"Of course," Pierre said. He didn't smile.

"You will accompany us," the skinhead commanded.

Pierre nodded his understanding. He went to the door behind the desk. Reaching around the wall into the small office, he took the big ring with the master key from its special hook above the desk that had been his grandfather's.

Key in hand, he came out from behind the desk and joined the trio of neo-Nazi soldiers.

"Have you men eaten?" Pierre asked.

"No," admitted the German soldier.

The party entered the small elevator. Pierre reached up to grab the gate.

"In that case I invite you to dinner. I will prepare the meal myself."

He pulled the old-fashioned metal gate down with a resounding clank.

SMITH HEARD THEM coming down the hallway. They were stopping at each room in turn.

It had become obvious to the people staying there what was going on in the hotel. The objections tapered into a dull acceptance. Guests submitted their rooms and their personal belongings to the indignity of a search at the hands of the brutish skinhead soldiers.

When they at last came to his door, Smith had been sitting patiently for more than an hour.

He heard the footfalls on the old carpeted floor. There was not a rattle of keys as he expected. Just the sound of a single key sliding into the lock.

Smith got hastily up from the chair and reached for the briefcase on the bed.

The door sprang open into the room. Smith was caught like a deer in headlights. He was leaning over the bed, his frozen hand extended over the battered briefcase with its portable computer. He glanced at the door with a look of desperation.

Coming in from the dingy hallway, the neo-Nazis immediately sensed they had stumbled onto something valuable.

"Move away from there!" one of the soldiers ordered in French.

"Non!" Smith said. He lowered his hand farther. The briefcase was enticingly in reach.

Three machine guns raised threateningly.

"I will not tell you again," the skinhead in command said with sneering coldness.

Defeated, Smith withdrew his hand. Shoulders hunched, he stepped obediently over to the far side of the bed.

The three men hurried across the room. At the door Pierre LePotage looked mournfully at Harold Smith. This was terrible for business. He apologized to his guest with a wordless shrug.

Smith responded with an odd look. He was edging farther to the wall. He glanced down at the floor.

It was the subtlest of gestures, but Pierre somehow caught the meaning in Smith's eyes at once. With a casualness that would have impressed the greatest living actor, the desk clerk eased himself back out into the hallway. He disappeared beyond the wall.

"What do you suppose it is?" one of the skinheads said to his fellow soldiers, intrigue and greed in his voice.

"Probably more junk," said the lead soldier, studying the metal hasps. He glanced at Smith. "How do you open these?" he demanded.

"They are on a spring. You simply have to twist them," Smith explained.

The soldier placed his thumbs against the pair of locks. He pressed against them, hard. The split second he did so, Smith threw himself to the floor.

Only one of the men saw Smith go down. He watched the American drop from sight behind the bed the instant a wall of flame erupted around all three storm troopers.

The sound was no greater than that of a loud firecracker, but the result was far more violent. Behind the protective shield of the bed, Smith was safe from the brunt of the explosion.

He came up off his stomach a moment later, moving rapidly around the bed.

Pierre came in from the hallway. On the bed a small fire burned atop the charred comforter. The Frenchman expertly pulled the ends of the bedcovers up over the fire, extinguishing the flames.

Coldly rational now, Smith went over to the German soldiers. Only the one who had opened the briefcase was dead. His face and hands were reddish black masses of gore. The other two had been severely wounded. They lay dying on the old hotel rug.

Smith detested killing. But he also was a man who didn't shy away from doing what was necessary.

Smith didn't know if he would have to ration bullets. He drew a knife from a scabbard at the waist of one soldier. With the dispassion of someone carving a Thanksgiving turkey, Smith plunged the knife into the hearts of the dying men.

Gathering up the soldiers' Walther MPL German submachine guns from the floor, he dropped them to the bed. Smith stripped the guns of their ammunition. He was about to damage them beyond use when Pierre stopped him.

"I believe I will have need for them," the Frenchman said levelly.

Smith glanced at the concierge. Quickly he handed

over two of the guns. Dividing the ammunition into two equal amounts, he gave half to the desk clerk.

"*Merci,*" Pierre said. "Now we must get you to a safe place."

"I will be fine," Smith insisted.

Pierre glanced down at the three dead skinheads. When he looked back up, he wore a faint smile. "I have no doubt," said the desk clerk. Carrying his two submachine guns, the Frenchman left the room.

Smith hurried to the bathroom door.

"It is safe, Maude," Smith said. "Please close your eyes before you come out."

Mrs. Smith did as she was told. The door crept cautiously open, and Maude stepped back into the hotel room. She appeared shell-shocked.

"I heard an explosion, Harold." She trembled, eyes screwed tightly shut.

He knew that any lie he might come up with would be pointless. After all, his wife wasn't stupid.

"We must hurry," he urged firmly.

Taking her by the arm, Smith led her hastily past the bodies and out into the hall. She didn't ask to bring her luggage.

25

Remo hot-wired a Mercedes on Oxford Street and drove maniacally through the empty streets of London, finally flagging down the first British Army jeep he encountered.

After a brief discussion with the lieutenant in the army vehicle, during which the officer relinquished two front teeth and his sense of smell for the next six months, the soldier agreed to escort Remo and Chiun to the English end of the Channel Tunnel.

They flew at speeds in excess of 120 miles per hour down the M20, turning off in Folkestone five miles inland from the famed cliffs of Dover. Remo and Chiun left the stolen car and gap-toothed soldier behind, hurrying aboard the first Le Shuttle train.

Thirty-one miles and fifty-seven minutes later, the train emerged into the dwindling yellow sunlight in the French terminal at Coquelles near Calais, two miles inland.

Remo liberated a car from an English businessman who had brought the vehicle over on the train and tore out onto the A26 motorway. He pointed the car toward Paris.

A LONG SECTION of Boulevard Mortier had been closed down during the occupation. DGSE headquarters was in the hands of the enemy. Helene Marie-Simone skulked through the streets of Paris, alone.

A light drizzle had erupted shortly after nightfall. She held the collar of her leather jacket tight at her neck. Though it didn't provide much in the way of warmth, it kept out most of the rainwater.

Alone.

Helene hadn't set foot in her apartment since returning to France. If DGSE was in the hands of the neo-Nazi occupying army, there was no telling how much secure information they had gotten hold of. If her superiors had no time to destroy all that was sensitive before relinquishing command of France's premier espionage service, they would have an alphabetical listing of all DGSE agents.

She cursed herself for not informing Remo of the telephone call.

It had been from Director Remy Renard himself. He told her in hushed tones of what appeared to be a coup attempt at the Palais de l'Élysée. Agents who had been sent to liberate the palace had never returned. There was no word from the president, but he was believed to be inside.

Of course, all of this was hours before news broke of the fall of Paris. Helene had blundered back into the city at the worst moment of crisis. The capital had been locked down tightly before she had a chance to flee.

She was trapped. A prisoner in her own city.

Helene had been wandering the streets for hours, waiting for nightfall. Now that it had finally come, her stride became more purposeful. Keeping to the shadows, she walked down the damp sidewalk along the Champs-Elysées toward the presidential palace.

Barricades had been placed before the gates. Bags filled with sand were stacked atop one another. Before them, huge concrete slabs had been dumped in order to prevent suicide runs by explosives-laden trucks.

Armed guards knelt behind the barriers, chatting among themselves. From the shadows Helene scanned the fortifications.

There did not appear to be many guards. The force they had used to take the city was small. They must have expected reinforcements to come once the mission was under way.

Only two men were behind the sandbags. Occasionally a third man would stroll into view within the gates. A vicious-looking German shepherd walked at leash length before the final guard.

She watched the scene for half an hour. The rain grew heavier, pasting her brown hair to her face in thick sheets. She tugged it away from her eyes with impatient, shaking hands.

The guard with the dog completed his circuit every

ten minutes or so. Within that interval the two guards were completely alone.

She waited until the dog guard returned one last time. As she watched his rain-slick back disappear beyond the high columns beside the gate, Helene moved out of the protective shadows. Her hand felt inside her coat, reaching for the butt of her gun.

She walked briskly across the wide street to the palace.

Her shivering now had nothing to do with the cold.

THERE WERE NO LIGHTS on inside the ground floor apartment. The windows were dark, the shades tightly drawn.

The figures approached from the east, up the dimly lit side street to the alley door. Rain dripped down from the roof three stories above, splattering in furious, uneven bursts against the pavement.

Somewhere distant two cats shrieked a sudden argument at one another. Afterward there were voices. A single loud laugh followed by a bawdy German shout. More laughter.

The dark, drenched shape in the lead came up to the old door, hugging the wall. A single knock, followed by three in rapid succession. Silence ensued.

"Résistance," a voice called in a hoarse whisper.

No response.

The rain continued to drain loudly into the alley. The German voices grew louder. They were coming closer.

Another knock.

''It is Smith,'' the dark shape hissed in English.

Footfalls. Louder now. They were in the alley. But they were unhurried.

At the door a brief pause was followed by the sound of a dead bolt sliding back. The door opened an inch and a watery yellow eye peered out into the alley. All at once, the door swung open wide.

The Germans were nearly in view.

Without a glance down the alley, Smith hustled his wife inside the small apartment.

The door shut and locked once more.

Seconds later the German patrol strolled past the unlit apartment. They continued on without a glance at the silent alley door.

THE FRENCH ARMY HAD placed roadblocks around the city of Paris. The only people being allowed in so far were members of the press. By order of Führer Schatz no one was being allowed to leave. Beyond their barricades, French authorities were helpless to do anything to liberate their capital city.

The president had been allowed to speak via direct satellite transmission to those members of the French senate and national assembly who hadn't been caught in the neo-Nazi web during the spate of kidnappings.

He informed them that he had indeed signed the document of surrender. He also told them that he was against their taking any action at this time to liberate the city. Of course, he was surrounded by eager young skinheads with plainly visible firearms, so the sincerity of France's chief elected official was suspect.

Of one thing, there was no doubt. France was facing a constitutional crisis.

The leaders of both houses of parliament were being held captive. The prime minister had been out of the city at the time of the takeover and had assumed control of what was left of the government. However, he was having difficulty rallying support among the remaining legislators.

In absence of a plan or a functioning government to support that plan, a vacuum had developed. And in that void nothing was getting accomplished, giving Nils Schatz and his tiny band of fascists more time to solidify their stranglehold on the famous city.

On one of the northwestern roads leading into Paris, a heavily armed convoy of French soldiers had stalled at the city's outskirts. Concrete barriers lined the road.

French army soldiers milled helplessly around trucks and jeeps on their side of the partition. On the other side a woefully outmatched force of neo-Nazi soldiers stood smugly at attention.

The French forces could easily have overrun the band of invaders, but hadn't yet been given instructions to do so. The Germans knew this. Like neighborhood milquetoasts given licence to taunt the local bully, the skinheads were milking their newfound power for all it was worth.

The Germans jeered and spit toward the French soldiers. The French could do nothing but stand back and stand down.

The standoff had gone on like this for several hours when Remo and Chiun finally drove up in their stolen Fiat.

They were waved to a stop by French guards.

"We're in kind of a hurry," Remo pressed, leaning out the window as an armed French soldier approached.

"You are American?" the soldier said in English.

"Yep," Remo replied. "Hey, Frenchie, could you move that tank?" he called up ahead. He beeped the car's horn.

"I am Korean," Chiun said to no one in particular.

Sensing he had a couple of potential lunatics on his hands, the French soldier took a step back from the car.

"Could you wait a moment, please?"

As Remo's car idled, the soldier walked briskly over to his commanding officer. The officer—a colonel—looked suspiciously at Remo and Chiun. He, in turn, went off to find his commander.

For a few long minutes, Remo tapped the dashboard anxiously. There seemed to be a dozen large vehicles in their way along with a dozen more huge concrete barriers.

He turned to Chiun.

"You want to walk?" he asked.

"It would be preferable to sitting here," Chiun admitted with a curt nod.

The two of them got out of the car and headed up the road alongside the stalled column of army vehicles.

By this point word of the car and its strange occupants had gotten up to the general in command of this particular detachment.

The general's name was Adrien Cresson. He was a wiry man with thick curly hair and a deep baritone that belied his size. He was also in a foul mood.

Suspecting they might have a pair of Nazi sympathizers on their hands, General Cresson had come personally down from his command post to Remo's parked car.

"Traffic into the city is restricted—" the general started to say as he approached the car, his hand perched on his side arm.

He stopped short. The vehicle was empty. General Cresson glanced angrily back at the colonel and private accompanying him.

"Where are they?" he demanded.

The men only shook their heads in confusion.

Furious, he ordered the platoon to spread out along the road, searching under trucks and around the sides of tanks.

The scurrying French army soldiers located their prey in a matter of seconds. The two men from the car were seen strolling calmly through the barren stretch of road between the convoy and the first of the concrete barriers.

"No one stopped them?" General Cresson boomed, furious.

"No one *saw* them, sir," begged the colonel.

Cresson wheeled on his men. "Level weapons on those two!" he yelled.

The French soldiers obeyed.

On the other side of the line, the arrogance of the German soldiers melted into deep concern as the weapons of the French army detachment were pointed in their direction.

Remo and Chiun felt the pressure waves of rifles aimed at their backs.

"Beautiful country, isn't it?" Remo said.

"It reeks of fermented grapes," Chiun commented.

They strolled past the French barriers and over to the German end of the road.

"Halt!" an angry, French-accented voice shouted from behind them.

In front of them the Germans were at a loss what to do—with either the French army or the two men approaching.

Until now, the kidnapping of the French president had awarded them a sense of impunity. Now it seemed as if that air of privilege had evaporated.

Rather than flee, the half-dozen skinhead soldiers raised their own weapons at the approaching men.

BACK AT THE FRENCH lines, General Cresson had been ready to give the order to shoot. But when the occupying soldiers raised their machine guns at Remo and Chiun, he ordered his men to hold their fire.

Anxiously the French line watched the drama that was playing out before them.

"HALT!" the leader of the German troops called in English, echoing the command he had just heard the French general give. He was an unregenerate old Nazi. One of the men Schatz had brought with him from the IV village. He and his comrades were crouching alertly behind their protective wall of four-foot-high barriers.

"Wo ist die Toilette?" Remo asked, using a German phrase he had picked up from a guide book on Le Shuttle.

The neo-Nazi soldiers frowned. Was it possible this lunatic had broken through the French lines and was risking his life approaching occupied Paris simply to locate a bathroom?

The German in command decided that it made no difference.

"Turn around slowly and go back the way you came," he ordered, aiming his gun at Remo's chest.

"No can do," Remo said, shaking his head. "It's an emergency. I just had a big plate of snails at a little outdoor café that specializes in health-code violations.'' He continued toward the German defensive barriers.

"Stop!'' the Nazi officer called one last time. His curled finger closed within a hair of his trigger.

Remo and Chiun kept coming.

That was enough for the officer. Without further preamble the German opened fire. His men followed his lead an instant later.

German machine-gun fire erupted on the road into Paris for the first time in more than half a century. But unlike then, the bullets had no hope of finding their marks.

The instant the soldiers' fingers began caressing their triggers, Remo and Chiun split away from one another. Remo moved left, Chiun right.

They vaulted over the barriers in half a heartbeat, landing amid the startled squad of skinheads. Before the men were aware of what had happened, they felt their still-firing guns being wrenched from their hands. Fingers accompanied weapons—ripping free as if held in place by nothing stronger than air. Machine guns and detached digits soared high above them, landing with clattering finality on the vacant expanse of road between the two warring camps.

Spinning on the nearest disarmed soldiers, Chiun became a swirl of vengeful blue in his soft robin's egg kimono.

The Master of Sinanju launched back and forth, battering the foreheads of the stunned troops, crushing skulls and launching deadly fragments of bones into brains. Metal battle helmets rocketed backward off of the men, so great was the concussive force. The dead men crumpled to the road a split second after their useless headgear.

On his end of the line, Remo had taken out the first pair of skinhead soldiers with blows identical to the ones employed by the Master of Sinanju. Remo's third and final soldier bared his teeth as he grabbed for a side arm on his baggy uniform.

He was an older man. Obviously a product of World War II. Swearing in guttural German, the man pulled his gun free and wheeled on his attacker, only to find that his target had vanished. In fact, everything around him had vanished. The world had grown incredibly dark.

And then the pain began.

Outside the confines of the helmet, Remo had clapped his hand down atop the old soldier's head-gear. He pushed.

There was a crunch of metal, like a beer can being crushed, followed by a snap-snap-snap of bone as the old Nazi's spinal column was compressed from above.

The man's startled eyes disappeared beneath the helmet. These were followed by his nose, his mouth and, finally, his chin. When Remo was finished, there was no sign of the thug's shaved and tattooed pate. He looked like a doughy mannequin's body with a greenish mushroomlike head.

Remo jammed two eye holes into the front of the

helmet. With his blunt fingertip, he created a smiling crease in the thick metal beneath the two holes.

He held the soldier at arm's length, examining the makeshift smiley face.

"Have a *bien* day," Remo said with a smile of his own. He dropped the soldier to the road.

The Master of Sinanju came over to join him. He looked down at the helmet-head of the soldier.

"The eyes are crooked," the old Korean said, tipping his head to one side thoughtfully.

Remo shrugged. "Spur of the moment," he said. "I'll do better next time."

Chiun nodded his approval.

They were about to leave the scene when something from the French lines distracted them.

It was soft. Barely audible at first.

It was a single feeble clap.

Remo turned.

General Cresson was standing alone just beyond the French barriers. He was at full attention; back erect, chest jutting forward proudly, staring directly at Remo and Chiun. His jaw quivered almost imperceptibly as he brought his hands together in a deliberate, repetitive motion. There was a faint hint of moisture in his flint black eyes.

All at once the entire platoon of French army soldiers on the other side of the road exploded in a spontaneous burst of cheers and applause. The sound thundered up the motorway.

Remo cast a wary eye toward the city. He looked back at the cheering French forces.

"Hey, you wanna keep it down?" Remo called. "Sheesh," he complained to Chiun as they began walking, "no wonder this city keeps getting invaded. No one knows when to shut up."

They continued up the road for Paris.

26

Nils Schatz watched the reports out of Germany with something approaching pure, undiluted rapture.

Everything was going exactly according to plan.

Before the Berlin Wall came down, IV had worked for many years to establish a network of people sympathetic to the cause within the borders of both East and West Germany.

That fool Kluge had back-burnered the project, concentrating the organization's resources on technology and foreign investment. But the men were already there. Most of them would have worked for nothing, so great was their hatred. Indeed, many of them had been without funds since Adolf Kluge had assumed control of IV.

But Schatz had seen to it that they were paid. With the money he had been stealing all these months, he had gotten them supplies, weapons. And they were ready.

Neo-Nazi groups were already massing on the other side of the Rhine. They were ready to march through France and on to Paris.

The army of this new Germany had vowed to keep

its people on the other side of the border, but Schatz knew that that would be impossible to do. Eventually there would be too many of them and they would come spilling over the border into France, sweeping across the country in a bloody wave so magnificent it would be impossible to stop.

The movement had its sympathizers within the regular army, as well. Schatz was certain that, before the week was out, the German army would be on his side, as well.

History was being made. Finally.

The shameful stain that was the Nazis' ignoble defeat in World War II was on the verge of being finally and completely erased.

The promise of IV would be realized in his lifetime. The Fourth Reich. The beginnings of a Teutonic empire that would span a thousand years.

And he—Nils Schatz—would be its führer.

At the moment the leader of the reich was seated on the dais in the small auditorium of the Palais de l'Élysée.

Sitting on the floor against one wall were the city's elite, including the president of France himself. They were being guarded by a group of handpicked skinheads.

These were the ones with hope. He saw a piece of him in each of them. Every one of these young skinheads had the same love for blood that young Nils Schatz had had. He would train them to be his personal SS.

For now it wasn't yet safe for Schatz to tour the streets of this conquered city. He had spent much of the day and long hours into the night watching the televised reports of the fall of Paris, reveling in his bold accomplishment.

On the table before him was his walking stick. As he stared in wonder at the television screen, he rolled the cane back and forth absently between thumb and forefinger.

He was aware of sharp footfalls coming in from the hallway. They came to a scuffling stop on the auditorium floor beneath the stage.

"Führer," Fritz called up to him.

The newly promoted field marshal had a disturbed edge to his voice. Schatz held up a staying hand, not turning away from the television.

Suddenly the CNN coverage he had been watching cut away for an interview with a former United States secretary of state. Schatz snarled, shutting off the television with the remote control. At last he turned his attention to Fritz.

His assistant was not alone. With him were two skinhead guards. Between the pair of men was a beautiful young woman. She wore a set of handcuffs and an expression of utter hatred.

"What have we here?" Schatz asked, amused.

"This traitor was apprehended within the palace walls, Führer," Fritz said crisply. "She has murdered several soldiers of the reich."

Schatz gathered up his cane and stepped purposefully down from the stage. He walked over and stood toe-to-toe with Helene Marie-Simone.

"How many men?" Schatz asked, looking at the girl.

"Three guards," Fritz announced hotly.

Schatz stared deeply into Helene's eyes. He didn't tear his gaze away as he issued orders to Fritz.

"Pull two more from duty on the street. Place them at the place our brave men were murdered."

"We have not many men to spare, Führer," Fritz said nervously. "It is important that we have some presence on the streets. If the people were to realize how few men we actually have—"

"Would you perhaps prefer that a lone terrorist like our young lady friend here were to steal in here in the dead of night and assassinate your führer?" Schatz asked. The words were said playfully, but there was a cold undertone.

Fritz snapped to attention. *"Nein, mein Führer!"*

"Go," Schatz ordered.

Spinning on his heel, Fritz marched dutifully back out the auditorium door.

"You are the one from Guernsey," Schatz mused. "You were in the company of the Master of Sinanju. Tell me, my young assassin, is he with you now?"

Helene was not sure what a Master of Sinanju was. However, she had a sinking feeling that he was referring to either Remo or Chiun. She refused to play his game. Helene remained silent.

Schatz continued to stare into her eyes. As if he

could see through to her brain and read her every flitting thought.

Helene's eyes strayed from his gaze only once. She shot a look to the president of France over against the wall. He seemed none the worse for wear.

"I will tell you what I think," Schatz said when it became clear she would not answer voluntarily. "I think you are alone. I think that if the Master of Sinanju were with you, he would have made it inside with far greater ease than you. He does not come now, nor will he in the future. For he sees his superior in me."

As he spoke, Schatz's eyes grew more and more wild. They held the look of a madman.

In that instant DGSE agent Helene Marie-Simone had an epiphany. She knew with a certainty beyond simple knowledge that the psychotic old man before her intended to kill her.

With great deliberateness Schatz ran the bronze end of his cane delicately beneath Helene's flawlessly shaped chin.

"Permit me, my dear, to show you how the Fourth Reich deals with murderers."

27

The light drizzle had ended in a ten-minute-long downpour. Afterward many of the storm clouds scudded east, revealing a spotty tapestry of distant stars.

A few tenacious clouds remained above the city. Large, uncertain droplets of rain splattered to the wet ground as Remo and Chiun walked along the vacant sidewalks of Paris.

They had encountered few neo-Nazis since entering the besieged capital. A few foot patrols. Infrequently a truck with a painted swastika on its side would rumble past.

Obviously there were not many of them. The two hundred or so men Remo and Chiun had seen on television marching so proudly beneath the Arc de Triomphe must have been nearly the entire invading force.

"It doesn't make sense," Remo mused as they walked. "Let's say for the sake of argument there are double the number of soldiers here than were on TV. That still only gives them an army of four hundred. Even I can't believe the French would turn over their capital to four hundred men."

"There is more here than meets the nose," Chiun said.

"Nose?" Remo asked. He turned to the Master of Sinanju. Chiun remained silent.

Remo's eyes narrowed. As they continued down the street, he concentrated his olfactory senses on the minute particles suspended in the air around them.

It took him a moment to locate what Chiun was referring to. When he did, he was annoyed at himself for not noticing it, as well. The rain had cleaned much of the odor from the air, but some of it still remained.

"Mustard gas," Remo said with a somber nod. "I can smell the rotting canisters, too. They've got the gas and probably the bombs stored in the city somewhere."

"Of that there is no doubt," Chiun said.

"Which direction is it coming from?"

"Every direction," the Master of Sinanju answered seriously. "These villains have turned this entire city into one gigantic boom device. That is why the French conceded defeat so readily."

"This time," Remo clarified.

"True," Chiun admitted. "But whatever their past history, they have in this instance recognized a true threat. We must tread lightly."

"You don't have to tell me twice," said Remo.

"We must tread lightly," Chiun repeated.

"What was that for?" Remo asked.

"In case you blow me up before I have a chance

to warn you yet again,'' the Master of Sinanju explained simply. They continued on through the dimly lit streets of the City of Lights.

FÜHRER NILS SCHATZ of the German Fourth Reich watched over the shoulder of one of his young SS apprentices. The skinhead was trying to show the old Nazi how to navigate through the uncomplicated computer system that had come already installed on the machine.

"This is a mouse, *mein Führer,*" the lad was saying. He rested his hand atop a palm-sized piece of plastic to the side of the computer. "With it, you move the small arrow on the screen."

"The cursor," said Schatz.

"Yes, *mein Führer,*" the skinhead said brightly.

Schatz detested technology. But although he was loath to admit it, it would be necessary in the new order. Others would have these devices. He could not allow the Fourth Reich to be outstripped by other nations in the infancy of its thousand-year life.

On the screen was a detailed map of Paris. Square red blocks indicated areas where explosives had been planted. Blue triangles showed the places that had been used for mustard-gas storage.

"One need only move the cursor to either a triangle or a square," the skinhead explained.

As he spoke he moved the cursor onto a red spot. Depressing the left mouse button with his index finger, the young man called up a computerized sheet that listed in detail the amount of ordnance that had been placed at that particular location.

"It is quite simple," the youth offered.

"Yes," Schatz said, lips pursed in a look of perpetual distaste. "Let me."

The youth obediently stood, allowing Schatz to assume the seat before the computer. Leaning his cane against the side of the desk, Schatz sat down.

He pressed the button on the mouse. Immediately the image on the screen changed to that of a gray background. Lines of text ran up the right side of the screen.

"What did I do?" he asked sternly.

"Nothing, *mein Führer*," the skinhead explained. "That is the help function. You merely have to—" He reached over Schatz's shoulder in order to take control of the mouse.

"No," Schatz snapped. "*Tell* me."

Hurried footsteps racing into the room from the corridor interrupted the lesson. Schatz cast an angry eye over his shoulder.

It was Fritz. Panicked once again. Fritz always seemed panicked about something lately. He was standing between the two skinhead guards Schatz kept with him at all times.

"*Mein führer,* Herr Kluge—" Fritz began.

Schatz cut him off with a raised hand. He did not even look his way. As he spoke, he used the mouse to roll the cursor around the screen. The small arrow of light twirled drunkenly on the computer screen.

"Do not speak of Kluge. Not in this, our finest hour. Kluge is a nothing, an infant. A coward. He has squandered the invaluable resources of IV on what? On economic matters. We are an organization for conquest. That fool in diapers never understood our true purpose."

"I understand now that I should have put you in restraints."

The cursor stopped dead. Schatz's withered old hand had frozen upon the smooth plastic mouse. He turned slowly around in his seat.

"Kluge," he said with an almost imperceptible nod.

The leader of IV stood just inside the door to the small office next to Fritz. His blue gray eyes were more enraged than they had been in the small village in Argentina. He had just spent two hours traveling through the empty streets of Paris and had seen the lunacy of Nils Schatz firsthand.

"What were you *thinking,* you fool?" Kluge demanded.

"I was thinking of that which you never dared think," Schatz answered. He picked up his cane from its resting spot beside the desk. Still seated, he toyed with it, slowly twirling the walking stick on the carpeted floor.

"What? Of suicide?" Kluge snapped. "You pathetic old imbecile, you are out to ruin us."

Schatz slammed the blunt end of his cane down

on the floor. As quickly as it struck, he was pulling
it up in the air, aiming it at Adolf Kluge.

"Us?" Schatz snarled. His yellowed teeth ground
viciously together. "I am not out to ruin *us*." The
cane stabbed toward Kluge more violently. "However you, Herr Kluge, are an altogether other matter."

REMO AND CHIUN MET their first real resistance
within the borders of Paris on their way into the part
of the city that housed its most famous tourist attractions.

They were walking south on Rue de Clichy when
they encountered a convoy of neo-Nazi vehicles. The
entire column consisted of two stolen Hertz rental
trucks that had been badly painted over in the colors
of the Nazi flag.

Remo and the Master of Sinanju continued padding down the damp sidewalk as the trucks slowly
approached.

"Shall I find out from these?" Chiun asked.

"I suppose we're going to have to ask sometime,"
Remo said glumly.

"It is preferable to wandering the streets aimlessly
for the foreseeable future."

Remo nodded. "I don't smell any explosives in
them."

"Nor do I," said Chiun.

Remo stopped on the sidewalk, crossing his arms.
As he did so, the Master of Sinanju stepped out into

the road. The old Asian walked over into the middle of the wet street and turned to face the oncoming truck.

DOWN THE ROAD the driver of the lead truck caught sight of the wizened figure in the amber glow of the truck's headlights.

The truck wasn't going fast—only about fifteen miles per hour. The old man had plenty of time to get out of the way. In point of fact, he shouldn't have even been outside. It would be good to give him a little scare.

The skinhead behind the wheel beeped the horn.

The old man refused to budge.

The skinhead depressed the horn harder this time, holding his palm atop it for a solid ten-second burst.

The old man picked a piece of lint off his kimono sleeve.

That was all the skinhead needed. There was a curfew in Paris. And he was under orders to enforce that curfew.

With more force than was necessary, he clomped his heavy black boot down onto the accelerator. The truck lurched obediently forward.

He watched the old man grow larger in the headlights as the truck bore down on him. The stranger still made no move to get out of the way.

The skinhead felt a swelling tingle of excitement as the truck ate up the last few feet between him and his target.

It was only at the last minute that he noticed another man standing on the sidewalk. No matter. He would attend to the second one later. Perhaps they would enlist him to scrape his old friend's remains from the front of the truck.

The driver had only gotten the big truck up to twenty-five miles per hour before overtaking the tiny Asian.

The wrinkled old face disappeared below the level of the dashboard. There was an instant where the skinhead behind the wheel swore he heard the crunch of brittle old bones.

Then suddenly there was a painful shriek of wheels and the windshield was coming up very fast to meet him. And he realized in a blinding flash that he had been flung from his seat and that the old man had somehow stopped the truck as solidly as if it had struck a concrete wall.

The glass shattered against his face—shredding his pasty skin. He was propelled forward out of the truck.

The skinhead soared over the head of the wrinkled old man, who held his hand against the front of the truck in a gesture so weak it looked like it would not have stopped a fistful of daisies.

He landed on the pavement, skidding several yards before coming to a stop against a pair of fine leather loafers. The young skinhead looked up, blood running into his eyes.

Looking down from above was the upside-down

face of the man who had been standing on the sidewalk.

"OUCH," REMO SAID with a smile. "That looked really painful."

There was a screech of brakes, followed by a crash from the direction of the stalled truck.

Remo glanced up in time to see Chiun bounding over to the sidewalk, robes billowing around him like an insanely inflating parachute.

He had held the first truck just long enough for the second to plow into it, releasing his hold the instant the next driver slammed on his own brakes.

The driverless vehicle careered forward, flipping over onto its side. It crashed headlong into a darkened building, half on the street, half on the sidewalk. Its wheels spun crazily as its engine continued to race.

The next truck driver got control of his vehicle seconds after plowing into the rear of the first truck. He gripped the steering wheel for dear life as he slammed soundly on the brakes. Leaving a dozen yards' worth of black treads, the truck skidded across the wet street. It finally came to a gentle stop against a lamppost. High atop the pole, the faint yellow streetlight quivered ever so slightly from the truck's soft touch.

The skinhead on the road pushed blood from his eyes with shaking hands as he watched a pair of men spill from the cab of the less damaged truck.

As the men ran across the street, Chiun flounced up beside Remo.

"Nice work," Remo said.

"Of course," Chiun acknowledged, his tone indicating that he was surprised that Remo would have expected anything less. "Do you wish to save these pinheads for any reason?" he asked of the pair that were approaching.

"No, this one will do," Remo said, nodding to the man on the ground.

Wordlessly Chiun whirled forward to intercept the advancing skinheads.

They had their weapons drawn and aimed at the Master of Sinanju, ready to open fire. Chiun plowed straight into them faster than they could squeeze their triggers.

In a blur visible only to Remo, Chiun dropped his hands atop the helmets of the two men. A pair of simultaneous hollow plop-crunch noises followed. Their old-fashioned headgear collapsed like folding beach chairs around their ears. Quick as a flash, the Master of Sinanju carved a pair of smiley faces into the fronts of both helmets. Unlike Remo, he made certain his eyes were even.

He turned, holding the bodies by the necks for Remo's inspection. The helmet faces stared, unblinking, at Remo.

"Maybe you should try a nose," Remo suggested.

"You must develop an appreciation for minimalism," Chiun replied. He released the helmet-headed

corpses. Leaving them in the street, he joined Remo
and the injured skinhead.

The young man was suffering from only a few
superficial wounds. He grew more frightened as the
Master of Sinanju approached.

"Keep him away!" he begged fearfully.

"Not to worry," Remo said. "It's my turn."

Grabbing a knotted fistful of neo-Nazi shoulder
muscle, Remo squeezed tightly. The young man's
eyes bulged so hard they looked as if they might pop
from their sockets. The pain was too intense to even
scream. Though his mouth was open wide, no sound
emerged.

"That's level one," Remo said, easing back on
the pressure. "Now tell me, who's behind this?"

"The führer," the young man gasped.

Remo shot a look at Chiun. The Master of Sinanju
stood more erect upon hearing the German title.

"Do better than that, sausage breath," Remo said.
He squeezed harder.

"Nils Schatz!" the man cried in pain. "He is an
old leader! From the time of the first führer!"

"Now we're getting somewhere," Remo said en-
couragingly. "Where can we find this Shits guy?"

"At the presidential palace," the skinhead answered.

Remo turned to Chiun. "You know where that
is?"

"You refer to the Palais de l'Élysée?" Chiun

asked the skinhead. The young man nodded. "I know the place," Chiun said to Remo.

Remo turned his attention back to the bloodied skinhead.

"When you meet the first führer, tell him Sinanju says to keep a seat warm for his understudy."

He drove two hard fingers into the frontal lobe of the whimpering neo-Nazi.

"YOU ARE NOT in command," Kluge said. "I demand that you return with me to Argentina at once, before you further jeopardize our anonymity."

"We are no longer anonymous," Schatz sneered. "No thanks to you. Because of your cowardly leadership, we have squandered decades scurrying like frightened rats at the periphery of the world. I have accomplished that which you were afraid to do."

"I was not *afraid,* idiot!" Kluge screamed. "You've accomplished nothing. A stupid old man with a stupid old scheme of revenge against the world. *'Der Geist der stets verneint.'*" Kluge spit the German words out like a curse. "'The spirit that never dies.' Pah! *You* should have died. Along with these insane hopes of military domination."

Schatz had remained seated since Kluge had arrived in this small office in the Palais de L'Élysée. But at this last outburst from the IV leader, he pushed himself to his feet. Though it was unnecessary, he used his cane for support. He stared icily at Kluge.

"This insane hope is a reality," he said with cold simplicity.

"And what of Sinanju?" Kluge demanded. "Oh, yes, I know that both Masters of Sinanju have been here, on this very soil. And they were involved in your little—" he waved his hand impatiently "—foray into England."

Schatz shot a look at Fritz. The old man held his leader's glare for a few seconds before finally turning away. It was as good as an admission of guilt. Scowling, Schatz turned back to Kluge.

"They have yielded before the might of the reich."

"Hah," Kluge spit venomously. "They do not yield. They *never* yield. Do you have any idea the intricacies involved in our last encounter with those two? Whoever they work for in America tried to trace us through PlattDeutsche. I managed to throw up a few computer roadblocks barely in time to keep them at bay. We lost that entire company. It was nearly a billion-dollar loss."

"Economics," Schatz snapped. "Technology. Your two mistresses. They have brought us to ruin."

"No, *you* have brought us to ruin. Face the truth, Schatz. *I* am the future of IV. You are its past."

"Do not be so certain of yourself, Adolf," Schatz said. He pointed to the pair of skinhead guards standing inside the door. "Take him," he ordered blandly.

Immediately the guards grabbed Adolf Kluge by the arms.

"Are you insane?" Kluge demanded, shocked.

"Have you not said so yourself?" Schatz asked with a simple shrug. He turned to his guards. "Put him in with the French prisoners. I will decide what to do with him later."

Kluge was too stunned to protest. The skinhead guards led him from the room and down the corridor.

"*Mein führer,* I am sorr—" Fritz began with a helpless shrug of his bony shoulders.

The cane was up in an instant, resting against Fritz's pointy chin. The old man was too afraid to push it away. The cold end sat there, held aloft by Nils Schatz's trembling hand. Fritz could see a faint film of dried blood and gore on its bronze tip. He swallowed in fear.

"Be relieved that you are not joining him," Schatz said menacingly. He lowered the cane to the floor.

Fritz closed his eyes and heaved a sigh of relief.

The second his eyes were shut Fritz felt a tremendous pressure against the side of his head. A blinding flash of light crashed in a furious wave from a point just behind his left ear.

Fritz reeled.

His eyes opened for a moment and he saw the room in a tilted haze. It took him a second to orient himself.

He realized that he had fallen to his knees. In the process he had somehow grabbed on to the chair that Nils Schatz had been sitting on in front of his computer.

His führer and lifelong friend was before him, holding his favorite walking stick in a two-handed grip. To Fritz it seemed as if everything were moving in slow motion.

Schatz swung again. The metal end of the cane connected with a hollow crack.

Again the blinding pain.

Fritz lost his grip on the chair. He fell spread-eagled to the floor. With desperate hands he tried to push himself up to his creaking knees.

Above him Schatz swung a final time. The heavy tip of the cane landed square in the back of Fritz's head. At last the skull cracked obediently and the old Nazi fell once more to the floor. This time he didn't move.

Schatz withdrew a few steps from the corpse, panting excessively. He had to lean against the wall from his great exertion.

"In the future," Schatz said to the body, as if Fritz were still alive, "I would advise you, Fritz, to ask your führer before giving out privileged information."

The young skinhead who had been aiding Schatz with the computer was still in the room. He stood at attention by the small terminal.

Schatz pointed at the body with his cane.

"See the field marshal to his quarters," he instructed. "I believe he is ill." He walked from the room and up the long corridor.

Schatz had spoken it with such seriousness that the

neo-Nazi standing at the computer was uncertain whether or not his führer was joking. However, not wishing to be on the receiving end of a punishment like the one Field Marshal Dunlitz had just gotten, the skinhead stooped dutifully to collect the body.

He carried the old dead Nazi to his room.

28

He didn't enjoy the prospect of leaving his wife in such a dangerous climate, but Harold W. Smith had no other choice. For the moment he knew that she would be safe.

He stole quietly down the soggy streets of Paris in a borrowed black overcoat. Beneath it was hidden the gun he had taken from the dead skinhead back at his hotel. He held it awkwardly as he walked stiffly through the late-night air.

Aside from the dull glow from its many street-lights, Paris was dark. The lights in the public and private buildings had been doused in accordance with a decree issued by the city's new military ruler.

The inhabitants of Paris had been remarkably submissive over the past twelve hours since the occupation had been announced. Smith had learned that this was due in large part to the fact that the elected president had appeared on neo-Nazi controlled local television and instructed citizens to stay indoors during this early part of the occupation. He had informed the population of the bomb and mustard-gas threats and told them that the leader of the group responsible had vowed to kill one hundred randomly chosen French civilians for every single neo-Nazi soldier killed. It was too dangerous for them not to comply.

And so the population remained as they had been told to remain. In hiding in their darkened rooms.

Of course, it wouldn't last. Smith had known many fine men on the streets of this very city who would die before shrinking away from doing that which was right. At this very moment, one of them watched over his wife.

France would fight back.

When the time for rebellion finally came, there was no telling what the madman in command of this insane scheme would do to stop it. With his finger on the trigger of so many explosives, the resulting deaths could quite easily be tallied in the hundreds of thousands.

That was why Smith was on the streets alone now.

For he had learned something in his youth that had been a cornerstone of his belief system his entire life. It was what he had tried to tell Remo a few short days before.

One man could make a difference.

Smith's footfalls were tiny clacks against the damp sidewalk. He walked as quickly as possible toward the president's palace.

He knew that there were patrols out. He had avoided two since leaving his wife several streets back. Just a few more blocks to go, and he would be home free.

Smith stepped down from the sidewalk and was hurrying across 4 Septembre Reaumur when he heard the sudden rumble of an engine.

He hadn't heard it coming soon enough.

Heart quickening, Smith ran across the street, still trying to conceal the awkward shape of the machine gun beneath his coat.

Too late.

All at once a large truck rolled into view around the corner from Sebastopol.

Smith was trapped in the headlights like a fly in amber.

There was a shout in German as the truck picked up speed, barreling toward him.

All hope of avoiding confrontation before reaching the palace was gone. Ever rational, Smith realized he had only one option open to him.

As the truck ate up the space between them, Smith pulled the machine gun from beneath his long coat. Without hesitation he raised the weapon and fired.

A short controlled burst shattered the windshield on the driver's side. The truck immediately began decelerating.

At the same time Smith saw a dark shape hang out of the passenger's-side window. A series of fiery bursts exploded from the darkness behind the bright headlights.

The bullets fired from the truck missed their mark. As Smith had expected, it was difficult for the man in the passenger's seat to aim while the vehicle was moving.

Smith had no such problem. He redirected his fire, this time at the skinhead with the gun. Bullets pinged off the truck's metal body, sending small ricochet sparks into the night.

Unlike before, however, his target was no longer where it had been.

Just as Smith opened fire, the passenger ducked back inside the cab as the truck continued to slow. Blind luck kept him from being shredded by gunfire.

Through the shattered window, Smith could barely make out the slumped form of the driver. He was obviously dead. The second man pushed the body out of the way and climbed in behind the steering wheel.

Smith fired again, but he saw at once that it was futile. His target was staying hidden beneath the dashboard.

By this time the truck was nearly upon him.

Jamming the gun close to his chest, Smith ran the rest of the way across the street. He ducked inside a protective alcove between two buildings just as the truck careered past.

It squealed to a stop a few dozen yards beyond the spot where Smith had taken refuge.

He heard a voice hissing a stream of furious German. Most likely into a radio.

It was over. There would be dozens of reinforcements here in no time. Smith had failed.

Distantly he heard the truck engine shut off.

The German was creeping toward him. Although the man was walking lightly, Smith heard the occasional scuff of a boot heel against the wet street.

He was a sitting duck. The alcove he was hiding in went back only a few feet. If he tried to run, he would be plainly visible to his stalker.

Smith felt his heart thudding beneath his rib cage. It ached. As if someone had kicked him in the chest.

His breathing from his exertions was ragged. He was an old man. Not suited to this sort of activity.

It wouldn't matter much longer.

Smith didn't consider himself to be a heroic man. He only ever did that which he thought was necessary. To "go out fighting" was an axiom that he felt was intended for fools. It had always had very little meaning to him.

But for the first time in his life, Smith found that he was out of options. And for the first time Smith realized the truth behind the words.

Back braced against the wall, Smith raised his gun level with his chest. He prepared to fire on the skinhead the instant he came into view.

As he stared out into the street, gunfire suddenly erupted from beyond his field of vision. Bullets raged against the side of the old building, spitting out jagged red chunks of brick and small puffs of mortar.

Smith ducked farther back, plastering himself against the wall. He blinked to clear the dust from his eyes. And in that instant, he saw a dark shape glide into the alley beside him.

Wheeling, Smith turned the gun on the shadow. Before he could fire, he felt the weapon being pulled gently from his hands. He grabbed for it with arthritic fingers.

"You could hurt someone with that," Remo's familiar voice said. Smith spun to the sound. The face of CURE's enforcement arm was serious. Remo handed the weapon back over his shoulder.

The Master of Sinanju stood beyond Remo. He took the gun by the barrel, holding it at arm's length between his thumb and index finger.

"All hail, Emperor Smith," Chiun intoned. "Shooter of Guns. Vanquisher of the Pinheads."

Chiun twisted the gun into a U-shape before tossing the weapon out into the street. It clattered loudly against the damp pavement.

"There is a Nazi soldier out there," Smith stressed, nodding to the street.

"I kind of figured," Remo said, "seeing as how he just tried to kill me and all." He ambled out toward the sidewalk.

"I believe he may have used a radio to signal others," Smith called after him.

"There aren't that many to signal," Remo said as he slipped from the alcove.

Chiun appraised Smith. A tiny hint of approval played in the light that reflected dimly in his youthful hazel eyes.

"You are looking well, Emperor," Chiun said.

"Thank you, Master of Sinanju," Smith replied tensely.

"In future, however, I would beg that you refrain from the use of firearms. They reflect poorly on both you and your humble servants." He bowed slightly.

Smith returned the bow with a faint nod. "I will do my best," he said.

Smith was waiting to hear the inevitable gunfire that would sound when the German soldier at last spotted Remo. As he strained to hear, however, the only noise that drifted into the alcove was a groan of metal and a dull cracking sound. Afterward there was silence.

"Remo has cleared a path for your noble self," Chiun announced, motioning to the street.

Smith knew better than to doubt the Master of Sinanju.

Chiun trailed him out to the road. Remo was trotting back from the body of the fallen skinhead.

The young man's remains didn't look right. From the angle Smith was viewing it, it looked as if the skinhead's helmet had swallowed up his head. Obviously it was a trick of the light. He was distracted from his observations by Remo.

"What are you trying to prove, Smitty?" Remo demanded, coming up to meet them. "You're going to get yourself killed."

"That was not my intention," Smith said brusquely.

"I'll tell that to your widow," Remo replied. "Where is she, by the way?"

"She is in the care of an old friend."

"Since when do you have friends?"

Smith's lemony voice became more tart. "That is irrelevant," he said sharply. "We must hurry. The architect of this nightmare is at the Palais de l'Élysée."

"We were already on our way there when we heard this nonsense," Remo said, waving to the bullet-riddled truck.

"In that case, let us continue."

Smith started down the street. Remo stopped him with a firm hand on the shoulder.

"Look, Smitty. Your wife is probably scared out of her wits right about now. Go back with her and sit tight. We can handle things from here."

"Remo, this is too serious," Smith pressed. "We cannot leave things up to chance. Parisian television is broadcasting scenes from Germany. This new fascist takeover has spawned a blood lust in that country. Even if you stop this new führer, if he manages to first detonate his hidden stores of explosives, he could inspire his followers to further acts of violent aggression.''

''The emperor is correct,'' Chiun said, nodding his agreement. ''The Hun have been kept at bay for many years, but that will not last forever. Their desire for conflict originates in the womb. However dormant it might have been, a victory here could inflame it anew.''

Remo sighed. ''So what are you saying?'' he asked Smith.

''Get me inside the palace. If there is a computer system or some other technological means used for detonation, you and Chiun will be out of your element. Perhaps I can stop the bombs before they go off. Without an explosive finale, those negative elements within Germany's borders might not have inspiration enough to attack.''

''Can't you access it from outside?'' Remo asked.

Smith shook his head. ''My laptop was destroyed.''

''Figures,'' Remo said, shaking his head. ''Okay, we'll get you inside. But promise me, Smitty. No more of this Schwarzenegger crap.''

''I promise to do only that which is necessary,'' Smith said tightly.

''A typical nonanswer,'' Remo sighed. ''Let's go.''

The three of them headed for the parked German truck.

29

The deaths of the three soldiers at the Hôtel de LePotage were reported by radio to the Palais de l'Élysée.

After the treatment old Fritz had received, the aged Nazi who was manning the radio station would have been happier to keep this information from Nils Schatz. But since the führer was standing directly behind him when the news came in, that proved impossible.

"Send in reinforcements," Schatz ordered.

"We haven't many men to spare, *Führer*," the old man said. "Several patrols have failed to report in."

"How many are at the murder scene now?"

"Only two, *mein Führer*."

"Give me that," Schatz said, grabbing the microphone from his henchman. The old man at the radio hurried to stab the Transmit button. "Listen to me," Schatz intoned. "This is your führer speaking. I want everyone in that hotel shot as a traitor to the fatherland."

Four staticky words came back over the old-fashioned radio setup.

"The hotel is empty."

"What?" Schatz demanded.

"That is why it took so long to find them," the radio operator explained. "No one reported the crime."

Schatz's face twisted into an angry scowl.

"Burn the hotel to the ground!" Schatz ordered.

"Yes, *mein Führer!*" came the scratchy reply.

Schatz threw down the mouthpiece.

In the instant before the portable transmitter that the skinheads at the hotel were using cut out, the radio operator swore he heard a surprised shout and a sudden burst of machine-gun fire. He glanced at Schatz.

Stomping down from the stage, the führer hadn't heard. The radio operator decided to remain silent.

Schatz marched back and forth in front of the dais, his cane tucked up beneath his armpit like a swagger stick. He finally stopped on the side of the room where the hostages had been forced to sit since they had been taken captive.

Some of the men were asleep. Many more sat on their haunches, hugging their knees to their chests. Adolf Kluge sat silently behind the president of France, trying to remain inconspicuous.

"See how the Fourth Reich deals with murderers and saboteurs?" Schatz said to the president.

The president said nothing.

"Soon a legion of brave Aryan soldiers will swarm across your borders," Schatz sneered. "Perhaps if you behave, I will reinstall you as puppet president."

The leader of France spoke softly.

"I assure you that sovereign France will never allow those men to cross into this country."

Schatz laughed. "We will see."

"Even if it were true, NATO will not stand idly by," the president added. "You would be wise to surrender now."

"NATO?" scoffed Schatz. "NATO is nothing without the United States and Great Britain," he said dismissively. "At the moment England has its own problems with which to contend. As for the United States, it would perhaps have been wise if your predecessor had allowed the Americans to fly over your country on their Libyan bombing raid. Since that time it has been difficult for the giant in North America to rouse itself to French causes."

The president agreed privately that the words had some validity. The current president's party had not been in power at the time. If it had been up to him, French planes would have joined their American allies in the bombing of the terrorist Arab state.

"We will see," the president said simply.

The radio on the stage suddenly crackled to life.

Schatz abandoned the president, marching back across the floor to the dais.

Behind him the president of France heard a soft voice.

"You would be advised not to incite him," Kluge whispered in English. His accent was distinctly British. "He is unstable."

The president was surprised. He had thought Kluge to be a subordinate who had lost favor with the Nazi leader.

"You do not work for him?" the president whispered.

Kluge managed a sour laugh. "Hardly," he said. "I was sent to help by your good friends across the channel. Have you heard of Source?"

The president didn't have time to admit that he had. All at once Nils Schatz thundered loudly from atop the dais.

"This is an outrage!" he screamed. The radio operator cowered beneath him. "How many are dead?"

"We do not know yet," the radio man said. "Two trucks have been located on Rue de Clichy. Their drivers are both dead. One gruesomely."

"How?" Schatz demanded.

"His head was crushed beneath his own helmet, Führer." He hesitated a moment. "I received news of similar deaths at one of our checkpoints earlier in the evening. Forgive me, Führer, but I assumed these men who are working for us were inebriated. After all, what force could collapse a skull this way?''

Schatz's mouth had become an angry, bloodless line. He spun away from the radio operator, looking down on Kluge.

On the floor Adolf Kluge's expression remained bland. He knew what must be going through the old man's crazed mind.

Sinanju. They were on their way.

It was his folly that had brought him to this. Kluge wasn't about to risk exposure by telling the self-titled führer this in front of half the French government. Sitting cross-legged behind the French president, Adolf Kluge remained mute.

Schatz turned his wild-eyed attention from Kluge to the French president. He was silent for a long moment, reeling in place. Pale blue veins throbbed frantically beneath the dry skin at his temples.

So agitated did he appear, Kluge actually thought he might drop dead on the spot. Sadly it was not to be.

Finally, Nils Schatz spoke.

''Your people will be taught a lesson for this—'' from the stage he aimed his cane at the president ''—for this...this...*outrage!*'' He screamed himself hoarse, wheeling around to his skinhead attendants.

''Collect one hundred prisoners for every murdered soldier! I will give them a demonstration of our might at the primary target. When they see it destroyed, the world will know not to trifle with the Fourth Reich!''

He pushed away young hands that wished to help him down from the stage. Waving his cane like a bare flagpole, Nils Schatz stormed from the room.

His insane shouting echoed down the empty corridors of the Palais de l'Élysée.

30

As they drove up in their borrowed truck, Remo was surprised to find that someone had moved the line of concrete barriers that had been placed before the gates of the presidential palace. They were resting now to one side of the road. The bulldozer that had pushed them there sat quietly beside them. Huge tears had been made in the road, scraped up by the heavy concrete slabs.

"Maybe someone already took care of things," Remo suggested from the driver's seat.

A hail of bullets against the front of the truck a second later told them otherwise.

Smith was crouched down in the rear of the truck. Chiun had been riding shotgun. When the men on the grounds of the palace opened fire, Chiun sprang from the truck and raced up the path that led inside the huge mansion. Remo paused only long enough to advise Smith to keep out of sight before he joined the Master of Sinanju outside the vehicle.

There were a few more bursts of automatic-weapons fire from inside the grounds. Soon these fell silent.

After a minute Remo returned to the side of the truck.

"Coast is clear, Smitty," he called.

Smith got up from the floor and climbed into the cab. Remo helped him down to the ground.

At the front of the truck they met up with Chiun.

"How does the emperor wish to proceed?" he asked.

"The fastest route inside," Smith stressed.

"Of course," Chiun said. "But it is customary at this time to do either one of two things. You may wish to rule from this place—which, as palaces go, is not without its charm. Or you may opt to sack the priceless artifacts from within and burn the building to its foundation."

"Neither," Smith said urgently. "We are not here as conquerors."

"Be advised, Emperor," Chiun said slyly, "the French are known the world over for the courtesies they extend to those who plunder and enslave. It is the only time they shine as a people."

"No, Chiun," Smith said firmly. He sidestepped the Master of Sinanju and ducked through the gates.

Remo shrugged and trailed Smith inside.

Chiun shook his head in disapproving bewilderment.

"Americans," he muttered to himself. He wandered inside the palace grounds after Remo and Smith.

THEY HAD GONE a few dozen yards up the drive when Smith literally stumbled across the first body. Remo grabbed him before the CURE director toppled to the ground.

Smith looked down at the dead skinhead. Presumably he was one of those who had fired on them upon their arrival. The young man's head appeared to have shriveled up beneath his helmet. An indented smiley face had been pressed into the drab metal exterior.

There were two others lying nearby who had been similarly dispatched.

"That is unnecessary," Smith said, looking down at the helmet with a displeased expression.

"Hey, I don't tell you how to do your job," Remo remarked, defensively. He walked past Smith.

They encountered no more resistance between the spot where the bodies lay and the palace.

"Hang back, Smitty."

Remo approached the door first. The Master of Sinanju came up from behind, standing protectively next to the CURE director.

They could see Remo pause on one side of the staircase that led into the palace. He tipped his head oddly, looking over the side railing into a small landscaped garden beyond.

Abandoning the stairs, Remo slipped over the railing and disappeared from sight.

"What butterfly does he chase now?"

Perturbed, Chiun led Smith to the base of the stairway. They skirted it, going around the far side.

The smell of death hit them immediately.

Smith saw dozens of bodies lying in a tangled bunch amid the roses and rhododendrons. They were French soldiers. The men who until yesterday had successfully guarded the palace.

Remo crouched at the edge of the pile of corpses. He was looking down at a particularly mangled body.

The face was unrecognizable. It had been smashed repeatedly with a fierce glee that was clearly unnecessary. The first few blows had done the job. Most of these wounds had been inflicted after death.

When he stepped around Remo, Smith was surprised to see that it was the body of a woman.

Remo looked up, face hard.

"You knew her?" Smith asked.

"I borrowed her phone a couple of times," Remo said tightly.

Smith understood immediately. "We must stop him before he kills again," he said softly.

Remo glanced back at the corpse. Nodding, he got to his feet. They left the body of Helene Marie-Simone in the small garden and continued inside.

ADOLF KLUGE SPOKE in German. Lest any of the French officials present understood the language, he pitched his voice low.

"You realize now that this operation is doomed to failure," he whispered.

The old radio operator glanced at the pair of skinhead guards near the door. Swallowing, he looked back at Kluge.

"We did not know it would come to this, Herr Kluge," he admitted sadly. "He promised glory."

"The time for glory has passed, old friend," Kluge said. "The best we can hope for now is simply to survive."

He could see that he almost had the man on his side. Schatz had left ten minutes before. Kluge had been working hard to get the old Nazi radio operator to see the futility of this insane campaign.

"I did it all for the fatherland," the old man said. His bloodshot eyes were moist.

"I'm sure you think that," Kluge replied. "But I assure you that you have done more harm here than good. Please help me to undo some of that damage. While there is still time."

The old man cast a glance at the pair of skinhead guards who were standing over near the dais. Each of them held a Gewehr assault rifle. Proud of their rather limited role in the neo-Nazi occupation, they stood at attention. They stared blankly ahead. Kluge suspected they were on some sort of drug.

The old radioman had made up his mind. Turning

away from the soldiers, he unclipped the single silver snapper on his hip holster. He was about to reach for the gun in order to turn it over to Adolf Kluge when he was distracted by the sound of gunfire down the corridor.

The soldiers at the stage immediately grew alert, spinning toward the open door.

Kluge would never have a better chance.

He ripped the gun from the old Nazi's holster, twisting the man around and using him as a human shield. To the French it looked as if his long secret conversation with the radioman had caused the old soldier to drop his guard.

"Get down!" Kluge yelled in French to the diplomats seated on the floor.

As the men and women flung themselves to the carpeted aisle, fingers interlocked above their heads, Adolf Kluge opened fire on the pair of Nazis at the front of the stage.

He took two shots at the nearest skinhead. The first bullet caught the man in the rear of his left shoulder. He tried to turn on his attacker, but only made it halfway around when the second bullet caught him with a violent thwack in the temple. He toppled over, bouncing first off the stage and then crumpling to the floor.

The second skinhead managed to get off a couple of shots from his rifle.

Kluge felt a few rounds pound against the body of

the old man. The Nazi groaned no louder than if he had just awakened from a nightmare. He grew limp in Kluge's arm.

Another shot.

A single bullet ripped through Kluge's bicep. Lip curling in pain and anger, he flung the body of the dead Nazi to the floor, at the same time tossing the gun from his injured arm to his good left hand. He caught the weapon and squeezed the trigger once.

The bullet snapped into the chest of the skinhead. The force of impact was so great, the man swirled around toward the stage, flinging his gun to the floor. He sprawled across the stage, arms thrown wide. He didn't move again.

Ignoring his bleeding arm, Kluge turned on the gathered diplomats, including the president of France.

"Stay there," Kluge instructed.

The politicians weren't about to move. They looked on in fear as Kluge moved swiftly across the auditorium. On the way he gathered up one of the discarded rifles.

Kluge propped his back against the wall inside the open door. He took a deep breath. Thus steadied, he jerked his body around, sticking the muzzle of the gun experimentally into the hallway.

Instantly a hand that extended into a thick wrist reached into the room from the corridor.

"I'll take that," Remo said, coming into view.

He pulled the rifle from Kluge's hands, taking it in his own. Holding the barrel in one hand and the stock in the other, Remo brought the middle of the gun down across one knee. The rifle snapped obediently in two neat halves. Remo tossed them away.

"All clear," Remo called behind him.

As Remo ambled into the room, Smith came in from the corridor in the company of Chiun. Smith immediately spied the computer that Schatz had had moved up on the stage after the death of Fritz. Leaving the others, he hurried up the steps, sliding in before the screen.

On the floor Kluge suppressed his surprise at seeing for the first time the man he knew to be the Master of Sinanju. When he saw Adolf Kluge, Chiun's eyes narrowed.

"You do this?" Remo asked, nodding to the bodies lying around the room.

"I did what was necessary," Kluge said. With difficulty he pulled his attention away from Chiun. He pulled a handkerchief from his pocket and held it to his bleeding arm.

"You're English," Remo said, noting Kluge's accent.

The head of IV nodded in response. "And you are American presumably," Kluge said.

"That's the first thing about me everyone seems to notice lately."

"I presume the palace is secure?"

"It looks that way," Remo told Kluge. "There were only a couple of guys outside and a couple more inside. It looks like everyone else bugged out before we got here."

"It is safe, Mr. President," Kluge called back to the assembled French officials. "They are Americans."

The crowd of people on the floor across the room became animated for the first time in almost a day. They pushed themselves up on cramped legs, rubbing aching backs as they tried to shake away the feeling of pins and needles in their lower extremities. Some left to find a bathroom. Not one of the lesser dignitaries expressed thanks for his release. Alone, the president came over to greet them.

"You have my gratitude," he said happily.

Remo was about to say "you're welcome" when the Frenchman grabbed Adolf Kluge by the hand and began pumping madly. His face beamed appreciation.

"Hello," Remo said, perturbed. "Palace liberators this way." He waved his hand in front of the president's face.

"Ah, yes." The president reached for Remo's hand.

Chiun interjected. "This one is German," the Master of Sinanju said, his nose crinkling unhappily. He nodded to Kluge.

"Non," the French president said, his hand withdrawing. "He is with British Intelligence."

"That is an oxymoron," sniffed Chiun, "and beside the point. He has the stink of a Hun."

"Look, Chiun," Remo said, "he was helping out the good guys. Right now that makes him a good guy." He turned to Kluge. "So do you work for Source?" he asked.

"You've heard of it?" Kluge said, trying to sound surprised.

"Who hasn't?" Remo asked.

"Yes," Kluge said, uncertainly. "In point of fact, I cannot really say."

"Then it must be MI5. If you were Source, you'd say so."

Smith suddenly interrupted their conversation. "Remo, Chiun, come here," he called from the stage.

Remo immediately turned away from the others, hopping up atop the dais. He was followed by Kluge, the French president and a still suspicious Chiun.

"I have gotten into their system," Smith said excitedly as the others gathered around. "It is really quite simple." He punched a few keys. A screen of text was replaced by a map of Paris. "Everything is here. Locations, amounts stockpiled. Everything."

"Those blue and red dots are the bombs?" Remo asked.

Smith nodded. "They indicate both regular explosives and mustard-gas shells."

"It looks like a hell of a lot of bombs," Remo said worriedly.

Smith shook his head. "That is true," he admitted. "However, they have been placed in the subway, as well as government buildings and cultural centers. From what I have learned, all of these places are virtually if not completely abandoned at present."

"Can you tell from this what might be their primary target?" Kluge asked. "Schatz threatened to destroy it, as well as murder hundreds of civilians when he stormed away from here."

Smith looked back at the computer. "Possibly," he said. "I believe there is a numbering system." He used the cursor to initiate the proper commands. A ripple effect passed down the screen, leaving numerals in its wake. When it disappeared from the bottom of the computer, each dot was left with a small white number superimposed on it.

"Oh, my god," the French president said when he saw where number 1 was located.

Smith frowned. For confirmation he moved the cursor arrow up to the dot marked "1." When he depressed the plastic button, a fresh screen of text flooded the computer face. The text supported the conclusion of the president.

"I would guess that is the primary target," Smith said.

"So we know where he's headed," Remo said. He started for the stairs.

"Wait!" the French president called. He looked desperately down at Smith. "Is German occupation so bad?" he asked. "Can we not give him what he wants?"

Smith's face steeled. "Need I remind you, Mr President, that he wants to murder and enslave your countrymen?"

"Yes, but..." The president indicated the information on the computer screen with a helpless wave of his hand.

Disgusted, Smith turned his attention away from the Frenchman and back to Remo.

"The Métro is likely cleared of all civilians," he said. "As are the buildings on this list. The worst he can inflict on the city is a cultural black eye. Get him."

"Stop!" the president cried, flinging himself at Remo, blocking his exit. He turned his attention on Smith. "Who are you to issue orders in sovereign France?"

Remo looked at him distastefully. He took the president by the shoulders, lifting him off the floor. He placed him between Kluge and the still seated Smith.

"We're the good guys," Remo said. Without another word he and Chiun headed down the stairs and raced out the auditorium door.

The president tried to go after them once more, but Kluge interceded.

"It is necessary, Mr. President," he said with a somber nod. His voice was funereal.

The president's shoulders slumped in defeat. The fight drained out of him.

"*Oui,*" he said sadly. He sat down at the long table atop the podium, eyes downcast. Kluge patted a supportive hand on his rounded shoulder.

After Remo and Chiun had left, Smith had turned back to the computer. His nimble fingers were typing madly away at the keyboard.

Once, unseen by anyone in the small auditorium, Adolf Kluge glanced up from consoling the president of France. He eyed Smith suspiciously.

31

The führer of the Fourth Reich marched back and forth in front of the wide iron support column. Above him, illuminated by powerful floodlights, the latticework structure of the Eiffel Tower jutted almost one thousand feet into the postmidnight Paris sky.

There were two dozen men around him. A mixture of both old-time Nazis and modern skinheads. They formed a protective phalanx around their leader.

As he paced between them, Nils Schatz banged his cane against the ground, creating angry dents in the dull bronze tip. He noted with displeasure that the walking stick had lost its luster. He would have to have someone polish it when he returned to the palace. Perhaps the president of France himself. He whirled.

"Where are they?" Schatz demanded hotly, pacing up to a nearby subordinate.

"They radioed half an hour ago, *mein Führer,*" the skinhead said helplessly.

"I know that," Schatz snapped. He walked a few

steps in the opposite direction before twirling back around.

They were awaiting the arrival of the first hundred French victims. Chosen at random, the civilians would be shot in retaliation for the murder of only one skinhead. Afterward, Schatz intended to destroy the tower in order to demonstrate to the world the seriousness of his purpose.

He could see the pile of rusted old ordnance stacked beneath the nearby column. There were crates of shells as well as loose aerial bombs and mines, the latter being too large to box. Schatz had been assured that this one blast would take out the supporting leg above it, after which the tower would topple like a three-legged horse. A small digital detonator glowed red from a shadowy spot between the pile of explosives. It was the same kind of manually set device that was on all of his cases of stored ordnance.

He would not allow his dream to slip away from him. Not now. Not when it was so close to becoming a reality.

Paris was only the beginning. Soon the rest of France would fall. Germany would certainly join him then. After that it would take only a push to force the rest of Europe into line. And afterward…?

Schatz knew. This modern world wasn't like the one that had given birth to him. These people were weak. They were crying out for a leader. For him.

He turned again on the skinhead.

"Raise them!" he commanded, pointing at the portable radio set with his cane.

"As I told you before, I have been unable to, *mein Führer,*" the skinhead said.

"Do not make me angry, boy," Schatz sneered, striding over to the young man. He pushed the skinhead viciously in the chest with the end of his cane.

Schatz was distracted by the sudden rumble of an engine. It came from the Seine side of the tower. He rose to his full height, glaring unhappily at the approaching two trucks.

"At last," he snorted. He marched over between the line of men to meet the vehicles.

Coming in one after the other, the trucks were approaching fast.

Schatz saw as they barreled toward him that the cab of the lead truck was empty. His face puckered unhappily as his twisted brain attempted to understand the significance of two empty trucks.

The vehicles didn't slow.

Teeth clenched in a rictus of fury, Schatz jumped from the path of the oncoming vehicles just in time, landing in a heap on the ground. The nearest skinheads pulled him to his feet, brushing the dirt from his clothing. He pushed their hands aside, spinning around in time to see the speeding trucks slam into the Eiffel Tower.

The first truck crashed into the base of the column

beneath which the ordnance was stored. Even as the lead truck's nose crumpled painfully, the second truck was slamming it from behind, twisting the first truck to one side and toppling it over onto the base. The engines of both vehicles hummed softly.

Schatz stormed over to the trucks. He saw immediately that the undamaged second vehicle was empty. The Parisian men, women and children who were to be an example to their fellow citizens not to challenge the glorious Nazi Reich were nowhere to be seen.

"What is this?" Schatz demanded, whirling on his men.

"It's goodbye, schnitzel face," said an American voice.

The führer's blood turned to ice.

As Schatz watched in horror, the two of them appeared out of the shadows. Like avenging angels.

It was them. The ones from Sinanju.

The young one who had threatened Schatz over the Guernsey video camera grabbed a pair of skinhead soldiers by their necks and slammed their heads sharply toward one another. The resulting sound was like two pots being banged together. When he was finished, two helmets were fused together as if by a welder's torch. The skulls beneath were pulverized to mush.

At the same time the Reigning Master of Sinanju had leaped in front of four startled German soldiers.

His arms shot back and forth like pistons, piercing the foreheads of the men with deadly talons. The men dropped like wet bags of potting soil to the damp ground.

Schatz stumbled backward as the two Masters of Sinanju fell on his remaining skinhead and Nazi guards.

This couldn't be happening. Not now. Not when he was so close to success.

A single gunshot exploded behind him. There was a shriek of pain as the Nazi who had fired the weapon fell, his neck spurting blood from a wound inflicted by a sharpened fingernail.

The firing weapon sparked an idea in the back of Nils Schatz's perverted mind.

Exploded.

There was still a chance.

"Protect your führer!" Schatz ordered the porta-ble-radio operator. He hurried past the idling trucks toward the stack of explosives.

REMO JERKED the barrel of the gun around, forcing it back into the face of the attacking Nazi. The old man's teeth cracked to splinters as the muzzle tore through his mouth, continuing on into the back of his throat. It exited the rear of his neck.

"You'd have thought some of these guys would have called it quits after the last world war," Remo commented as he went to work on another old Nazi.

"Madness does not admit defeat," Chiun said. He cracked the kneecaps of two nearby skinheads.

"Remind me to embroider that on a pillow," Remo said, finishing off Chiun's wounded with two precise toe kicks.

The area around them was littered with the dead of the Fourth Reich. There was only one man left alive. It was the skinhead radio operator.

Remo grabbed him by the throat. "Where's that old guy that was here a minute ago?" he demanded. "Shits."

"Führer Schatz...is...there," said the man, his face turning deep red beneath Remo's squeezing hand. He pointed beyond the trucks to the base of the Eiffel Tower.

"Thanks," said Remo.

A final squeeze snapped the skinhead's spine. Remo dropped him to the ground. Running, he and Chiun headed for the tower.

SCHATZ HAD SET the digital timer on the stack of explosives to go off in four minutes.

Luckily for him, he had insisted that the detonators they had purchased with stolen IV funds be modeled after the small digital alarm clock that sat beside his bed in the sleepy IV village in Argentina. Schatz wasn't good with many of these new contrivances, but he certainly knew how to operate an alarm clock.

He was running now in the direction opposite the men from Sinanju.

Schatz had no idea how far he could get in four minutes. He hoped it would be far enough. One thing was certain, though. There was no way the two Masters of Sinanju would be able to escape the blast.

He ran for half a minute before realizing that he had left his treasured walking stick behind. It was too late to return for it.

He would get another. When the bomb exploded and the tower fell. Once the world recognized that the Fourth Reich would not be trifled with. The führer would have his choice of the finest walking sticks in the world.

His aged lungs burned as he ran. His arms and legs moved in pained, jerky motions.

How much farther would be safe?

He fixed his gaze on a tree far ahead. That would be the point. Surely if he reached that, he would be free of the blast zone. And he would most certainly reach it.

That certainty vanished a few seconds later when it occurred to Schatz that the scenery before him wasn't getting any larger. Was that not what generally happened as one approached something?

Another moment and he realized why.

He looked down at his feet. They were several inches off the ground. Though his legs pumped madly, they pushed against empty air.

Schatz looked back over his shoulder. He saw a hand that extended into an abnormally thick wrist. Beyond them both was a familiar cruel face. It was the same face that had mouthed the words "I am going to kill you" on the camera at the Guernsey air base.

"We had a date. Remember?" Remo said coldly.

Holding the old German by the scruff of the neck, he carried Nils Schatz back to the Eiffel Tower.

"DO YOU NOT KNOW how to disarm it?"

"Do I look like I know how?" Remo asked.

"You are American," Chiun insisted.

"So?"

"So true Americans know such things."

"Look, they don't teach bomb disarmament in Catholic school," Remo said.

"They do in Ireland," Chiun suggested.

Remo ignored him. He studied the wires running from the bottom of the detonator. They were multicolored and ran into one of the largest of the rusted shell casings. The timer was ticking down to the one-minute mark.

Behind them, virtually ignored, stood Nils Schatz. Remo had deposited the old Nazi near the front of the broad iron support column before he and Chiun turned their attention to the bombs.

Schatz glanced over at one of the crashed trucks. It was still in good shape. Its engine hummed softly.

"I think I should cut the red one," Remo decided, reaching for a wire.

"Why?" Chiun asked, stopping him with a long-nailed finger.

"I saw in a movie where they cut the red wire to stop a bomb," Remo explained.

"I once saw a movie in which a man flew. I do not believe, Remo, that men can fly."

"Hmm," Remo said, sitting back on his haunches.

As Remo studied the bomb, Nils Schatz began inching toward the parked truck. Along the way, he collected his treasured walking stick.

"Sever the blue one," Chiun said authoritatively.

"Why?" Remo asked.

"Blue is my favorite color."

"So what?" Remo asked. "Red is my favorite color."

"That is because you lack taste."

They heard the sound of the truck engine revving desperately. Both men looked over in time to see the big rented vehicle back away from the second damaged truck.

Nils Schatz sat in the driver's seat, eyes wild. He spun the wheel furiously, turning the truck away from the tower. Stomping on the gas, he began speeding away.

Remo looked at Chiun. He shrugged helplessly.

"Shits is right, Chiun," he said. "I'm stumped."

The Master of Sinanju frowned. The timer continued ticking down. As they watched, it slipped below the thirty-second mark. Chiun shook his head.

"Let us make haste," the Master of Sinanju said.

Swirling, he and Remo raced from the base of the tower.

SCHATZ WAS GOING to survive!

He would live, and along with him the dream of a thousand-year Teutonic dynasty.

His foot pressed heavily on the accelerator as he raced away from the tower. His heart thudded loudly in his narrow chest. He could see the Eiffel Tower's massive shape illuminated in his side-view mirrors by floodlights.

The fools from Sinanju would perish after all. The old one would finally pay the ultimate price for the shameful death he had forced on the first führer.

His heart and lungs ached from his exertions.

Any second now. And afterward the world would never again question the power of the Fourth Reich.

Schatz glanced in the side-view mirror once more.

He saw something that made his desperately beating heart stand still.

The young Master of Sinanju was running down the road after him.

He glanced in the mirror on the far side of the cab. The old one was reflected there. And he was coming closer.

Impossible!

Schatz pushed harder against the accelerator. It was already to the floor.

He glanced in the side-view mirror once more.

Remo was almost upon him.

Schatz glanced frantically around the cab for a weapon to use against them. All he saw was his beloved walking stick.

The driver's-side door suddenly popped open. Schatz noted it dully.

A second later, the passenger's-side door opened. The Master of Sinanju slid into the front seat. He didn't even look in Schatz's direction.

Schatz felt Remo's strong hand on his shoulder. They passed one another at the door frame. Somehow, in the wink of an eye, Remo was seated behind the steering wheel and Nils Schatz was hanging by Remo's left hand out over the flashing roadway.

"Thanks for keeping my seat warm."

With a flick of his wrist, Remo flung the new führer backward.

Schatz sailed through the air, landing on the seat of his pants in the middle of the road. Remarkably he was not killed. Friction burned the flesh of his backside painfully away as he slid in a seated position all the way back to the stack of ancient ordnance.

Smoke poured from his trousers as he landed with the gentlest of touches against the explosives.

Schatz looked up at the digital counter.

Ten seconds left.

As he reached for the timer, he glanced back in the direction from which he had just come. The truck continued speeding away.

He saw a hand appear from the driver's-side window, throwing something back in his direction. Whatever the object was, it was long and dark. It flew at him slowly, end over end. Moving almost hypnotically.

Five seconds.

His hand froze over the timer as he realized what it was Remo had thrown. In the cheerful glow of the floodlights, he could see the bronze tip of his cane.

Two seconds. Still time to stop the countdown.

The slowness was an optical illusion. The cane flew in at supersonic speed. The metal end of the walking stick impacted with the shell casing of an old artillery shell.

The collision sparked the combustible material within.

Fire swelled from a single spot, bursting out around the screaming, bitter old Nazi.

"Noooo...!" Nils Schatz shrieked as the pile of old ordnance erupted in a massive conflagration that shook the ground for miles around.

And as the fire consumed him, another, greater fire welled up around the self-proclaimed führer. To Schatz, it felt as if the very earth had opened up and the flames into which he slipped and which took firm hold of him burned unquenchably for a thousand years. And beyond.

REMO SLOWED the truck to a stop. He and Chiun looked back on the flames burning at the base of the Eiffel Tower. A gift shop had caught fire, as well as several trees. However, the tower itself had weathered the blast remarkably. It remained fully intact.

"They just don't build eyesores like that anymore, Little Father," Remo commented.

Putting the battered truck in gear, they drove back through the silent streets to the presidential palace.

32

For several blocks before the Palais de l'Élysée they had begun encountering French troops. At more than one stop along the Métro line, *demineurs* in protective gear were hauling ancient ordnance up from the subway system.

"I smell Smitty's hand in this," Remo said.

At the palace itself they encountered little resistance. Remo and Chiun made their way into the small auditorium where they had left Smith. Everyone but Smith was gone.

The CURE director lay unconscious on the floor.

Remo and Chiun hurried over to him. After a moment of Chiun's ministrations, Smith came around.

"Stop him, Remo," Smith said weakly.

"Stop who, Smitty?" Remo asked gently.

"That man who claimed to be a British agent. After I faxed the pertinent details of the planted bombs to the French authorities, he knocked me out." With Remo's help, Smith climbed uncertainly to his feet. "It is as I feared," he said, inspecting the computer.

The monitor had been pushed to the floor and was smashed. The chassis of the drive system had been pried open. Parts had been wrenched from inside.

"He has taken the hard drive," Smith said, looking into the guts of the system. "Anything we might have recovered from it is lost."

"Did I not mention that he was a Hun?" Chiun sniffed in an I-told-you-so tone.

"That information would have been invaluable to us," Smith said. "With it, I would have been able to track down this elusive IV organization."

Remo shook his head. "Whoever he was, he's long gone now," he said. "We'll have to get them another way. I think your big concern right now is your wife."

"Maude," Smith gasped. He had forgotten all about her.

"That was her name, last I heard," Remo said.

Smith glanced around, suddenly realizing the significance of where they were. "Remo, you must get me out of here. I cannot be discovered in the presidential palace of France. There would be too many questions to answer."

"Okay, Smitty, on one condition."

"What?" Smith asked warily.

"Before you finish your vacation, could you pick me and Chiun up a snow globe of the Eiffel Tower?"

"One each," Chiun said quickly.

"One each," Remo agreed with a nod.

"I will see what I can do," Smith said.

Smiling, Remo escorted Smith from the palace. For the first time in days, he felt good.

EPILOGUE

Adolf Kluge glanced furtively around the airport terminal in Antwerp, Belgium.

He didn't think he had been followed. Although, he realized bitterly, the men who would be following him would be invisible to him until it was too late.

He had destroyed the hard drive with its crucial IV financial information before leaving France. That would buy him some time. If not for the arrival of French officials on the scene, he would have finished off the man known as Smith.

As it was, Smith was old. It was possible that he would die as a result of the vicious blow Kluge had given him.

He hoped this was so.

Kluge was traveling now under an assumed name. His flight would take him to Spain and then on to Venezuela in South America. From there he would take a short flight to Argentina.

He hoped the men from Sinanju weren't waiting for him when he arrived. Thanks to Schatz, he had much to do in preparation for their inevitable visit.

A voice in French called out his flight on the public-address system.

He still saw no sign of either Remo or Chiun.

They were not following him. Now.

Hurrying, Adolf Kluge made his way to the departure gate.

Iran ups the ante in Bosnia with new weapons of terror....

STONY MAN™ 37

TRIPLE STRIKE

A kidnapped U.S. advisor and a downed recon plane pilot are held in a stronghold in Muslim Bosnia, where Iranian forces have joined with their Bosnian brothers to eradicate the unbelievers.

The President and Stony Man must use their individual powers of influence to bring the agents of doom to justice—if there's still time....

Available in November 1998 at your favorite retail outlet.

Follow Remo and Chiun on more of their extraordinary adventures....

THE

Destroyer™